*The Most Lovable Detective
You'll Ever Meet . . .*

Heron Carvic's
MISS SEETON

Don't miss a single misadventure of
the marvellous mistress of mystery!

PICTURE MISS SEETON
A night at the opera strikes a chord of danger when Miss
Seeton witnesses a murder . . . and paints a portrait of the
killer.

WITCH MISS SEETON
Double, double, toil and trouble sweep through the village when Miss Seeton goes undercover . . . to investigate
a local witches' coven!

MISS SEETON DRAWS THE LINE
Miss Seeton is enlisted by Scotland Yard when her paintings of a little girl turn the young subject into a model for
murder.

MISS SEETON SINGS
Miss Seeton boards the wrong plane and lands amidst a
gang of European counterfeiters. One false note, and her
new destination is deadly indeed.

Continued . . .

This book contains a preview of the new upcoming Miss
Seeton mystery: *Miss Seeton Undercover.*

ODDS ON MISS SEETON

Miss Seeton in diamonds and furs at the roulette table? It's all a clever disguise for the high-rolling spinster . . . but the game of money and murder is all too real.

ADVANTAGE MISS SEETON

Miss Seeton's summer outing to a tennis match serves up more than expected when Britain's up-and-coming female tennis star is hounded by mysterious death threats.

MISS SEETON BY APPOINTMENT

Miss Seeton is off to Buckingham Palace on a secret mission—but to foil a jewel heist, she must risk losing the Queen's head . . . and her own neck!

MISS SEETON AT THE HELM

Miss Seeton takes a whirlwind cruise to the Mediterranean—bound for disaster.. A murder on board leads the seafaring sleuth into some very stormy waters.

MISS SEETON CRACKS THE CASE

It's highway robbery for the innocent passengers of a motor coach tour. When Miss Seeton sketches the roadside bandits, she becomes a moving target herself.

MISS SEETON PAINTS THE TOWN

The Best Kept Village Competition inspires Miss Seeton's most unusual artwork—a burning cottage—and clears the smoke of suspicion in a series of local fires.

HANDS UP, MISS SEETON

The gentle Miss Seeton? A thief? A preposterous notion—until she's accused of helping a pickpocket . . . and stumbles into a nest of crime.

MISS SEETON BY MOONLIGHT

Scotland Yard borrows one of Miss Seeton's paintings to bait an art thief . . . when suddenly a *second* thief strikes.

MISS SEETON ROCKS THE CRADLE

It takes all of Miss Seeton's best instincts—maternal and otherwise—to solve a crime that's hardly child's play.

MISS SEETON GOES TO BAT

Miss Seeton's in on the action when a cricket game leads to mayhem in the village of Plummergen . . . and gives her a shot at smashing Britain's most baffling burglary ring.

MISS SEETON PLANTS SUSPICION

Miss Seeton was tending her garden when a local youth was arrested for murder. Now she has to find out who's really at the root of the crime.

Available from Berkley Books

MORE MYSTERIES FROM THE BERKLEY PUBLISHING GROUP . . .

THE HERON CARVIC MISS SEETON MYSTERIES: Retired art teacher Miss Seeton steps in where Scotland Yard stumbles. "A most beguiling protagonist!" —*New York Times*

SISTERS IN CRIME: Criminally entertaining short stories from the top women of mystery and suspense. "Excellent!" —*Newsweek*

KATE SHUGAK MYSTERIES: A former D.A. solves crime in the far Alaska north . . .

DOG LOVERS' MYSTERIES STARRING HOLLY WINTER: With her Alaskan malamute Rowdy, Holly dogs the trails of dangerous criminals. "A gifted and original writer." —Carolyn G. Hart

TREWLEY AND STONE MYSTERIES: Even the coziest English villages have criminal secrets . . . but fortunately, they also have Detectives Trewley and Stone to dig them up!

STARRING MISS SEETON

HAMILTON CRANE

BERKLEY BOOKS, NEW YORK

STARRING MISS SEETON

A Berkley Book / published by arrangement with the author and the Estate of Heron Carvic

PRINTING HISTORY
Berkley edition / January 1994

All rights reserved.
Copyright © 1994 by Sarah J. Mason.
Excerpt from *Miss Seeton Undercover*
copyright © 1994 by Sarah J. Mason.
This book may not be reproduced in whole or in part, by mimeograph or any other means, without permission. For information address: The Berkley Publishing Group, 200 Madison Avenue, New York, New York 10016.

ISBN: 0-425-14044-X

BERKLEY®
Berkley Books are published by
The Berkley Publishing Group, 200 Madison Avenue, New York, New York 10016.
"BERKLEY" and the "B" design
are trademarks of Berkley Publishing Corporation.

PRINTED IN THE UNITED STATES OF AMERICA

10 9 8 7 6 5 4 3 2 1

"CINDERELLA" CAST LIST

FAIRY CRYSTAL	:	Miss Alice Maynard
JASPER, *a Broker's Man*	:	DC Foxon
MARMADUKE, *another*	:	PC Potter
INJECTA, *an Ugly Sister*	:	Dr. Knight
INSTRUCTA, *another*	:	Mr. Jessyp
BARON STONEYBROKE, *their stepfather*	:	Charley Mountfitchet
BUTTONS, *his page*	:	Nigel Colveden
CINDERELLA, *his daughter*	:	Emmeline Putts
FAIRY GODMOTHER	:	Mrs. Elsie Stillman
PRINCE CHARMING	:	Maureen
DANDINI, *his friend*	:	Bert the Postman
FOOTMAN ONE	:	Trevor Newport
FOOTMAN TWO	:	Kevin Scillicough

PANTOMIME PRODUCTION TEAM

DIRECTOR	: Lady Colveden
PRODUCER	: Miss Molly Treeves
SCENERY	: Miss Emily Seeton & Co.
STAGE DRESSING AND PROPS	: Mabel Potter & Co.
PROMPT	: Miss Seeton
LIGHTING AND SOUND	: Admiral Leighton, Sir George Colveden
WARDROBE	: Martha Bloomer, Miss Armitage & Co.
PUBLICITY, FRONT OF HOUSE, TREASURER	: Major Howett

chapter

-1-

LADY COLVEDEN STABBED a brooding knife into the breakfast butter. "I do wish," she said, in a plaintive tone, "that casting wasn't always so difficult . . ."

Hoping for sympathy, she glanced at what she could see of her menfolk. Behind the local paper—*The Brettenden Telegraph and Beacon* (*est. 1847, incorporating [1893] The Iverhurst Chronicle and Argus*)—her husband was invisible. Sitting next to his father, Nigel munched toast in a daydream, deaf to all entreaty.

Lady Colveden coughed. "Casting," she repeated, rather more loudly. "Why do I—why does everyone—find it so horribly hard to get right?"

Nigel swallowed the final mouthful, and reached for his third slice. In gazing round for the butter, his eyes met those of his parent, wide with silent—or not-so-silent—suffering. Nigel widened his own.

"Are you dropping hints that you'd like a few lessons? I'm surprised at you, Mother. If the water bailiffs caught anyone from this family fishing for game slap bang in the middle of the close season as we are, the very least that would happen is a hefty fine and Dad's magisterial—or do I mean judicial?—buttons being snipped off. That is, assuming it's trout or salmon you're after, and not—"

"Nigel, don't be silly." Wide eyes narrowed to a frown. "You know perfectly well I don't mean fly fishing—or with bait, either, if it comes to that." She wrinkled an elegant nose. "Ugh! When I remember how you and Julia used to dig worms

1

in the garden and raid my needlework box for bent pins—not that they were bent to begin with, of course, but by the time you two had finished with them they were certainly no good for anything else—"

An explosion of mirth erupted in stereo from behind the pages of the *Beacon* and from the young toast-butterer beside them. Meg Colveden's menfolk knew her well.

Sir George left his son to put their shared, unspoken thought into words. "Mother darling, it's you who should be told not to be silly. You can't fool us. *You* know perfectly well that Julia and I had more use out of those pins in one summer than you've had in all the years since we graduated to a proper rod and line. And I don't recall offhand that we ever needed to bend a single one—you're hardly the world's most, er, skilled sempstress, you know."

"I'm sure there's no need to rub it in. I do the best I can," returned his mother, trying to sound hurt at this brutally unfilial judgement; but her air of wounded dignity was marred by a dancing light in her eye as she suppressed a giggle. "Well, perhaps it isn't *quite* as good as some other people can do— which is why," loftily, "it's Martha Bloomer who's making the costumes—with Miss Armitage, of course, because she has such a marvellous sense of colour; but Martha is absolutely brilliant with her needle—and you needn't try to pretend you think I mean fish, because after last night I should have thought it must be obvious to anyone that I don't—er, didn't."

Nigel at last allowed light to dawn. "Oh, the pantomime rehearsal—hey!" His knife clattered on his plate. "Mother, I warn you—if this sudden onrush of doubt and uncertainty over the casting heralds a plan to switch parts on me when I've spent all the time when I haven't been ploughing, or sowing winter wheat, or muck-spreading, or laying hedges, sweating away at Buttons until I'm blue in the face—"

"Nigel, as if I would! Well, not you, anyway—you're absolutely perfect in the role." There was a quaver in her ladyship's voice, and a corresponding quiver in the pages of the *Beacon* being ostentatiously perused by her husband. The tendency of the Colvedens' son and heir to suffer unrequited love as easily as, at this time of the year, others suffered attacks of the common cold, made him the obvious choice for Buttons: the term *typecasting* might have been invented for his benefit.

"And even if you weren't," went on his mother hastily, "you're far too good-natured, Nigel, to start fussing if you don't end up with the part you want—or any part at all," she added, absently spooning a second dollop of Oxford marmalade on her plate before passing the dish to her son: who chuckled.

"Mrs. Skinner and Mrs. Henderson, of course—York and Lancaster, as it were. I don't suppose they'll ever really bury the hatchet after that business of the church flower rota, will they? And to hell—begging her pardon—with anything Miss Treeves might have to say on the subject." Molly Treeves, sister to Plummergen's Reverend Arthur, had spoken out very forcefully at the time of the original quarrel between the village's pair of would-be Constance Sprys, so that the combatants now no longer dared to hurl face-to-face insults or indulge in slanderous gossip about each other, but rather maintained a state of pointedly armed truce: the sharpness of the point depending on the physical proximity of Miss Treeves. Pantomime Producer to Lady Colveden's Director, Molly had been unable to attend last night's preliminary read-through, leaving her partner to exert every ounce of self-control she could muster throughout two most tortuous hours.

Nigel nodded cheerfully as he spread marmalade. "And, to introduce a biblical note, let me add that Solomon and his Judgement come a very poor second to you, my dear Mother, in your Producer-and-Director role. I should say you turned in the best performance of the lot. Very impressive—and effective. I'd never have dreamed of giving the Fairy Godmother to Mrs. Stillman . . . though she was pretty good as the housewife in that Onion Seller sketch of Mr. Jessyp's, now I come to think of it."

Lady Colveden nodded. "Actually, Mrs. Stillman was our first choice, if she wanted the part, but you know what Mrs. Skinner and Mrs. Henderson can be like if they imagine one of them has a better chance at anything than the other. When neither of them can act to save her life! It wasn't so much Solomon as Agag, if it's Agag I mean. He was the one who walked delicately, wasn't he? Well, I felt exactly like Agag the entire evening."

"It didn't show." Nigel gestured hopefully towards the teapot. His mother lifted it, judged the weight, and nodded. As he passed his cup, her son went on: "Everyone else was happy with the way things worked out, weren't they? Except me, of course, having to nurse a broken heart for love of Emmy Putts—though I suppose you don't care about how ridiculous that makes me look—"

"No, I don't, because it doesn't. It's only a pantomime, for goodness' sake. I don't believe the village will think Emmy's your type any more than they'll think you're hers." Lady Colveden hid a smile. "Poor Emmy—it's typecasting, really. That girl's a born Cinderella, always dreaming of becoming a film star . . . and she has that lovely long blonde wig, too. It will look marvellous under a spotlight . . ."

Nigel's expression fleetingly suggested that he had not found the appearance of Emmeline Putts, reinstated at this year's summer fete to the throne of Miss Plummergen, any more appealing for having worn her crown on top of artificially lengthened and lightened locks which had been skilfully pinned to her original crowning glory, which was short and dark. Nigel was, however, a good sport, and managed to suppress his inevitable groan at the idea of making unrequited love to young Miss Putts on stage, in full view of approximately four hundred and fifty persons, three nights running in Christmas week. He smiled.

"Emmy may not be particular friends with me, but she does get on well with Maureen, doesn't she? Prince Charming on a motorbike might sound slightly odd, to the uninitiated, but—"

"The motorbike isn't Maureen's, as you know very well. It's Wayne's," said Lady Colveden, pouring herself a second cup of tea before remembering to enquire, with a lift of her eyebrows, whether her husband's cup was empty. Nigel gently raised the nearest corner of the *Beacon*, and found that it was. He eased it along the cloth, bypassing cutlery, crockery, and the as-yet-unread copy of *Farmers Weekly* which lay in its path before picking it up to hand to his mother. Sir George emitted a vague grunt which could have been either a magistrate's opinion of those who rode motorbikes, or an expression of thanks; as the *Beacon* remained resolutely in place it was hard to tell. It did, however, move just enough for its evidently enthralled reader to turn another page. Morning was not the best time of day for Major-General Sir George Colveden, Bart, KCB, DSO, JP—as his nearest and dearest had long ago accepted.

"I trust," said Nigel, as he reinserted his father's cup beneath the *Beacon*'s bottom corner, "that Wayne has no plans to play Prince Charming. For one thing, his legs won't look nearly as good as Maureen's in tights, and Prince Charming in black leather simply wouldn't do."

"Nigel, what a ghastly thought." Lady Colveden shuddered. "This pantomime is strictly traditional, and if anyone tries to— to modernise it, both Molly and I will resign in protest. Prince Charming played by a man instead of by the Principal Boy! It doesn't bear thinking about—why," as a strange noise erupted from behind the pages of the *Beacon*, "even your father thinks it would be perfectly dreadful."

The noise came again, proving to be more a chortle of mirth than a snort of exasperation. "Could be a good deal worse," gasped Sir George, choking. "Being modern, I mean. The Ugly Sisters—women . . . two of 'em . . ."

He broke off, unable to say more. Nigel, who like his sire had at times what some might consider a warped sense of humour, pursued the unspoken thought to its logical end, and himself burst out laughing. Lady Colveden gazed from the shaking shoulders of her son to the palpitating pages of the *Beacon*, and suddenly understood why her menfolk had been so stricken.

"George—Nigel! It's very unkind of you to make fun— to . . . to talk about . . . Oh dear, it's too . . . too . . ." And then it was her turn to give way to aristocratic hysterics.

"Too, too bad of us," gurgled Nigel at last, while Lady Colveden fished for her handkerchief and Sir George began unpleating pages creased almost beyond recognition in his frenzied grasp. "Too, too b-bad—as the Hot Cross B-bun herself would no doubt say . . ."

"Nigel, sometimes you can be very wicked." Lady Colveden dried the last few tears, and replaced her handkerchief. "Mrs.

Blaine and Miss Nuttel as the Ugly Sisters—goodness, don't
set me off again . . ."

"Wonder what they'd call themselves." Nigel had sobered
sufficiently to be able to discuss the unlikely casting of the
Lilikot ladies in a voice that was almost steady. "It'd have
to be something in pairs, wouldn't it—like Euthanasia and
Asphyxia, or Valderma and Germolena. I know! How about
Belladonna and Digitalis? No," he amended, before anyone else
could object. "Rather too obviously poisonous, even though—
oh well," as his mother frowned, "perhaps not. Er—how about
Hazel and Almond?"

Miss Erica Nuttel and Mrs. Norah Blaine, who have lived
in Plummergen a dozen years or more, are still unaware that
they are known to the village at large as the Nuts, a nickname
that has evolved in part from their aggressively vegetarian
lifestyle, in part because the pair are, their critics—and indeed
some of their allies—would insist, as nutty as fruitcakes. Mrs.
Blaine, who is plump and given to flashes of temper followed
by long, brooding sulks, is also known as the Hot Cross Bun,
a play on the pet name of Bunny bestowed on her by Miss
Nuttel: who has been referred to, at times, as Nutcrackers.
Nigel's suggestion for suitable names for the Ugly Sisters was,
therefore, more than apposite, even if his choice of players
was not.

"This is a *traditional* pantomime, don't forget." Lady
Colveden smiled. "Dr. Knight and Mr. Jessyp will make
wonderful Dames, I'm sure—and if you'd been listening
last night you'd know that they've already decided to call
themselves Injecta and Instructa. I think that's rather clever."

Dr. Knight, who had retired from Harley Street to take over
Plummergen's Nursing Home, was, like village schoolmaster
Martin Jessyp, a keen member of the Amateur Dramatic Society. Dressed as a hippopotamus, the doctor had sung a rousing
chorus of "Mud" at the recent *Comical Capers* review in aid of
the Organ Fund, while his teaching colleague had written, and
co-starred with the postmaster's wife in, a risqué little dialogue
dealing with the antics of a French onion seller. Mr. Jessyp
had immersed himself in his part, contriving a highly realistic
costume of striped T-shirt, scarlet neckerchief, blue trousers,

and beret, and with an enormous string of onions draped across one shoulder. He had arrived at last night's *Cinderella* rehearsal with the earnest request that all the lady Padders (as the Plummergen Amateur Dramatists were known) would in future save—rather than throw away, stuff in soft toys, or turn into rugs—all their laddered stockings, for the benefit of the enormous bosoms which he and his fellow Dame, Dr. Knight, intended to affect.

Nigel was struck by another inspiration. "Suppose," he gurgled, "Dr. Knight and Mr. Jessyp hadn't been any good. Dad and the Admiral might have suited instead—if you'd managed to persuade them to shave, that is." General Sir George sported a natty little moustache, which, on occasion, he was prepared to grow to wax-pointing length for the purposes of (discreet) fancy dress, while the features of Bernard "Buzzard" Leighton were adorned by a neat, nautical ginger beard. "They could," suggested Nigel, above the protesting huffs of his father and his mother's evident amusement, "have called themselves Balaclava and Trafalgar, couldn't they?"

"Wrong century," said Sir George, hoping his son didn't really think him so ancient. "Catch the Buzzard losing his beard, even for the pantomime! Leave my moustache alone, as well . . . Wouldn't have minded a shot at Baron Stoneybroke, though," he added, with a sigh that shivered the pages of the *Brettenden Beacon* and made Meg Colveden smile. There was a strong sense of the theatrical in her husband, though he kept it well under control out of consideration for the dignity of the bench. A magistrate, he felt, should set an example: but not too much of one. Community spirit was the ticket—providing you didn't indulge to excess . . .

"Well, George, if Charley Mountfitchet decides in the end it isn't a good idea to have the landlord and one of the waitresses missing from his pub every night at exactly the same time, you might just be in with a chance." Lady Colveden smiled again as the *Beacon* trembled, and her husband's embarrassed coughing rose from behind its pages. "Charley says he can really do justice to the Stoneybroke role, the way business seems to have fallen off at the George and Dragon over the past few weeks. But it's odd, when you think about it. I should have said, with the number of reporters we've had around the place—and you know how most of them enjoy a drink, especially when it's on expenses . . ."

"The most recent influx of the Press," Nigel hurried to point out, "was all of two weeks ago, when we had that . . . that spot of bother on Bonfire Night. Things have quietened down no end since then. I doubt whether, even for the sake of Charley's profits, she'd be too willing to stir them up with that umbrella of hers when the season of peace and general goodwill is practically upon us . . ."

There was a thoughtful pause. Lady Colveden said: "But it doesn't seem to matter whether she's willing or not, does it? I mean, whether or not she *intends* to stir things—because they just seem to stir themselves, don't they? When Miss Seeton's on the loose."

"They certainly do," said Nigel, recalling previous occasions when Miss Seeton and her unwitting umbrella had *stirred things up* to a remarkable degree. "So we'd take it as a particular favour, Mother darling, if for the next month you could keep a very tight rein on the Battling Brolly—very tight indeed. Let her occupy herself with designing the posters and scenery, and learning how to use the prompt book just in case—but don't let her anywhere near the props, or the lighting, and certainly not near the star traps. Just for once, I should like a nice, peaceful few weeks with nothing else to do but make public love to Emmeline Putts three nights on the trot . . ."

"Amen to that!" cried Sir George, dropping the *Beacon* in the butter dish. But there came no expostulation from his wife as she watched yellow-gold and newsprint-black mingle in greasy smears: for Lady Colveden had been unsettled by Nigel's frivolous words. She couldn't help wondering whether the pantomime committee had, after all, been wise to involve Miss Seeton quite so closely in the production of *Cinderella* . . .

And she found herself staring at her uneaten portion of toast, silently echoing the fervent prayer of her husband and son for a Christmas free from untoward events—and yet rather fearing that they all three prayed in vain.

chapter

-2-

THE DAYS ARE short in December; the evenings are long, and eminently suited to indoor rather than outdoor pursuits. Pantomime rehearsals—always provided that the road to the rehearsal room is not blocked by blizzard or flood or fallen tree—are a splendid way of passing the time in the run-up to Christmas, with its many attendant festivities and social occasions. No more than three weeks after the previous conversation, *Cinderella* was well on the way to taking shape, and those Padders who had failed to win the parts for which they had auditioned were beginning to brood about such failure with less intensity, and to dispute the director's decisions with less vim.

About one part there had been no brooding, and not even a hint of dispute. Who else but Miss Maynard—almost fully recovered from her recent bad back—should play Fairy Crystal? As deputy teacher to Mr. Jessyp's head, she was one of the very few—other than their parents—Plummergenites who had the slightest control over the village schoolchildren; and the wise pantomime producer will use plenty of children. Children, after all, have older friends, and families, less financially embarrassed than themselves, only too happy to pay to watch their cherished treasures dance and strut their hour upon the stage . . .

Fairy Crystal was always onstage when such dancing and strutting took place, beating discreet time with her wand or using it to point when some overanxious elf missed a step. At the request of Lady Colveden and Miss Treeves, Alice

Maynard, whose musical abilities were highly thought of in the little community, had strung together a few popular classics in a tuneful piano medley and recorded them on tape, to be played over the loudspeakers of the village hall during performances, and to be used for rehearsals during free periods at school. She worked out a few simple steps, sorted the children into groups according to height rather than age, and taught the entire school the same basic routine, with minor variations from group to group, depending on which music was being used at the time. The different costumes, she agreed with Miss Treeves and Lady Colveden, were sure to hide from all but the most observant eyes the very makeshift nature of the fairy interludes . . .

Scene One: A Woodland Glade. On tripped Fairy Crystal, followed by a train of excited little ones who shuffled into more or less their right places about the maypole and grasped their ribbons with sticky hands. Miss Maynard flourished her wand, stepped forward, and addressed the audience.

> "No empty talk, no mighty paradoxes
> Shall puzzle pit, or gallery, or boxes—
> Tonight we act, in simple prose and rhyme
> Our good old, joyous English pantomime.
> We tell a tale you've doubtless heard before,
> Though none the worse for that, I'm certain sure.
> I wave my wand—let it not be in vain:
> Beneath my spell, be children all again!"

Another flourish, and from the wings came the tinkle of Fairy Crystal's tape, worked by Admiral Leighton: who, with the assistance of Sir George, had volunteered for the twin duties of Lighting and Sound. While the music played, the fairies threaded, as skilfully as three weeks of practice would allow, their path around the maypole until they had twined themselves into the central lovers' knot with fewer mistakes than might have been expected from children so young. Grouped prettily about the maypole base, they sang a little song guaranteed to have every parent in the audience reaching for proud handkerchiefs, then let fall their ribbons, tried not to giggle, and made

their exit in Fairy Crystal's wake as the Broker's Men entered
from the other side of the stage . . .

There is much more to the art of panto than just the storyline.
There must be terrible puns, and topical allusions; there must
be popular songs, and speciality acts which may have nothing
at all to do with the plot; there must be double entendres and
personal comment and in-jokes to help the audience enjoy
themselves even more. Making Plummergen's Constable Potter and his Ashford colleague, Detective Constable Foxon, play
the parts of Jasper and Marmaduke was sure to raise one of
the loudest laughs of the evening, and Lady Colveden never
ceased to congratulate herself on her selection . . .

The Broker's Men entered from the left, in accordance with
the theatrical tradition that "good" always enters from the
right, and proceeded to bemoan the fact that they were lost
in the middle of a wood, miles from anywhere, with no idea
how much farther it might be to their destination. PC Potter,
who had sung "A Policeman's Lot Is Not a Happy One" to
great acclaim in *Comical Capers*, warbled to the same tune
a mournful ditty about blisters, while Foxon (who couldn't
sing a note to save his life) hammed it up frantically at his
side before both headed for a stream—in the wings—to cool
their feet, leaving the stage clear for the entrance of Injecta
and Instructa.

The Ugly Sisters were as pleasing a contrast as one could
wish to see. Dr. Knight was a jovial man who had filled his
hippopotamus suit with the need for hardly any extra padding;
Mr. Jessyp was of slight build and medium height, precise
in both his habits and his normal appearance. As Instructa,
however, he sported outlandish pince-nez on the end of a
nose he intended, on the night, to extend with putty, and
proposed forcing his wiry frame into an exaggerated S-shape
of bust and bustle once a sufficiency of laddered hose had
been accumulated. His costume, he insisted, should be in
pedagogic shades of grey, black and white, the only hint of
colour in his appearance the tumultuous scarlet wig he had
elected to wear.

Injecta was to have an even larger bust than her sister,
and hair of similar fiery hue, styled in enormous corkscrew

curls. As a finishing touch, Dr. Knight had persuaded Martha Bloomer to make him a Red Cross cap, which would only be removed—Pantomime Dames often wear a different outfit for each appearance—when a tiara was required for the ball-room scene. Both men looked forward to enjoying themselves immensely on the night, and threw themselves into rehearsals with a will.

They entered now, squabbling as the Ugly Sisters have squabbled since pantomime began.

"Carrots! Carrots! You've got red hair!" And Injecta tugged at Instructa's Titian curls—Martha Bloomer had unravelled a monumental woollen sweater—before slapping cheeks which on public evenings would be heavily made up.

"Carrots yourself, you beast!" Instructa roundly boxed her sister's ears. "There's nothing wrong with having red hair—and even if there is, I can't help it any more than you can. It's hair-red-itary!"

The wrangle continued. Injecta was spiteful, her tongue as sharp as her needle namesake. Instructa, between flashes of temper, sulked. Lady Colveden, watching from the floor of the hall, giggled as she always did, then wondered yet again whether she ought to suggest, as tactfully as possible, that Mr. Jessyp might water down his imitation of Mrs. Norah Blaine, Dr. Knight his impression of Miss Erica Nuttel. But, as always, she decided that the Nuts would never recognise themselves: people who were caricatured so publicly seldom did, especially when it was so very over the top, and (Lady Colveden giggled again) so very, very funny . . .

The Ugly Sisters lurched at last into a bitter, off-key duet in which they insulted each other with most ingenious rhymes, then flounced to opposite ends of a fallen treetrunk to sit facing firmly in opposite directions. There followed a nifty little bit of stage "business" whereby the treetrunk, lying across a broken branch, behaved as a seesaw, with the slighter Instructa Jessyp being catapulted up into the flies—more ingenuity, also courtesy of Admiral Leighton—three times before the heavyweight Injecta settled herself in comfort.

Into the brooding silence came the Broker's Men once more, their aching feet soothed by the offstage stream, refreshed and

ready to be about their business. The Ugly Sisters, observing
them, expressed their delight in tones audible to everyone
except Marmaduke and Jasper. Men! Two of them, as well—
one each! But so very shy . . . too shy to approach face-to-
face—such good manners! And talking of *courting,* too—what
could be better than that?

The Broker's Men gave tongue in praise of their work,
which they enjoyed above everything else. Serving writs on
people, taking them to court—what could be better than that?
Jasper and Marmaduke were plainly oblivious to the echoing
counterpoint of the Ugly Sisters on their treetrunk, from which
they now rose at the same time—the seesaw effect twice, the
Dames had agreed, would have quite ruined the joke—and
headed with rapacious arms outstretched for the still-unwitting
Broker's Men. They heard Jasper and Marmaduke speak of
Stoneybroke Hall; they announced, with pleased surprise, that
this was their home. They did not properly take in the Broker's
Men's remark that Stoneybroke in name was Stoneybroke in
fact, and that by the time they'd done their work and handed
over their writ the Baron would be lucky to have two farthings
to rub together . . .

Courting—rubbing along together—asking for hands . . . it
was clear to the Ugly Sisters that Marmaduke and Jasper had
been instantly smitten with their charms, and were about to ask
their father for permission to marry them. This permission they
would, naturally, give . . .

Their squeals of maiden modesty penetrated the hitherto
deaf ears of Jasper and Marmaduke, who blinked, froze, did
a double-take, and ducked desperately beneath the approaching
rapacious embraces to escape, babbling of the only *safe* place
being *a bank,* to the wings . . .

Cinderella was indeed taking shape very well. Miss Treeves
and Lady Colveden expressed themselves publicly as far less
unhappy with the production than they might have been; and
members of the cast began to browbeat or blackmail their
nearest and dearest into buying tickets or, at the very least,
into promising to do so.

There was, of course, the usual rivalry among the Padders
as to who would sell the most tickets, and much grumbling that

Emmy Putts, in the title role, had what her fellow thespians considered an unfair advantage over everyone else. Working in the post office as she did, Emmy needed to make no great effort to entrap prospective purchasers: no knocking on doors for Cinderella, no waylaying people in their gardens or claiming the next seat on the twice-weekly Brettenden bus for the purposes of blandishment and cajolery and the application of moral force. Miss Putts, without stirring from her daily place of employment, could almost guarantee to encounter the entire ticket-buying populace of Plummergen within a week, for the village is deeply conservative in its habits. Though it does not scorn to shop at the butcher's, the baker's, the draper's, or the grocer's, it is Mr. Stillman's post office—with its larger floor area and its wider range of goods—which is the preferred location not only for the acquiring of life's little necessities, but for the exchange of gossip and the swapping of scandal as well: or, failing scandal, for the exchange of ordinary news . . .

As on the morning after a particularly successful pantomime rehearsal. Foxon, as Jasper, had introduced a series of elegant somersaults in order to escape the affections of Injecta; Potter, as Marmaduke, had been given an additional joke, concerning the invisible stream in which he and his colleague had cooled their weary feet, to follow his frantic cries about banks and places of safety. The whole cast was starting to feel more than confident, and Cinderella brandished books of tickets in a meaningful way.

"Talking of banks," said Mrs. Skinner, brooding defiantly on cheese rather than choosing to catch Emmy's eye, "there's that new manager over to Brettenden—I'll take three-quarters of a pound of Cheddar, and mind it's no more'n half an ounce either way on the scales, Emmy Putts—really gone and put young Jestin's nose out of joint, they say."

"Worked there since leaving school, so he has," said Mrs. Spice. "And allus put in for his bit of promotion when the chance come along—can't blame the lad for wanting to better hisself, can you? And along comes this new bloke—oh, I think it's a crying shame!"

Everyone agreed that you couldn't, and that it certainly was. The voice of Mrs. Skinner (had she not been the one to raise the topic in the first place?) prevailed above all other. "Well, if you ask me, he should've stood more'n a *chance* of it this time, too, being chief cashier already—not quite so much as that, thanking you, Emmeline—only what do the high-ups do but bring in some furriner nobody's ever seen before! It don't make sense, to my way of thinking . . . And I suppose that'll have to do, if you can't cut it no closer, though I'm sure I don't know how the recipe'll turn out now with it being under like that—no, nothing else today, ta." And Mrs. Skinner averted her gaze from the pantomime tickets young Miss Putts had pushed casually forward with the cheese over the counter.

Mrs. Henderson said at once: "I'll take three tickets, Emmy love, now you've time—and a pound of Cheddar, but not to worry if it goes a bit off the scale—oh, and a box of cream crackers, as well. And if it comes to making sense, I'd've thought anyone oughter know you don't put youngsters like Perce Jestin in top jobs, not with all that money lying about, a regular responsibility, I should think. Not till they've proved theirselves proper, which you can't say as he's rightly done, only having the job in the first place on account of that chap as embezzled the funds all them years ago, and strangled his fancy piece over to Ashford . . ."

Mrs. Skinner smirked. "Well, if it isn't *proving yourself* to've stopped him strangling a Certain Other Party of our acquaintance as well as that Polstead female, then I'd like to know what is!"

Her look spoke more than could be expressed in a hundred words, though there was no need now of even one. The entire post office knew the identity of Mrs. Skinner's *Certain Other Party*, though the tale of Miss Seeton's little adventure had become garbled over the years, as tales in Plummergen are wont to do, despite the case having been widely reported at the time. It had caused a sensation when the chief cashier of Brettenden's City and Suburban Bank, having faked his own death and murdered his mistress, in brazen disguise then entered the branch from which he had absconded and came upon Miss Seeton, quietly queueing to deposit a cheque. The cashier had, it is true, applied subterfuge and untruth to persuade Miss Seeton to ride with him in his car to the

country house previously purchased from his ill-gotten gains—
but he had never had any thought, despite the assertions of
Mrs. Skinner, of strangling his victim. He had simply lured
her up to the roof, planning to push her over the low parapet:
a plan which the providential arrival of the police had thwarted,
though Miss Seeton herself never realised that she had been in
any danger.

A general muttering greeted Mrs. Skinner's remark, and
it was tacitly conceded that she had won this point. Mrs.
Henderson tossed her head, and told Emmy she'd asked for
one pound, not two, and she'd thank her to slice it a bit more
careful in future, and about those tickets she wasn't quite so
sure, with time to think it over and not knowing which was the
best night. She supposed she'd be in later, when she'd made
up her mind . . .

Mrs. Skinner, observing her rival start to retreat, smirked
all the more; but then Mrs. Henderson, remembering, rallied.
"Furriner nobody's seen?" she remarked, returning to finger
Emmy's pile of tickets with a careless finger. Mrs. Henderson
had been in the Brettenden branch of the City and Suburban
last market day at what she now realised must have been a
most (for her purposes) propitious time. "I can't for the life
of me make out how nobody could miss *seeing* that great
moustache, and his hair all slicked down with oil the way it
was—ah, and the watch-chain across his stomach, too. More
like a manager than young Jestin'll ever look, to my mind,
for all he's a furriner and Perce is Brettenden born and bred.
Trouble with these youngsters is, they want everything far too
soon, for my liking, before they know what's what. But mark
my words, our money'll be safer nor it's ever been, locked
away in the bank . . ."

chapter
-3-

"BANKS," REMARKED A weary voice in an office on the ump-teenth floor of New Scotland Yard, "are not as safe as once they were. Given the events of the past few weeks, I am sorely tempted to remove my modest savings and stuff them inside an old sock." The voice hesitated, sighed, and added: "Or perhaps a mattress. Either hiding place must, I feel sure, be preferable to the so-called security currently on offer from our financial institutions."

Having made which startling announcement, Detective Chief Superintendent Delphick slammed shut the latest bulky folder, sighed again, scribbled his initials on the cover, and tossed it on top of the teetering heap of official documentation already crowding his in-tray. It landed with an ominous thump. The Oracle did not move as the heap of jumbo-sized files teetered still more, hesitated, and then with its own, monumental sigh of rustling paper, spilled in a slow cascade from the heights of the wire basket to spread itself all over his desk.

"Damn," said Delphick, watching the avalanche with fatal-istic calm. "Now look at what I've made me do. Tut, tut, how very careless."

Detective Sergeant Bob Ranger, who had glanced up from his own paperwork as Delphick uttered that initial despairing remark, had watched with wide-eyed amazement and dismay his chief's apparently unheeding action, and the chaos which resulted from it.

"Sir," ventured Bob, once the paper at last seemed to have stopped advancing, and the pink of Delphick's blotter was completely buried, "do you—excuse me—feel all right, sir? A spot of flu coming on, or something?"

It was, after all, the middle of December; germs which had lain dormant during the summer, and had flexed their waking muscles warily throughout the autumn, were now at the height of their sinister powers, and making their presence felt wherever anyone looked. Bob's wife, Anne, daughter of a doctor and herself the nurse/receptionist in a group medical practice, reported daily on the lengthening queues of sniffers and sneezers who appeared at the surgery, on the growing band of croakers and coughers who telephoned for personal visits.

"If you're not feeling well, sir—"

"I am not sickening for influenza, thank you, Sergeant." Delphick favoured his anxious subordinate with a bleak look. "I am, in fact, in the rudest of health." He cleared his throat experimentally, took a deep breath, and slapped himself twice across the chest. "Hear that? Clear as a bell, Bob. No need to fuss over me—I feel perfectly well—or rather, no, I don't. I feel," confessed the Oracle, subsiding, "thoroughly fed up, as I'm sure you must, too. It is a wearisome thing indeed to be the sole prop and stay of an ailing metropolitan constabulary . . ."

With his loudest sigh so far, he leaned forward, pushed both his hands in a scooping motion against the base of the invasive documentation, and thrust the whole heap away from himself with so much force that it shot, blotter and in-tray and all, over the farthest edge of the desk to the floor.

Bob, staring, was speechless. The Oracle, he knew, had never been much of a one for paperwork; but chucking it all over the floor was—well, was taking things a bit too far. Besides (the sergeant's gloomy thoughts all too quickly added) what was the betting it wasn't going to be His Nibs who ended up collecting the scattered bumf and stuffing it back in the right folders . . .

Delphick and Bob had worked together for many years. It didn't need an Oracle to guess what must be going through the sergeant's mind as he gaped across at the litter of paper and cardboard on the carpet. The chief superintendent burst out laughing at his expression.

"My word, I feel better for letting off a little steam." He exhaled luxuriously, stretched, then slowly pushed back his chair and strolled to the front of the desk to survey the wreckage at his feet, the smile still lingering in his grey eyes. "No, Bob," as Sergeant Ranger, blinking, shook himself and prepared to rise. "This mess is entirely my fault, and mine, therefore, must be the hand which sorts it out. You've enough reports of your own to struggle through, heaven knows—or rather," stooping from his great height to start sweeping the scattered files into a more manageable heap, "enough reports belonging to, or at least originating from, other people. As, of course, have I—which is not the least of our problems . . ."

He rose, and stirred the riot of files and folders with a thoughtful foot. "Comrades in adversity, Bob, that's what we are—not so much Seven Against Thebes as Two Against Germs." Pleased at the witticism, he bent again, chuckling, to his now-tranquil sorting of the violently unsorted files. "Two Against Microbes, maybe—or maybe against Bugs? What causes influenza, do you know—a bacterium, or a virus?"

He scooped his first selection back up to the desk, dusted his hands, and looked decidedly pleased with himself. "Bacteria, or viruses—vira—virids? It is a common error, Sergeant Ranger, to suppose that *bacteria* is the singular. It is not, of course."

"Of course, sir," mumbled Bob, bewildered, as Delphick gathered up more documents and dropped them on the desk with but a cursory glance. If it hadn't been the middle of winter, he'd have said the Oracle must have got a touch of the sun. Perhaps, despite his denials, he *was* sickening for the flu, and this weird carry-on was because he was running a temperature and'd gone light-headed . . .

Bob left his desk and tried to appear unobtrusive as he made his way across to assist in the final scoopings. Unobtrusiveness, for someone standing six-foot-seven in his socks with breadth in proportion, wasn't easy, but the Oracle's loyal sidekick did his best: he had to find out if the Old Man was radiating excess body heat or hiding shivers he wouldn't want ordinary people to know about, seeing the Yard was already so short-staffed with the pre-Christmas epidemic and he'd feel guilty about dumping even more work on his hard-pressed sergeant . . .

The sergeant pressed as close to his superior as decency would permit, gathering more folders in one huge hand than Delphick could manage in two: and shook his head, baffled. The Oracle was neither hot, nor shivering: he wasn't clammy with perspiration, nor scarlet-faced from fever—though the healthy pink flush of one who has been stooping and lifting gave Bob a few uneasy moments before he realised its cause. He dropped the final folders on the chief superintendent's desk, and turned with a baffled shake of the head back towards his own.

Delphick stopped him. "Thanks, Bob, though you really needn't have bothered—I told you, I enjoyed that." Sergeant Ranger ventured a quizzical lift of the eyebrows which his superior did not miss. "And I haven't, in case you were wondering, suddenly gone stark staring bonkers—although if we're lumbered with any more of this routine stuff I've no doubt I soon shall—but, as a safety valve, I would definitely recommend a little mild documentary deconstruction, as opposed to destruction, from time to time . . ."

The Oracle chuckled, waving his sergeant to the visitors' chair, himself taking his rightful seat. He said nothing more for a while, but began to sort through the muddle of files and folders, starting by turning them all the same way round. Bob, in silence, watched him.

"Soothing," murmured Delphick at last, as he checked cover reference numbers and made the occasional note. "From order to chaos, and back again—what might be called the palindromic overview of life . . . And it was an overview I wanted, Bob." Suddenly, he was entirely serious. "A different view, anyway—like shaking the pieces in a kaleidoscope and finding the most pleasing pattern. Since there was no pattern, whether pleasing or otherwise, that either you or I could discern despite all this tedious study—what I might call this boring poring . . ."

He permitted himself a dry chuckle, then continued his task of reconstruction by setting one disordered file neatly upon another while Bob, realising the truth behind the uncharacteristic behaviour, leaned back in his chair with a sigh of relief to watch.

He ventured his own chuckle, less dry and more thankful, as Delphick began to disappear behind an edifice of folders erected four-square on his blotter. "If you build that much higher, sir, you won't get a . . . a proper overview, not without standing on tiptoe, anyway."

Delphick grunted an absent acknowledgement, added one more folder to the pile, pushed the whole heap warily to one side, and began another. "I hate paperwork," he remarked.

The rawest recruit would have known that after less than five minutes working for the Oracle: Sergeant Ranger had had eight years. "Er—yes, sir. But . . . well, it's got to be done—and as you said yourself, there don't seem to be that many people left in the place to do it—"

In one pithy sentence, Delphick gave Bob his views on the general health of Scotland Yard, and then pointed out that he—and his sergeant—were supposed to be policemen, not pen-pushers. Their job was to go out catching crooks, not—he brandished the latest file, and added it glumly to the others—to read their blasted biographies . . .

Bob thought he might risk it. He grinned. "Couldn't agree more, sir, but with what feels like half the building home sick, and not making any sense on the telephone when we try talking to 'em, there's not much else we can really do, is there? Except, well, to read the reports and try to make sense of 'em—and then, perhaps it's a sort of compliment, sir. To have been asked, I mean, when it isn't really a chief super's job unless somebody's been killed, which they haven't—so far," he had to add, uneasily wondering whether he'd tempted Fate with his words.

Delphick dropped the final report on top of his second heap, surveyed both through narrowed eyes, sighed, and shook his head. "Nothing," he announced, with yet another sigh. "I had, you may have inferred from my—perhaps unorthodox—actions, hoped for inspiration to strike—but all that my efforts appear to have achieved is further confirmation that I would rather be out on the streets chasing chummies than sit going through report after report which, to all intents and purposes, might have been written about precisely the same crime each time. Only the names," he added, with a frown, "have been changed. To protect the innocent? Goodness alone knows." He picked up the sheet of paper on which he had, from time to time, scribbled his notes.

"The method would appear to be identical in every case. One gang member waits in the getaway car, which is almost invariably a stolen Ford Escort—dark blue for preference, though black has been used on occasion. Two of this gentleman's colleagues, wearing masks and armed with sawn-off shotguns, threaten bank staff and customers respectively, while the fourth member of the gang, also masked, loads his two haversacks with loot while the others keep watch—and there," throwing down the paper in disgust, "you have it, Bob. The same old story, all-too-successfully repeated all too often. And no leads that anyone—including us, working our trousers to the bone for hour after interminable hour—is able to ascertain."

There was a thoughtful silence. Bob broke it. "I can't help feeling a bit sorry for the manager of that City and Suburban done last week, sir. What was it he said? The sixth time in two years, so now they're going to close the branch completely."

Delphick shrugged. "Comes of picking a prime site on a corner of a three-way traffic junction with another junction not fifty yards away. It isn't only the legitimate customers who are attracted to the premises—the chummies planning their getaway realise all too soon that they're spoiled for choice . . ." He stretched, and smothered a yawn. "Dear me. I suspect I'm starting to sound callous, Bob. Boredom has set in with a vengeance, and is bringing out the very worst in my character—which, with the season of goodwill almost upon us, seems hardly an attitude to be encouraged in a senior police officer . . ."

He stared at the reports in their individual heaps, and his hands, tempted, twitched: but he managed to resist temptation. After a moment, he chuckled. "So much for my hopes that a different overview would either produce a new angle for investigation, or at the least a modicum of mental relaxation. I'm as tired—or depressed—or uninspired—now as I was before.

We must consign these reports to temporary oblivion, Bob, in hopes that some underworld whisper will lead us to the truth before serious injuries or death should occur; and for now we will return to more pressing matters."

Bob, for once, did not respond to his superior's hints. Instead of pushing back his chair and heading for his desk, he frowned in thought. He said slowly:

"Talking of Christmas, sir . . ."

"Your leave—untoward occurrences or an intensification of the influenza epidemic always excepted—is assured, Sergeant Ranger. As, I devoutly trust, is mine, although one is always, of course, at the mercy of the telephone." Delphick favoured the instrument on his desk with a warning frown. "Will you be spending the holiday with your parents, or Anne's?"

"It's my sister's turn to stay with my parents, sir, so Anne and I are, er, going down to Kent." Delphick promptly diverted his attentions from the telephone, and sat up, his eyes narrowing. Bob forged gamely on. "Anne's father's one of the Ugly Sisters in the village pantomime, sir—they're doing *Cinderella*— and Anne seems to have been volunteered to help with the makeup, so—"

"No, Bob. Absolutely not." Bob tried his best to look bewildered, and failed. Delphick glared. "I said, Sergeant Ranger, that we must return to matters more pressing than shotgun robberies. So far, there has been no loss of life, and you should, after so long, be well aware that the work of this office is more normally concerned with murder than with . . . with mere mercenary machination. The very idea that we should involve others than ourselves in attempts to solve what has so far eluded our best efforts . . ."

As he ran out of steam, Bob tried again. "Well, sir, we *are* stumped—you said so yourself. And you also said you'd been trying for a . . . a different view, remember. Well, nobody could ever say Miss Seeton's view of life isn't as different as anyone's could possibly be—"

"No, Bob. Not this time." Delphick strove for a tone combining cool reason with dire warning. "Think, not just of my nerves, and yours, but of those of everyone who might happen to be in the fallout area when the worst occurs. Christmas,

Sergeant Ranger, is the season for peace on earth and goodwill to all men—not that I'm for an instant denying Miss Seeton's general goodwill. Far from it, indeed: I sometimes wish she were slightly less inclined to believe the best of everyone, no matter what the circumstances. But my idea of goodwill to all men would be to spare them the innocent attentions of Miss Seeton and her brolly for just a few days; and as to *peace*, now—I should say, given her past form, that anything less peaceful than Miss Seeton on one of her excursions would be hard to find."

He shook his head, and became even more grave. "Added to which, Bob, may I remind you that there has, so far, been no loss of life—but that criminals who parade sawn-off shotguns always present the possibility that they will, on some future occasion, use them. While not denying that Miss Seeton has a remarkably robust guardian angel—some of her escapes would be incredible in a work of detective fiction—I would nevertheless not care to risk involving her, unless absolutely necessary, in a case which could just be the time when the guardian angel's armour plating springs a leak, or blows a fuse, or whatever the technical term might be. Our tame art expert should be saved for more recherché crimes, Bob, where the risk is less and the rewards greater . . ."

He laughed. "Anyway, the Plummergen Pantomime Committee would tear me limb from limb if I removed MissEss from their immediate vicinity at any time during the next few weeks. My spies, remember, are everywhere—and they tell me that, with Miss Maynard's metamorphosis on a regular basis into Fairy Crystal, and Mr. Jessyp's transformation into Instructa the Ugly Sister, Miss Seeton has returned to her old employment and is teaching at the village school to give her colleagues ample opportunity to learn their lines and rehearse their parts. For once, Bob, we must try to solve a crime without the undoubtedly invaluable help of Miss Emily Dorothea Seeton . . .

"Although I can't help wondering, now that you've raised the possibility, whether we'll be able to manage it . . ."

chapter

-4-

As for Miss Emily Dorothea Seeton, she—as might have been expected by her friends and acquaintances—had no idea that her discreet person and equally—in her eyes, if not those of the aforementioned friends and acquaintances—discreet activities—activities which, ignoring all evidence to the contrary, she persists in believing are no more unusual than those of any other English gentlewoman—were at this time of particular interest to a pair of Scotland Yard detectives. However, utterly unlike any other English gentlewoman, had Miss Seeton learned of the Yard's interest it would not have surprised her in the least.

Miss Seeton is a remarkable, not to say unique, personality in the annals of detection. Now retired from her former post as a teacher of art, she brought herself first to the notice of the police when, having spent a peaceful summer's evening at the opera, she encountered a young thug indulging in less than courteous behaviour towards his female companion. Miss Seeton remonstrated with him for this discourtesy by employing the point of her umbrella to the small of his back, never dreaming that she had interrupted not so much a minor skirmish as a fatal stabbing. Her brief glimpse of the fleeing Cesar Lebel, reproduced on paper at the request of Superintendent (as he then was) Delphick, led to instant recognition of the murderer, attended by a long and complicated case before he was finally trapped, through Miss Seeton's own innocent actions, in Miss Seeton's own under-stairs cupboard.

The following spring, Miss Seeton became embroiled in a further long and complicated case concerned with—among other matters—a series of burglaries and a number of child murders, neither of which could have been solved without her artistic endeavours; in the autumn a third case, involving witchcraft and a sinister religious cult, resulted in Delphick's arranging, at the insistence of Sir Hubert Everleigh, Assistant Commissioner (Crime), to have Miss Seeton co-opted into the constabulary. It seemed to everyone (except, of course, to Miss Seeton, who remained in a state of blissful ignorance about the chaos her previous antics had caused) safer, as well as cheaper, to have her officially attached to the force rather than risk having her run around brandishing an unsupervised brolly, innocently stirring up trouble for all concerned.

Now on permanent retainer to Scotland Yard as an Art Consultant, Miss Seeton humbly regards herself as no more than an IdentiKit artist. She is, of course, entirely mistaken in this regard: her importance to her constabulary colleagues is immeasurable. Whenever a case has (in Delphick's own words) a recherché element—whenever the police confess themselves baffled—it is then that the telephone will ring, or a detective arrive on the doorstep of Miss Seeton's cottage (Sweetbriars, in the village of Plummergen, in the county of Kent). And Miss Seeton, as a paid employee (albeit part-time) of the Metropolitan Police, listens dutifully to the detective's tale—is perhaps escorted to the scene of the crime, or studies photographs of the evidence—and in due course will modestly offer what she can never quite understand is considered by her colleagues her expert opinion, in the form of one of her lightning sketches or strangely inspired drawings . . . whose inspiration she never quite understands, and of which—it being so strange—she is always a little ashamed.

But Miss Seeton currently had no cause to be ashamed of her activities, for her assistance in the matter of the Plummergen Pantomime was rightly, and vociferously, valued. A less self-effacing soul than Emily Dorothea Seeton might have become conceited at the words of praise and gratitude which were showered upon her from all sides; but Miss Seeton merely blushed, and smiled, and murmured that it was indeed a great pleasure for her to be able to repay, in some small way, the many kindnesses shown her as a relative newcomer to the little community.

She sat now in the village hall, the promptbook on her knee, her pencil in her hand, as she jotted down variations in the lines and acting business as directed by Lady Colveden or suggested by appropriate members of the cast.

Baron Stoneybroke bustled into the woodland glade and came, breathlessly, upon his stepdaughters, bewailing the loss of the Broker's Men and blaming each other for their flight. The Baron, whose habitual helplessness in the face of so monstrous a regiment of women had been somewhat modified by Charley Mountfitchet—after all, was Prince Maureen not employed by him at the George and Dragon? No need to give the girl ideas that he was too soft a touch—roundly scolded Instructa and Injecta for squabbling, and asked them where their sister Cinderella might be.

Injecta tossed her head. "Off looking for kindling, of course. How can anyone be expected to have a decent cup of tea if the water isn't boiling properly—and how can they make toast without a fire?"

"Remember, Papa," chimed in Instructa, "it was your idea to dine al fresco, not ours. Dragging us out to this too, too horrid dirty old wood when—"

"Alf Rescoe?" Injecta turned upon the Baron. "Really, Papa, does this mean you've invited a *man* to share our picnic, and you didn't tell me? But you seem to have told Instructa—oh, it's not fair! If I'd known that Mr. Rescoe was coming too, I could have worn my very best dress!"

Before the startled Baron could reply, Instructa winked at the audience for her sister's ignorance, rolled her eyes, and adopted a pedagogic pose, peering over the gold-framed spectacles perched on the tip of her nose. "I never knew, sister dear, that you think I look so utterly adorable you have to be jealous of me—even when I'm wearing my everyday clothes, not my best. Too flattering for words!" Mr. Jessyp twirled daintily on one foot, simpered, then wagged an instructive finger at which Injecta scowled.

"Al fresco merely means *in the open air*, you juggins—too silly of you." Instructa's eyes gleamed like blackcurrants behind those gold-rimmed glasses as her sister sulked and pouted. "In this horrid dirty wood," went on Mr. Jessyp, "who could possibly want to wear her best dress and risk having it ruined? Cinderella should count herself lucky she doesn't need to worry about her clothes the way we do. I'm sure the brambles have snagged my nylons . . ."

She hitched up her petticoats to reveal a be-gartered calf boasting black-and-white striped stockings, full of holes, and flourished a froth of invisible lace which (Mr. Jessyp had already assured Lady Colveden) would look very well by the night of the dress rehearsal. Injecta, jumping back as the lace whipped past her nose, knowing she would find it hard to score over her sister, vented her annoyance on the poor Baron.

"You know I hate having to agree with Instructa, Papa, but I simply must, because for once she's right. This *is* a horrid dirty wood—it isn't nearly as comfortable as Stoneybroke Hall. Why on earth did you drag us all the way out here, when we could have eaten just as well at home?" She kicked crossly at the picnic basket on the ground. "If not better— because until that lazy Cinderella's lit the fire, everything's cold, when there's a lovely warm stove in the scullery back at Stoneybroke Hall. I'm sure Cinderella's being so slow from sheer spite, because she didn't want to come out in the fresh air when she could be sitting around toasting her toes." The Baron opened his mouth to protest, but was overridden as Injecta stormed on:

"Or, if you really didn't want to eat in the Hall, we could easily have gone to the George and Dragon. Even *their* food is better than stewed tea and soggy toast over a smoky camp fire, once it's been lit at last . . ."

Baron Charley Mountfitchet, landlord of Plummergen's leading hostelry, counted ten for audience laughter before going on to explain that, as he'd lost so much money of late, he was hoping to arrange in advance a Royal Pardon for the bankruptcy notice he very much feared was about to be served on him. Prince Charming and his court (he told the suddenly interested Injecta and Instructa) were rumoured to be holidaying in a hunting lodge nearby; and, if they should happen to come upon a happy family picnic, they might well wish to join

in the fun and frolic—the Baron cut a festive caper—and have
their royal hearts so softened that, by the time the Broker's
Men found their prospective victim, it would be too late . . .

"It *is* too late," came an awful interruption from the wings.
On marched Marmaduke and Jasper, trying not to limp,
brandishing enormous (and as yet invisible) parchment writs.
"Now, talking of *courts*," the horrified Baron was informed,
"we've just come from one—so here's a writ, wrote just for
you—and it's all perfectly legal," said PC Marmaduke Potter,
as Baron Mountfitchet recoiled in dismay. "D'you think I'm
so daft I don't know nothing about the due processes of the
law? Go on, take it!" And Marmaduke thrust his parchment
into the baron's unhappy hands.

"And take this!" cried Jasper Foxon, following suit. The Baron recoiled still further. "Take this!" repeated Jasper, viciously
pursuing his victim as he tried to shuffle backwards.

"And this!" echoed Marmaduke, entering into the spirit of
the thing: which so startled the Baron that he tripped on an
offshoot twig of the same log his daughters had used as a
seesaw. With a despairing cry, he tumbled to the ground. The
Broker's Men, pressing on with their pursuit, tripped in similar
fashion, but rather than tumble to the ground they performed
elaborate contortions so that they ended up, not on top of the
Baron, but sitting astride the log. Foxon's acrobatic abilities
and Potter's stolid presence here resulted in a pleasing little
interlude which ended when, satisfied their writs had been
properly served, Jasper and Marmaduke suddenly observed
the predatory approach of the Ugly Sisters, panicked, and
catapulted themselves, one after the other, into the wings either
side of the stage, pursued severally by Injecta and Instructa.

The Baron, still stunned from his fall, lay by the log in a daze.
This meant that when Buttons—played by Nigel Colveden in a
pillbox hat, a high-collared jacket and trousers with stripes down
the seams—entered for his soliloquy, he was uninterrupted.
Poor Buttons, with sighs and groans, lamented the unrequited
love he bore for Cinderella, praised her goodness and beauty
and gentle kindness, and only wished there were more he could
do to make life easy for her when the whole family treated her
with such cruelty. Her ignorant sisters (he said) he supposed

weren't as much to blame—being simply stepsisters—and how very simple (he interposed with a wink) they were—as her father, who'd had the good fortune to know Cinderella her whole life long and still didn't appreciate her . . .

This stern denunciation broke through the Baron's cloud of unconsciousness, and he awoke, to berate Buttons for being so uncomplimentary about his employer.

"Uncomplimentary, I agree," Buttons told him. "But *employer?*" His tone was incredulous, his expression scornful. "Says who? You can't *employ* people unless you pay them—and you haven't paid me for at least six months. Look!" He dragged the pockets of his trousers inside-out, and showed them to be completely empty. "Not a sausage! In fact," as he darted to the picnic basket and began rummaging within, "since we're talking of *sausages*, perhaps I'll find a string or two here—they'd be a good deal better than nothing at all, which is what I've been getting from you. If anyone says you *employ* me, then I say he's a liar, because you certainly don't—"

"No, I certainly don't," broke in the Baron. "You're fired, you cheeky young jackanapes!"

"Then you can pay me six months' money in lieu of notice," retorted Buttons brightly, slamming down the lid of the picnic basket and jumping to his feet, his outstretched hand thrust under the Baron's startled nose. "A nice little lump sum like that should be just about enough to set me up on a farm somewhere—I think I'd make a good farmer. After putting up with your stepdaughters, cows and pigs would make a pleasant change . . ."

Nigel grimaced in the direction of the seats where his fond parents were accustomed to sit, and in the time allowed for knowing laughter snatched up a fallen branch—failing a genuine branch at this stage of the proceedings, Miss Seeton's second-best umbrella had been borrowed for the purpose—which he held in exaggerated pitchfork fashion. He pushed his pillbox to the back of his head, mock-rustic, scratched his pate, stared, and frantically chewed an invisible straw. "Oh, ar," he said, sounding more like Stan Bloomer than Stan ever did. "Oh, aaaar!"

The Baron (it suddenly dawning upon him that he'd been insulted) snatched the pitchfork brolly from Nigel's hand, and began to chase him. Nigel, determined not to be outdone by DC Foxon, allowed Buttons to elude capture and/or skewering with a series of agile leaps back and forth across the log, until at last, both breathless, he and Baron Mountfitchet galloped into the wings.

"Thank you," called Lady Colveden from the floor, as the thump of footsteps ceased abruptly offstage. "That wasn't bad at all, Nigel. Charley, you were excellent." Not for worlds would her ladyship have told her son just how good she thought his performance really was: the true blue British blood of Plummergen's squirearchy never permitted more than the most temperate praise.

Nigel emerged from the wings and bowed gracefully, doffing his pillbox, while Baron Mountfitchet's gratified chuckle followed him. Miss Seeton, catching Mr. Colveden's eye as he made his second exit, smiled in sympathy, then suddenly recalled that she had meant to make a pencil note on her prompt copy as to the number of leaps and minor somersaults her young friend was to perform, and to time how long they were intended to take.

"Oh, dear." Miss Seeton stared down at the sheaf of type-written paper on her lap, and blushed. One's admiration for the sight of an expert—two experts—at work, she guiltily supposed. It had been such a delight to watch Buttons and the Baron, to realise that they knew their lines so well that her services ought not to be required—but it was most remiss of her, and a sad dereliction of duty, to have neglected to follow the entire scene as it was acted—and, good gracious, even more remiss of her to have started doodling on the opposite page from that on which the first lines of the scene were set out . . .

"Recto?" murmured Miss Seeton, frowning, as she flicked past her hasty doodle and tried to find the start of the next scene. "No, I don't think . . . yes, of course. Verso."

"Miss Seeton, I'm so sorry," said Lady Colveden, catching the final word. "With everything else, I must have forgotten to explain—we're missing out the children's verses and their

Fairy Dance at this rehearsal. Straight on to the entrance of the
Prince and Dandini, please."

Miss Seeton, blushing again, had all thoughts of the mystery
doodle driven from her mind as she watched Prince Maureen
and postman Bert, the Prince's best friend, start to struggle
through their first scene together, both in clear need of a prompt.
For the rest of the evening, Miss Seeton's attention never once
wavered from the action on stage. Her voice, accustomed after
so many years of teaching to carry as far as it was needed and
no further, was inaudible from the body of the hall, but easily
reached whichever member of the panto cast needed to hear
it. The notes she made were detailed, efficient, and as legible
as she could make them—in case, as she afterwards earnestly
explained to Meg Colveden, the influenza epidemic, about
which one had heard mention on the wireless and even, on
the occasions when one read them, in the newspapers, should
catch her in its toils . . .

"Not, of course, that I am not most fortunate in enjoying
splendid health, for my age . . ." Her purchase of *Yoga and
Younger Every Day* all those years ago had been, Miss Seeton
frequently told herself, the most worthwhile investment of her
life. "But this is, after all, winter, and one can never be *entirely*
sure. Coughs and sneezes," said Miss Seeton, with vague
memories of World War II, "spread diseases—and a number
of them have, as I expect you know, been coughing, although
Mr. Jessyp did remark that the latest delivery seemed to be
of sadly inferior quality, more like clinker, which might well,
when one thinks about it, be the real reason. The smoke, you
see, from the stove—and the coke, of course. At school. And
rubbing their eyes from time to time—which perhaps makes it
less likely that it is germs, or microbes, or whatever the cause
of it is—influenza, I mean, not smoke . . ."

Lady Colveden struggled nobly not to rub her own eyes as
she strove to sort out the coke, the smoke, the stove, the germs,
the schoolchildren's influenza (if, indeed, they were suffering
from it), and assorted pieces of World War II propaganda. "Be
like Dad," she responded, in desperation. "Keep Mum."

Miss Seeton nodded. "Is your journey really necessary?
Such crisp, telling phrases. Careless talk costs lives . . .

And the posters were indeed apt, particularly the one of him hiding—behind a wall, I believe. Hitler, as I recall, listening, though I suppose the correct term would be eavesdropping. One had always to be so conscious—which of course one could hardly fail to be, living, as I did, in the capital—the bombs, and the blackout, and the irregularity of the trains—so difficult sometimes to travel to work, or even, once one had made one's way in, to travel home again . . ."

Miss Seeton sighed, and shook her head; then smiled. "So many years ago now, of course, although—speaking of travelling home—if he could just let me have it back—dear Nigel, that is—I may travel homewards at once and delay you no longer. I believe that it is raining outside, and after your hard work this evening you must be looking forward to a rest and a quiet cup of coffee."

Lady Colveden's brain was by now whirling so fast that it was left to Nigel, who had been exchanging further ideas for the chase with Charley, Baron Stoneybroke, to come to his mother's rescue—to work out what exactly Miss Seeton meant—to return her umbrella—and, offering her a lift in his little red MG, to refuse to let her walk home through the chilly winter rain to her cottage at the end of The Street.

chapter

-5-

THE STREET IS Plummergen's main—indeed, almost its only—thoroughfare, running in a long, gentle curve over a half-mile distance from north to south, where it divides in two. To the right, it makes a sharp, ninety-degree bend and turns into Marsh Road, the farthest habitation of which is Rytham Hall, home of the Colvedens; to the left, it narrows abruptly between old, high-walled houses to run over the Royal Military Canal and on into the countryside. One of the old, walled houses on the left-hand side as one travels south is the vicarage, home of the Reverend Arthur and Miss Molly Treeves; that on the right, on the corner of Marsh Road, is Sweetbriars, home to Miss Seeton. It was therefore no great hardship for Nigel Colveden to run Miss Seeton home, though, being not only an old friend but a true English gentleman, he would have obliged had the rain been twice as heavy, and her cottage in quite the opposite direction.

In quite the opposite direction from Sweetbriars, looking northwards up The Street, the rest of Plummergen is laid out either side of that long, gentle half-mile curve. At a point almost exactly out of exact range of all but the keenest eye, on the eastern side of The Street, stands Mr. Stillman's post office; and it was in the post office, the morning after the rehearsal, that tongues were once more merrily wagging as everyone minded her—very, very rarely, in Plummergen is it "his"—neighbour's business.

Neighbour is an indefinite term. It can refer to one who lives in the next-door house—on the other side of the road—

in the nearby hamlet—in the not-too-distant town. The nearest
town to Plummergen is Brettenden, only six miles distant,
where the local newspaper is produced. And it was an item
in that morning's *Beacon* which—with it referring to a discovery virtually on Plummergen's doorstep—was so greatly
exercising the merry wagging tongues of the larger town's
smaller neighbour.

"Treasure trove, it is, no more nor less," announced Mrs.
Skinner, savouring the words. "Hundreds of years that box
has bin sitting in that there bank, full of gold and jools and
I'm sure I don't know what . . ."

"What it is, is just *medals*, the paper said—Napoleon, and
Wellington, and the . . . the Crimea and stuff," objected Mrs.
Henderson, who had read the article rather more closely
than her rival. "Historically important, it said—old regi-
ments, and . . ." Perhaps she hadn't read it as closely as
she'd thought. "Tell a lot," she went on hurriedly, "from
all that, the experts can, and *that's* why it's so valuable,
the paper said. Never said nothing about gold, or jools, or
treasure."

"Well, they wouldn't let on, would they?" Mrs. Spice, who
could never make up her mind which side of the Skinner-
Henderson feud she supported, decided to wade in this time
on Mrs. Skinner's behalf. "Stands to reason they don't want
to let folks know it's as valuable as all that, in case of it being
stole—"

"So who's going to steal from a bank?" demanded Mr.
Henderson, with scorn. "Locked away in the safe, a huge
great wooden chest like that, all heavy on account of iron
bands round, and the medals metal too—"

"Take the medals out, of course," snapped Mrs. Skinner,
with a grateful grin for Mrs. Spice. "These rich Americans,
they'll pay any price for a bit of history, them not having
much of their own, poor souls . . ."

An almost unanimous murmur showed that this was considered a score for Mrs. Skinner, who—perhaps unwisely—
decided to elaborate on her victory. "Mind you, no matter
how much money any of em's got, they'll find it no easy
task to smuggle a thing that size on an aeroplane, ships being

too slow and with time to search thorough on the way—"

The elaboration had indeed been unwise. "If he's money enough," interposed Mrs. Henderson smugly, "he'll have his own aeroplane, won't he? And no need to bother with the Customs—he could fly in and out anywhere, America being such a big place."

The resulting murmur, louder than before, was emphatically in favour of Mrs. Henderson. Mrs. Skinner scowled as her rival took her turn at elaboration, preening herself. "Not as I reckon there'll be any rich Americans allowed to get their hands on this lot, you can be sure of that. The paper said how the manager was . . . was consulting with his superiors, it being historical, and—"

"And—" Mrs. Skinner came bouncing back, just to prove that Mrs. Henderson wasn't the only Plummergenite who could remember a newspaper article—"didn't the paper say as how they'd be putting it up for auction? On account of them not knowing who might be the heirs after so many years of nobody asking to open it, and—"

"And," chimed in Mrs. Spice, "when things as is historical goes for auction, it's the rich folk as buys 'em—millionaires, or an American museum, or a . . . an archaeologist, or summat of the sort!"

This particular point seemed so deserving of the highest score of all that Mrs. Spice and Mrs. Skinner had started to smirk, when Mrs. Henderson countered with:

"I'd have thought an *archaeologist* was the last person as'd want to buy such stuff, seeing as how it's only just now bin dug out of the bank and surely not wanting it buried so soon as all that. An *archivist*, now, that'd be a different matter, being historical like the paper said, but . . ."

Mrs. Spice and Mrs. Skinner made mental resolutions to go home and reread the relevant pages of the *Beacon* again as soon as possible: it would be too late, of course, for today—but there was always tomorrow. For now, they chose to sulk, and fumbled for their shopping lists while they sought a change of subject, the military medal chest having proved too distinct a triumph—albeit, they trusted, a temporary one—for Mrs. Henderson: who was about to enlarge on this triumph when Mrs. Flax—a hitherto silent observer of the previous exchange—cleared her throat.

Mrs. Flax is Plummergen's Wise Woman, and as such is accorded much respect by a great part of the village. She has—she is always quick to remind the recalcitrant—Special Knowledge of the Old Ways: her herbal lore and store of proverbial wisdom is prodigious. When she chooses to speak, many listen, whether or not in their secret hearts they agree with what she says. Should they voice their disagreement, however, who is to know what ill luck might befall? Best not to run the risk of addled eggs, or blighted crops—or worse—by getting on the wrong side of Mother Flax, most of Plummergen opines . . .

"History enough around this place for any number of Americans," said Mrs. Flax. "Talk about Boney—why, there's the Canal, and all them towers, for a start."

Collective English memory goes back many centuries. The rivalry between Plummergen and nearby Murreystone, for example, dates from well before the Civil War of the mid-seventeenth century, when Plummergen took the Royalist, Murreystone the Commonwealth, side. Twentieth-century Cavaliers and Roundheads continue to fight their pitched battles in this corner of Kent at least once a year, during the annual inter-village cricket match, with lesser skirmishes randomly occurring at the slightest provocation.

Napoleon Bonaparte, dating from the nineteenth century, is an even more vivid presence than the shades of Charles I and Oliver Cromwell, Lord Protector of the Commonwealth. Against fear of Boney's invasion, the stout Martello Towers, many of which still stand, were erected along the Kentish coast, and the Royal Military Canal was dug—a canal which (Mrs. Flax now went on to remind her audience) could tell many a historical tale, if it chose.

"And some as aren't so historical, too," she enlarged, with a portentous nod. "That Hitler, for one. Cleared it of weeds right the way along, didn't they, in case of invasion? Some funny things happened hereabouts, in them days—dooodlebug bombs, and land mines, and parachutes—not that it'd be right to talk about it, even thirty years on, what with Official Secrets, and half of 'em not yet told . . ." She managed to give the impression that, of the chosen few knowing what secrets were still being kept, Mrs. Flax was of their number. "You youngsters, o'course, you've no idea what I mean, have you?"

She gazed with considerable condescension at young Mrs. Newport, born half a decade after VE Day; and Mrs. Newport, conscious of the need to propitiate the Wise Woman, blushed at being thus singled out. Standing beside Mrs. Newport her sister, Mrs. Scillicough, felt the eyes of Mrs. Flax sweep across her, and sniffed, and tossed her head. Since the day when she had asked Mother Flax for some herbal remedy to suppress the supernaturally high spirits of her obstreperous triplets—and, the remedy failing, Mother Flax had then worked her way with equal lack of success through her entire necromantic repertoire—Mrs. Scillicough had felt less than deferential in the presence of the local witch.

So Mrs. Scillicough sniffed, and tossed her head, and spoke with scorn. "If you ask me, we've heard enough about the War to last a lifetime. If we've heard our dad going on about it once, we've heard him a hundred times, for all he never went nowhere, with working on the land and being Reserved Occupation. But as for *secrets*, what about Rytham Hall, then? Dad says as it was—was requisitioned by the military, he says, barbed wire an' all round it, and soldiers on guard, with orders to shoot to kill. That's what I call a secret, what with nobody knowing to this day what it was they were doing there—"

"Ah," said Mrs. Flax, and closed one eye in a very slow, knowing wink which sent shivers down several spines. "Shoot to kill? They'd no need of that, not if they'd listened to me, only in their pride they wouldn't." In fact, the senior Army officer who had been buttonholed by the young (as she then was) Mrs. Flax had been hard put to it not to laugh in her face when she explained that she wanted to make a personal contribution to the war effort. It had surprised him greatly when, three weeks after having given her the brush-off, he'd been posted from his high-level security job in the danger zone of Kent to a far-flung tedium in the Catering Corps . . .

"Ah, yes—a few herbs," said Mrs. Flax, with another knowing wink, "and some ill-wishing, in a righteous cause, and there's nobody would've come near the Hall as weren't intended—but there, if they didn't choose to hear me, we won in the end, didn't we? In the end, mark you," with the air of one who could have brought about the downfall of Adolf Hitler in 1939, if she'd so chosen. "Not that I'm one to bear a grudge, o'course. It was all a long time ago . . ."

"Thinking of old times," ventured Mrs. Spice, with a wary look at Mrs. Henderson, "I can hear them explosions to this day, and see all the uniforms. Funny how one minute there was all them folk at the Hall, and the next they'd upped and gone again, isn't it?"

"They'd have given that Hitler a run for his money, I don't doubt," said Mrs. Skinner.

"If he hadn't drowned first," put in Mrs. Henderson, from whose kitchen window the fields ran gently down to the Royal Military Canal with an almost uninterrupted view.

"Talk of *drowning*," said Mrs. Skinner, "what about when Miss Seeton fell in, stealing all that silver, and young Hosigg helped her out and they both got roaring drunk on whisky? And what does Sir George do next but make him foreman, after carrying on like that with someone old enough to be his mother . . ."

The Second World War was indeed long over. Even for Plummergen, there was no particular amusement to be had in discussing, for the umpteenth time since 1945, what may or may not have been the purpose of the Army in occupying Rytham Hall for much of the duration: the Official Secrets Act being what it was, speculation had long ago lost its savour when everyone knew there was no chance of ever learning the truth. If Sir George, who had been much decorated during the conflict, knew it, he was not telling; the soldiers had mingled little with the village populace, and distance lends decided disenchantment to the brew of gossip, supposition, and surmise. It is far more enjoyable to exchange views on those who are our neighbours . . .

And, as it so often does, the talk in Plummergen's post office turned, once again, to Miss Seeton.

chapter

~6~

"A FINE START to the festive season," remarked Chief Superintendent Delphick, throwing down yet another report from a
microbe-ridden colleague. "Some poor devil of a bank clerk
tries to be a hero, and ends up in hospital fortunate indeed
not to be singing in the angelic choir with rather more realism
than he'd bargained for at this time of year. Loyalty to one's
employer is all very well, Bob, but no amount of loyalty could
compensate for the loss of a human life. The man is married,
with three children—and he's on the critical list . . ."

Sergeant Ranger, having reached the Yard a good half hour
earlier than his superior, had also read the report. He nodded
now as he quietly retrieved it from where it had slipped to
the floor, and added it to the bulging dossier on the Shotgun
Gang. "No doubt about it being the same crowd again, is there,
sir? Too many close similarities for it to be just a copycat
crime."

"A crime, with apologies to Gertrude Stein, is a crime, is a
crime, Bob. Incidentally, did you know that my misquotation
is such in more ways than one? She did not, in fact, use the
first indefinite article." Delphick, who had let his tongue run
on while his subconscious searched rapidly for the required
turn of phrase, permitted himself a pleased smile. "Mimetic
malfeasance or the thing itself, Detective Sergeant Ranger, this
office has no truck with it. We have done our best, understaffed
as we are, but our best is obviously not good enough. And not
even the least of hints from the criminal fraternity to help us on
our way . . . someone somewhere must have heard some sort

of whisper. Why haven't we heard it too?"

"Could be we'll get a whisper now, sir. Silver linings, and all that—I mean, it's rough on the bloke getting shot, but the chummies're great ones for the sanctity of home and mother. They won't take too kindly to the idea of widows and orphans, this near Christmas. Of course, sir," added Bob, never one to miss a good opportunity, "we could always try asking MissEss what she thinks . . ."

Delphick's grey eyes turned ever more bleak. "No, Bob. I've already told you I don't want her involved—and that was before they began using those guns instead of merely waving them in a threatening manner. Miss Seeton's forte is the freakish, the unorthodox—the unique, indeed, and certainly not the sordid everyday crime of bank robbery."

Bob cleared his throat. "I think you'll find, sir, that there are, well . . . less everyday ways of robbing a bank—when you read the rest of those reports, I mean. I'd've said myself it was a pretty unorthodox method—right up her—I mean your—street, sir. The green folder," he added helpfully. Delphick looked at him in silence. Sergeant Ranger grimaced. "Well, sir, with you saying a few days ago you were getting tired of forever reading the same sort of thing—I mean . . ."

"How mean," murmured Delphick, reaching for the green folder as Bob turned hotly red, "was my valley . . . Ah, yes." He stared at the first page of the report, and savoured it. "Yes, indeed—certainly unusual." He skimmed to the last page, nodded, and turned back to the beginning. "Yes, we are—or rather, the investigating officers were—in the vicinity of genius, Bob. What," he apostrophised the ceiling, "is genius but an infinite capacity for taking pains? How much time and effort must have been involved to get all the details absolutely right? How elaborate the scheme, and yet how simple!" He lowered his eyes, and fixed Bob with a steely stare.

"Bob, this could be serious. The Shotgun Gang, after all, have but a finite capacity—there are decided limitations to the success of their venture, dictated by the method they have chosen. They find it easier to rob a bank by merely walking in through the door and terrifying the staff into opening the safe, rather than tunnelling under pavements or blasting their

way through walls, with opening the safe an additional effort
of explosion. They must, of necessity, operate during normal
banking hours, when there will be plenty of witnesses—but
this . . ."

He turned again to the green-foldered report. "One man
could almost do this on his own, Bob. All he would need is
an ability to work metal, a telephone directory, a good map of
the area which he proposes to honour with his attentions, and
a means of transport. He has the darkness of the whole night
to conceal his activities, and no need to worry about laundering
dirty money, or marked notes . . . This system will work, Bob.
And I don't like it one bit."

"It *has* worked, sir. You've got to hand it to him, or them,
whichever—it's a pretty nifty idea—"

"Them? Ah, yes." Delphick looked thoughtful. "How I hope
you're wrong, Sergeant Ranger, about the plurality of this particular enterprise. The thought of one of these crooks is bad
enough, but if I thought there was a battalion of Night Safe
Men wandering the country . . . This"—Delphick tapped the
green folder grimly—"was, in my opinion, nothing more than
a trial run. It was successful, so he—or, heaven help us, they—
will certainly try it again—and on a far larger scale, since it
worked so well in this particular instance. With the run-up
to Christmas, shopkeepers' takings are on the increase—after
Boxing Day, there will be the Sales . . ." There was a brooding
silence. "Bob, you may—*may*—be right. We want to nip this
thing in the bud, and it seems we have no clue to help us . . .

"I wonder what Miss Seeton is doing now . . ."

Miss Seeton paused by the little table in the hall, and began
to cross items off her mental checklist. Strong scissors; a ball
of gardening twine; folded newspaper; a stout canvas bag, with
comfortable handles—yes, they were all there, as she'd laid
them out last night ready. Nobody had moved them . . . dear
Martha!

"Ready for the off, ducks?" Even as her image floated before
her employer's inward eye, Martha Bloomer, Miss Seeton's
invaluable domestic treasure and close friend, appeared from
the kitchen at the other end of the hall. It was one of Mrs.

Bloomer's regular days for "doing" at Sweetbriars, and she took her duties seriously. "Remembered your wellies, have you? Don't want you with wet feet from all that scrambling about in the mud, do we?"

Obediently, Miss Seeton pointed to the gumboots waiting beneath the table, and explained, with a smile, that she had indeed remembered them: in fact, she had been just about to put them on.

Martha smiled back. "Well, so long's you do, dear, then it won't matter how many puddles you hop over, will it? And there'll be summat hot for you in the oven by the time you get back, though, mind, there's no need to think on that account it'll be all right to freeze yourself to the marrow standing looking at birds, or trees, or anything. Hardly the weather for standing anywhere, after last night—all that rain, and a nasty damp feel still to the air—here," as Miss Seeton reached for her rainproof overcoat, "let me help you get yourself inside of that, dear."

The raincoat was duly buttoned. Miss Seeton's hat—one of her less exuberant efforts, a grey felt with a homemade blue ribbon cockscomb, of which she was rather proud—was pinned neatly on her head. Martha watched as her employer gathered up scissors, twine, and newspaper, and placed them in the outer compartment of the canvas bag; and she nodded.

"Can't think of nothing else you might need, not really. Just take care not to go snagging yourself on any brambles, won't you? And watch for the prickles once you've picked some— holly can be wicked stuff if you don't take care, but there's a fine crop of berries this year, I will say that—we can look forward to a hard winter when it comes properly, I suppose. Pity to leave 'em all to the birds, though."

"The scarlet, naturally, attracts them," said Miss Seeton absently, removing one of her second-best umbrellas from its clip on the wall beside the table. "I believe, Martha dear, from something Mrs. Ongar explained"—Miss Seeton's friendship with Babs Ongar of the Wounded Wings Bird Sanctuary had flourished of recent times—"that the berries might not so much be a sign of a severe winter to come, as of a fine summer past. Good growing conditions, you see, and nobody could argue that our weather has not been remarkably fine over the past few months, because even when it was warm and sunny, there was an adequate fall of rain to encourage plants to grow. Including," with a sigh, "the weeds . . . not that I am complaining, of course," she added, with a horrified, hasty blush for having thus inadvertently insulted another of her dear friends, Martha's husband Stan.

Miss Seeton's cottage was bequeathed to her by her distant cousin and godmother, Flora Bannet; but Sweetbriars itself is only part of the legacy—perhaps the lesser part, for Mrs. Bannet also handed on to her grateful goddaughter the various arrangements which, over the years, she had reached with Martha and Stan. These arrangements Miss Seeton was more than happy to inherit, seeing no need to change so successful a system of mutual self-help. Charging only a nominal sum, Martha cleans and cares for the cottage two days a week; for no charge at all, Stan tends the flowerbeds, vegetable plot, fruit trees, and chicken house. Miss Seeton and the Bloomers take their pick of all garden produce, including new-laid eggs; and Stan is permitted to sell, for his own profit, any surplus— which, since he is much gifted in matters horticultural, is generally considerable.

"Stan," said Miss Seeton, still blushing, "is so knowledgeable about these things, but I am ashamed to say that the difference between them is still too often a mystery to me— weeds, that is, and plants. Until they are grown, of course, when I have to confess, although Stan would no doubt scold me for saying so, that some of the flowers are almost as attractive as real ones—the weeds, that is. The flowers— except that they, too, must be regarded as real . . ."

Martha, who had known Miss Seeton for many years more than the seven she had spent in Plummergen, ignored (as she always did) her flustering, and handed her the canvas bag, giving her a gentle little push in the direction of the front door. "Bye now, dear, and if it looks like rain again you come right back, you hear? And never mind the kiddies and their handicrafts, it won't help anyone if you catch your death. Ta-ta!"

She stood at the open door to watch Miss Seeton trotting down the short paved front path to the gate, and waved as, having opened and passed through it, Miss Seeton turned to close it. "Bye!"

"Goodbye, Martha dear, and thank you," said Miss Seeton, who never ceased to rejoice in the wondrous good fortune which had brought her, with the sad loss of Cousin Flora, the happy ownership of her dear cottage in the country. She glanced back up the path to see that Martha had closed the front door and retreated inside, and patted the garden gate with a proud, proprietary hand; then she sighed with pleasure, stood for a moment watching the slow curl of smoke spiral lazily from her chimney to the leaden winter sky, smiled, and hurried off, her canvas bag over one arm and her umbrella over the other, along Marsh Road and out of the village.

She remembered, of course, to face the traffic as she walked: Marsh Road is a narrow, winding thoroughfare without benefit of kerb or pavement—a road used, fortunately for pedestrians, almost exclusively by local drivers, who alone know how to find it. Foreigners (and this term embraces, in Plummergen parlance, anyone who hails from more than a half-dozen miles distant) approaching the village prefer to do so from either the narrow over-canal southern end of The Street where it meanders in triumph from Romney, or from Brettenden, to the north. It is, therefore, generally accepted that any vehicle (slow-moving) you may encounter is more likely than not being driven by someone with whom you are acquainted: and, this being the case, it is considered no less than courteous to acknowledge the driver with a nod, a smile, or a wave.

Miss Seeton, as she saw the scarlet sports car emerge from a stately stone gateway and head towards her, did all three. Everyone in Plummergen knew Nigel Colveden's little red MG, and Miss Seeton was as fond of Nigel as anyone.

"Hello, Miss Seeton!" The car slowed to a halt before it had really got up speed, and Nigel leaned across to wind down the passenger window. "It's a chilly sort of day for birdwatching— or perhaps you have some other plan in mind. Is that your bins in that bag, or a picnic? Want me to come along and light the fire for you, or build a hide?"

"Picnic?" Miss Seeton blinked. "Binoculars? Dear me, no— as you said, Nigel dear, it is far too chilly today for exploits of that sort. Besides, the prickles would scratch the leather case, should I be successful in my little endeavour, and the berries, if squashed, would no doubt stain it, as well."

"You're out hunting for holly," deduced Mr. Colveden, who knew Miss Seeton of old and was often able to make sense of what she was saying. "Isn't it a little early—I say, I do beg your pardon, but—a little early to decorate your front door? We never have it at the Hall until Christmas Eve, and then my mother makes us put up masses all over the place. It makes such a jolly useful barricade against slugs afterwards, and she's too busy to pick it the rest of the year."

Miss Seeton, making a mental note to ask Stan his views on dried holly leaves as a deterrent for slugs, nodded, and remarked that dear Lady Colveden's garden was indeed a tribute to all her hard work, and that of course one would not presume to court ill luck—not that one believed in such a superstition, but it seemed only polite, when living in the country, to adhere as closely as possible to country ways—by decorating one's house for Christmas until the season was a little more advanced. Stan, if not dear Martha, would have a great deal to say on the subject if one did—decorate it early, she meant.

Nigel, who had known Martha since his infancy, grinned, and agreed that they would. "In which case, Miss Seeton—do say if I'm being too inquisitive, but what *do* you want the holly for? I can't believe Stan allows such things as the humble slug to work its evil way in your garden . . ."

"Good gracious." Miss Seeton paled at the thought: Stan was a perfectionist, and one insulted a perfectionist at one's peril. "There *are* slugs, of course," she admitted. "One can hardly avoid them altogether, can one? But Stan puts down soot, and salt, and saucers of beer, on occasion, which seem to work— and bread-and-milk at night sometimes, for the hedgehogs, which eat them—thrushes too, of course. Slugs, that is, not thrushes—the hedgehogs, I mean, and anyway of course they are hibernating now. I keep trying to remember to speak to Dan Eggleden about it. Or do you think I should try to buy a secondhand mattress instead?"

This time, Nigel was utterly flummoxed, and did not dare to reply. Was Miss Seeton proposing to buy a mattress for

the benefit of the hibernating hedgehogs—who would surely
prefer to roll themselves in bundles of leaves until spring—or
the slugs; or the thrushes, or even (his imagination boggled)
of Dan Eggleden, the village blacksmith? At any other time
of the year, he might have supposed Miss Seeton to have a
touch of the sun, but in December this was hardly probable.
On the other hand, it was, as he had said, a chilly day; there
was a lot of influenza about . . .

So Nigel gulped, cleared his throat, and asked gently:

"Miss Seeton, excuse me, but—are you sure you're feeling
all right?"

chapter

-7-

"WHY, YES, THANK you, Nigel, but—forgive me—do you? You seem to have a rather bad cough, and there is a great deal of influenza around, as I know only too well. Several of the children have been away from school—when Miss Maynard has worked so hard with them, and will be so disappointed— but we must, of course, hope for the best. Perhaps you could go home and ask your dear mother to make you a hot toddy? And it does mean, of course, that I shall not need to pick quite so much, although that is naturally small consolation for those who are ill. And, as you suggest, I can scatter the rest around my garden, for the slugs—or rather, not so much *for* them as against them. Unless, that is, dear Mr. Eggleden can help . . ."

Nigel felt that if he didn't get to the bottom of this, he would start to scream. He dared not clear his throat in case Miss Seeton began to babble again of epidemics; and so took a very deep breath instead. "Dan Eggleden," he said, in a voice he struggled to keep calm, "is a very helpful chap. You could do a lot worse than ask for his advice."

Miss Seeton looked anxious. "It is, perhaps, more the advice of dear Stan—that is, Greenfinger recommended this course of action, but Stan has told me he can see there is no harm in it, and it might just work, though he is not oversanguine. Stan, I fear, mistrusts books," said Miss Seeton, smiling fondly as she recalled how Stan Bloomer had chuckled at his first sight of the gardening tome she had bought, with such delight, in a London bookshop to take with her on her first excursion, as owner of a property in that county, to Kent. *Greenfinger Points the Way* had certainly been a guide—of sorts—since Emily Dorothea Seeton had forsaken her flat to move to her country cottage; the only trouble (Miss Seeton had told herself, more than once) being that Greenfinger and Stan, country born and bred (whereas one knew very little indeed about Greenfinger's origins) all too often pointed, or at least looked, in entirely opposite directions . . .

"And then," went on Miss Seeton thoughtfully, "always supposing that one could collect enough, there would be the problem of twisting it into a rope—or do I mean spinning? Wool, of course, would be far easier—but it is the sharp points, and the stiffness, which Greenfinger suggests make it so efficacious. Perhaps I might propose it to the children as a handicraft activity, instead of Christmas wreaths—except, of course," and she smiled at Nigel, who wore the air of a thoroughly baffled young man, "that I hope to find an adequate supply of holly this very morning, and may have to wait some days, or even weeks, for enough horsehair."

Nigel let out a long sigh of relief, smiled, and replied in a voice which amazed him with its steadiness: "Horsehair rope's a remedy for slugs I haven't come across before, Miss Seeton, and apart from asking Dan Eggleden I can't think of another way of acquiring the stuff—buying a mattress would be a little, well, extravagant, don't you think? But holly, now, is a different matter. We've lots of it in hedges and so forth around the farm and you're more than welcome to help yourself—don't worry," as she started to expostulate, "there'll be more than enough left for my mother, if all you want to do is fill that bag. And, I say, why stop at holly? Wouldn't some white berries make a good contrast? The odd sprig of mistletoe among all the red could look rather cheerful, I think."

Miss Seeton's eyes lit up at the idea, which appealed to her artistic sensibilities. But where, she asked Nigel, was any mistletoe to be found? One knew, naturally, that it was a parasitic plant, and as such entwined itself about the trunks and branches of sturdy trees, particularly apples and oaks; but she had no oaks in her garden, and the apple trees were sadly bare of anything save a few shoots of ivy, which for her part she thought looked picturesque, but which dear Stan considered would weaken the trees and pull them eventually to the ground. Greenfinger, on this point, was silent. What did Nigel think?

"About ivy on trees? Well, the Haunted Oak, which is where I was going to send you for the mistletoe, has great swathes of ivy over most of the trunk and some of the branches, and has done ever since I can remember. And they don't seem to have done the tree any harm—I mean, it looks as healthy now as it did when Julia and I were kids—but then a centuries-old oak's a rather tougher specimen than an apple tree, so if Stan disapproves, and he's the expert, I'd say you could do worse than listen to him."

Miss Seeton sighed; the ivy looked so attractive in her garden, creeping its way from a pair of weathered stone containers up the trunks of the closest trees: it produced, in leafless winter, a pleasing effect of green against grey which had caught her fancy on more than one occasion: she had even painted it, and pleaded with Stan to let it remain in case further inspiration should strike. But, with dear Nigel's words, she feared . . .

"Why," she enquired, banishing from her mind the doleful vision of herself at work with secateurs and shears, "do you call it the Haunted Oak? I have heard not a few local legends since I've lived in Plummergen, but nothing about any ghost at Rytham Hall."

"Oh. Yes, well . . ." And Nigel, to Miss Seeton's surprise, turned pink beneath his healthy outdoor tan. "There, er, isn't actually a ghost, as far as I know—the Haunted Oak was just the name Julia and I gave it as youngsters. Kids' stuff—books and films—you know the sort of thing."

Miss Seeton, whose years of teaching had given her a fair idea of how the juvenile mind worked, twinkled at him, and said that, if he cared to tell her, she would be most interested to know the type of ghost he and his sister had invented to make their home more, well, exciting in their childish eyes, so that she would know what to watch out for. Nigel grinned.

"What *didn't* we! A Grey Lady, of course—she was one of Julia's horrid contributions towards scaring us both into fits. She had long, cold fingers, and when the moonlight

shone on her bones, they gleamed with phosphorescence—
ugh! I always thought my White Knight was a far more
likeable character. He had silver armour, and a white crest
on his helmet—horsehair, I suppose," and Nigel chuckled.
"He had a white shield, and a silver spear, and was killed in
single combat with the Black Baron—a nasty piece of work
he was, believe me: ravished young maidens far and wide
throughout the county, and was in league with the ghastly
Doomed Abbot of the Chapel—another one of Julia's—to
abduct the maidens he'd ravished and lock them up in a
nunnery for their inheritance. They were always heiresses,
you see."

Miss Seeton saw, only too well. Nigel Colveden had as
romantic a heart, and as Galahadish a nature, as any young
man of her acquaintance; the seeds of this trait had obviously
been sown in his earliest youth. She smiled kindly on him as,
lost in reminiscence, he brought himself back to the present
and blushed once more. Could he—she earnestly enquired—
guarantee that, if she made for the Haunted Oak in search of
festive greenery, she would not be scared out of her wits by
any of the fearsome spectres conjured up by the imaginations
of the young Colvedens?

Nigel, who knew Miss Seeton to have no imagination worth
speaking of, grinned wryly, and assured her that he could.
"I'd come with you, if I had the time, but I'm on my way to
Brettenden for some tractor parts Jack Crabbe doesn't have in
stock right now. And, to be honest, I've never liked the place—
we never played there, that I can remember, even though it
looks splendid for climbing, and the spread of the branches
is just crying out for someone to build a treehouse. But there
was always something about that particular tree that made us
feel uncomfortable—which is why, I suppose, we decided it
must be haunted."

Miss Seeton assured him that she could manage very well
on her own, and had no wish to distract him from far more
pressing errands than the picking of holly and mistletoe for
the schoolchildren's handicraft project. As long as dear Lady
Colveden wouldn't mind—and if Nigel would explain how she
could find the, er, Haunted Oak . . .

"Good Lord, Mother won't mind at all. Half the village pinches the stuff anyway, for kissing-boughs and so forth—I'm sure she'd far rather you had first whack at it this year." Nigel was almost his old self again, infantile imaginings forgotten. He issued detailed directions to the ancient oak, watched Miss Seeton a few yards on her way, piped a farewell on his car horn, and was gone.

Miss Seeton walked on past the entrance to Rytham Hall for several hundred yards, until she came to the mossy milestone, half-buried in swirls of fallen leaves and dry grass, which marked the parish boundary. Nigel had told her that, though he and Julia had happily rambled the family acres starting from the Hall itself, it was far too complicated a route for one who did not know the lie of the land, and he hoped she did not mind taking a detour which was at least easy to follow. The milestone was the first mark; she must look for the gap in the hedge, and for the ditch which was the boundary between two fields. If she followed the ditch until it turned a sharp corner to run beside another hedge, there she would find a gate into another field. Let her open the gate, turn left, and walk along this hedge to the corner of the field . . .

Miss Seeton, glad she was wearing gumboots, arrived, in a slightly breathless state, at that corner of the field over which the great oak spread its branches. It had been a focal point almost from the moment she had left the road, though not while she was still on it. Miss Seeton being only five feet tall and the hedge, skilfully tended and "laid" by generations of farm workers, not only thickly branched, but of such a height as to block her line of vision.

It was a magnificent tree, silhouetted against the grey-blue winter sky, casting, even in the sickly December sunlight, a massive shadow on the ploughed earth beneath. Miss Seeton idly mused, as she approached it, on whether Nigel, with his dislike of the Haunted Oak, would have himself ploughed that field, or whether he had asked one of the men, or his father, to do so. But it was hardly her business, she reminded herself sternly. One did not care to pry into the feelings of others . . .

But it was a truly magnificent tree. Miss Seeton understood at once what Nigel had meant about its lower branches crying out for a treehouse: they were gnarled and strong, and even with the weight of centuries bowed very little towards the ground. Thickly draped with ivy, they could have concealed whole armies of cowboys and Indians, or (Miss Seeton smiled) cops and robbers—or, most likely (and her smile was even wider) King Arthur and his Knights . . . but Nigel and his sister had not chosen to play there, and the greenery had been allowed to grow undisturbed for who knew how many long years, except for the depradations of Plummergen youth in search of mistletoe for kissing-boughs. Miss Seeton turned gently pink, smiled, sighed, and shook her head as she drew closer to the Haunted Oak.

The base had an unusual appearance, and as she reached the edge of the massive shadow Miss Seeton realised that the trunk of the oak must be, at least in part, hollow: she could see right through to the other side. What was it she had heard Stan say of the English oak? One hundred years to grow, one hundred to live, one hundred to die . . .

" 'Or standing long an oak, three hundred year,' " quoted Miss Seeton softly, " 'To fall a log at last, dry, bald and sere.' " The Haunted Oak, while not yet fallen to a log, was past its prime, a dying tree: the smothering effect of ivy and mistletoe, perhaps? Miss Seeton, musing on Jonson's final lines, walked on.

Even a small woman makes a certain amount of noise when walking, wearing gumboots, in a muddy field along a hedgerow. There was a rustle of leaves, a sudden chattering, and a bird flew up from the haunted ivy to perch, bright-eyed, on a branch out of Miss Seeton's reach . . .

"Oh, dear." The magpie wasn't the only thing she saw to be out of her reach. Bunches of mistletoe, slim dark leaves pearled with white berries, hung down in tantalising fashion just a few feet above her head: above the heads of the villagers too, she suspected, since there appeared to be none growing lower down. Nigel's hopes of her having first whack had been sadly misplaced—but where there was a will, Miss Seeton reminded herself, there was nearly always a way.

She stood and stared up at the magpie, which glared back at her from its perch in a . . . an almost accusing manner, Miss

Seeton thought; then reproached herself for being fanciful; and then realised, as the bird spread its wings and flapped off in piebald indignation, that perhaps she hadn't been so fanciful, after all. Magpies, attractive to look at though they may be, are not loved by country dwellers. They rob the nests of other birds, and kill fledgling chicks. Gamekeepers shoot them as vermin . . . and Miss Seeton, with her long, crook-handled umbrella, must have looked, at a quick glance, as if she too had armed herself with a shotgun.

"Dear me, yes—but, of course, how practical . . ." And, with a pleased smile, Miss Seeton forgot about the magpie which still chattered at her from somewhere not too distant—draped her canvas bag over a convenient twig, and turned her umbrella upside down, grasping it by the spike. By standing on tiptoe on the swollen base of the trunk, leaning upward to clutch one of the thinner branches, and using the handle of her brolly as a hook, she could just about reach the lowest clump of mistletoe. With some energetic tugging, a few darting jumps, and a smattering of luck, the first bunch was ready for the canvas bag.

As Miss Seeton prepared to attack the next bunch, from deep inside the oak she heard a further rustling. Another magpie, perhaps? As she waited, she found herself quoting the old saw:

> "One for sorrow, two for mirth,
> Three for a wedding, four for a birth,
> Five for a christening, six for a dearth.
> Seven for heaven, and eight is for hell,
> But nine for the devil, his very own self."

She looked round for the first bird, and saw that the nearby tree on which it had decided to perch was a holly, scarlet and green against the brown of ploughed earth. The magpie, like Miss Seeton, seemed to be waiting for a second bird to appear; but the rustling stopped, and there was no further sign of life in the thick ivy covering of the Haunted Oak. It was, of course, unlikely to have been a ghost: ghosts, being ethereal spirit, have no need to move leaves as they pass. It might,

Miss Seeton supposed, have been some hibernating animal—
a squirrel, a vole, a hedgehog. She smiled absently, thinking
of Stan and the slugs, then remembered the holly, and glanced
towards the not-too-distant tree.

She had no wish to disturb the creature in the oak any
further. Animals roused too soon from hibernation have no
protection against the cold weather to come, and generally
perish. One bunch of mistletoe, she thought, would have to
do, if only she could ensure that there were enough holly
berries for contrast . . .

As she walked thoughtfully towards the holly tree, trying
to estimate the number of berries within umbrella-range, she
heard a louder rustling in the ivy behind her, followed by a
thump—which was almost immediately followed by an indignant chattering, as the magpie, seeing Miss Seeton coming
after it again, flapped crossly out of the holly tree and flew
off across the field. Miss Seeton turned to watch it, admiring
the dull green glint of its long tail in the pale sunlight . . .

And, turning, somehow loosened her grip on the canvas
bag—and in trying to take firm hold of it let it slip to the
ground. Automatically, she ducked to snatch at the handle—
if the bag fell, the few berries she had collected would be
squashed—but missed. Her umbrella slipped awkwardly down
her arm, its point stabbing into the ploughed earth of the
field—and Miss Seeton, with a little cry of annoyance, tumbled
over her umbrella facedown in the mud.

And heard, above the chattering indignation of the magpie,
a loud—a deafening—roar, and felt the earth shake beneath
her . . .

And felt unknown objects rain down upon her unprotected
back, and heard them land all about her . . .

And, hardly daring to raise herself from the ground, heard
the crackle and hiss of timber in sudden flames, and smelled
the acrid tang of smoke.

chapter

~8~

As NIGEL'S LITTLE car bowled Brettendenwards past the post office, his passing went unnoticed by those inside Mr. Stillman's establishment: everyone was too, too busy listening to the lament of Mrs. Norah Blaine.

The Nuts had not been much in evidence during the past few days—had not, indeed, been seen at all. Watchful eyes had observed lights burning at midnight in Lilikot, plate-glass-windowed home of Miss Erica Nuttel and Bunny Blaine; keen ears had heard sneezes, coughs, and spluttering sounds; more than one nose had caught the pungent whiff of Friar's Balsam, mentholated steam, and mysterious odours to which only Mrs. Flax claimed to be able to put a name. The Nuts, everyone concluded, must have succumbed to influenza . . . and Mrs. Blaine was out and about now for the first time in more than a week.

"Yes, poor Eric—two pounds of pearl barley, please—and when she is normally so much more *resilient* than I am—better make that three, I think. Fluid replenishment—such a raging temperature—and six lemons, Emmy. Large ones, of course—and to see her so ill—though I, of course, have greater difficulty in throwing off these things once I have given way to them. Too highly strung," sighed Mrs. Blaine, who for once, her plump form far slimmer than it had been in years, did not have to struggle to look frail. "Living off my nerves the way I do—it's too fortunate that we had the benefit of our healthy lifestyle to help us overcome the worst. I was the first to fall ill, and Eric made the most *marvellous* infusion for me—ipecac,

56

garlic, comfrey, chillies, elderflower, peppermint, and cloves, with water freshly drawn from our own well, of course. I felt better in minutes—too clever of her."

Someone enquired why, in that case, it had been so long since anyone had seen Mrs. Blaine up and about. Surely, if she'd been better in minutes—

"Better than I *had been*," Bunny broke in, "but as I was so ill to start with, it took far longer to bring me back to good health than it would have done for anyone less *sensitive* to germs—and then, too self-sacrificing, poor Eric was so busy taking care of me that she caught it. Such a terrible shock . . ." Mrs. Blaine gave the distinct impression that it had been a greater shock for her to see Miss Nuttel on a sickbed than it had been for Miss Nuttel to find herself there.

"Ah, now." Mrs. Flax cleared her throat portentously. "Shocks and sickness could well have bin spared you both, had you but come to me in good time. I'd have told you to dissolve garden snails in salt, and eat them with cream and sugar—powerful good for colds and sickness, so they are. Or adder-flesh and chicken broth's good for chests, if taken at the right time o' the moon—and if so be as any have a sheep to spare, why, cut out its lungs and bind 'em to your feet, and yours'll be clear as a bell by morning."

Mrs. Blaine began to turn pale. "Perhaps—perhaps larger, if you have them," she told Emmy Putts, absently pushing the lemons back across the grocery counter. "Poor Eric has set her heart on lemon barley water . . ." At the thought of what Eric, who went white at the very idea of blood and fainted whenever she saw it, would do should Bunny bind the lungs of a dead sheep to her feet, Mrs. Blaine shuddered. As for snails, and adders, and chickens—

"Eric and I," she reminded the Wise Woman with as much dignity as she could muster, "are the strictest of vegetarians, Mrs. Flax. We simply cannot believe that it is in the best interests of either our health or our . . . our moral fibre to . . . to eat flesh, or to cause undue suffering to any living creature."

Turning her back firmly on Mrs. Flax, Mrs. Blaine failed to notice the reaction of the rest of her audience, whose views on some of the suffering—albeit mental rather than

physical—caused by the gossip of the Nuts over the years
might have been, had they voiced them, forceful, to say the
least. To cover a burgeoning bout of hysteria, Mrs. Skinner
said quickly:

"Well now, Mrs. Blaine, you can't beat a good hot toddy for
the flu, if you ask me. A drop of whisky, hot lemon—weren't
you asking for lemons this very minute?—and honey—there's
the Admiral with his bees might spare you a jar, I daresay, if
you was to ask him."

Mrs. Blaine quivered, and almost dropped her shopping
bag. Admiral Leighton, who lived next door to Lilikot in
the cottage formerly owned by the Dawkin family of sinister
repute, was (in the eyes of the Nuts) an even more sinister
character than the late Susannah and her offspring. Lacking
the supportive presence of Miss Nuttel, however, Mrs. Blaine
felt quite unable to explain why accepting a jar of honey from
That Man—who knew on what poisonous plants his bees had
fed?—was something she simply could not bring herself to
do . . . and then she realised that Mrs. Skinner had given her
the perfect excuse.

"We are both, as you know, strictly teetotal—except for
homemade wine, of course, but that hardly counts as alcohol, does it? Too ridiculous!" Mrs. Blaine forced an airy
laugh.

Mrs. Skinner smirked. "Can be potent stuff, home brew,
whether 'tis wine or ale—hey, Mrs. Henderson?"

Mrs. Henderson scowled. She remembered, in depressing
detail, the occasion when her husband had decided that he was
spending too much money in the George and Dragon, and had
insisted that his wife should follow the recipe handed down
by his grandmother for Strong and Wholesome Barley Beer.
Having floated a yeast-enriched slice of toast on the heavy
"must" in the earthenware bread-crock, Mrs. Henderson had
waited the requisite length of time, then duly strained the
resulting liquor into bottles, and labelled them with great
pride . . .

The cost of replacing all the downstairs windows after the
explosion had been considerably more than the amount her
husband spent in the George in an entire year, and there were

still cracks in the walls which no amount of plastering seemed able to fill.

"Talk about making a party go with a bang," mused Mrs. Skinner, gleefully . . .

And went no further, as she was interrupted by the loudest bang anyone in Plummergen could recall having heard for over thirty years.

Mrs. Blaine's bag of pearl barley bounced off the counter and burst, with a noise like a million minuscule bullets, all over the floor. Emmy Putts, selecting lemons, squeaked with terror, and the lemons tumbled into the bin of oranges; Mr. Stillman's aluminium steps rattled against the wall in time with Mrs. Blaine's teeth. Mrs. Skinner and Mrs. Henderson stared as if each regarded the other as somehow responsible for what had happened . . .

"What—what's that?" cried Mrs. Spice, the first to regain her startled wits. Mrs. Flax, drawing in a deep breath, said darkly:

"Someone's bin meddling with what they don't rightly understand, that's what's happened, as I'd've thought should be obvious to all." Her eyes rolled ominously over each terrified shopper in turn. "Ah, and in their meddling pride they've stirred up Summat Best Left Hid, so they have . . ." A shudder of dismay ran round her hypnotised audience. "You mark my words, there's trouble a-coming, and worse—sounded from *her* end of the village, so that noise did . . ."

Mrs. Blaine, all set to cry: "Oh, Eric!" in panic, recalled that her friend and prop was ill in bed on the other side of the road, and collapsed in a quivering heap to the floor. She—everyone—knew who was meant by the Wise Woman's emphatic pronoun . . .

"Miss Seeton," breathed Emmy, thrilled; and was startled when Mr. Stillman—who, bearing in mind that shopkeepers depended on shoppers' goodwill, usually tried to remain silent—said crossly:

"Now that's more than enough o' your nonsense, Emmeline Putts." Although he'd only just recovered himself sufficiently to pick up the telephone, he banged it down again on the cradle, and prepared himself for some plain speaking. "And as for the rest of you ladies, you did really oughter know better—" He broke off in haste rather than adding the rider *at your age:* customers, after all, were customers. He coughed. "I mean, it's not as if none of you's never heard a bomb going off before, now is it?"

"A bomb?" Mrs. Blaine's squeal of alarm brought to mind the slaughtering of pigs. "A bomb—oh, it's really too bad! Not *again*—every five minutes, murder and kidnap and criminals and gassing—that nightclub man from London, setting bombs all over the place—and none of us safe in our beds—it's too— too dreadful!"

Above the excited babble which now arose, Mr. Stillman's stern voice held eventual sway. "You're a newcomer to these parts, Mrs. Blaine"—which was a decided hit below the belt. "You'd not remember, I daresay, just how bad things were in Kent during the war. Doodlebugs, and landmines, and planes shot down out of the sky in the Battle of Britain, not to mention bombers shedding their loads on the way back when it was too dark for 'em to find London—and what with the military taking over Rytham Hall and secret weapons and training and so forth, there was any number of explosions"—he picked up the telephone again—"and a good few of 'em sounding much like what we've just heard, to my mind." Glumly, he dialled nine-nine-nine. "Could be somebody's turned up an unexploded bomb with the ploughing, or digging over the vegetable patch or someth—Hello? Ah, yes, well, could be we'll need all three, I'm not sure . . ."

And so it was that, in response to the enquiry of the disembodied voice as to whether the caller wanted Fire, Police, or Ambulance, within ten minutes of Mr. Stillman's issuing his plea for assistance the bells and sirens of the emergency service vehicles could be heard rapidly approaching from the north. By this time, of course, everyone had debouched from the post office to the pavement, looking for clouds of smoke, tongues of flame, or any other indication as to the source of the explosion: which, now that Mr. Stillman had reminded them, the older inhabitants said they'd take bets on being a World War II bomb, if not older, and nothing to do with Miss Seeton at all.

• • •

Had they been witness to events at Rytham Hall, Mr.
Stillman's customers would have rapidly revised their views
on the innocence of Miss Seeton in what had just occurred.
Even as she was picking herself up from the ground, spitting
out a mouthful of loose earth, and dusting debris from her
raincoat in bemused fashion, the inhabitants and workers of
Rytham Hall were on their way to what was left of the Haunted
Oak to find out what had happened.

Sir George, driving the station wagon, with his wife an
anxious passenger, was first to arrive, followed almost at once
by young Len Hosigg, the foreman. Two of the farmhands
came next, and were promptly ordered back to work by Sir
George, on the grounds that they didn't want too many people
cluttering round the place, in case anything else blew up.
Better be safe than sorry—couldn't they see the flames, for
goodness' sake?

They could, and were glad to leave the matter in their
employer's capable military hands. Sir George, his wife, and
Len Hosigg, blinking as the wind drove smoke into their eyes,
hurried together to Miss Seeton's side and asked her urgently
what was going on.

"I'm afraid—I'm so sorry—I can't tell you," came the halt-
ing reply, as Miss Seeton, with her hat askew, its proud blue
ribbons no longer erect, falling instead into her eyes, tried to
scramble out of the mud to a standing position, and felt her
knees—yoga or not—turn to water. She clutched helplessly
at Lady Colveden's arm, staring about her in bewilderment.
"But—I don't understand—the Haunted Oak is on fire—it's
disappeared! This—this is dreadful—and that huge hole over
there . . ."

"Bomb crater," said Sir George, who had been for a quick
scout round while his wife ministered to Miss Seeton. "Have
half the county here before long, more's the pity. Len—on
duty at the road, there's a good chap. Keep out anyone except
the authorities—you know the drill. We'll head back to the
house and ring the barracks—Bomb Disposal. Nursing home,
as well," with a thoughtful look in the direction of Miss
Seeton, still leaning on Lady Colveden's arm, her whole body

trembling. "Shock," muttered Sir George, who was feeling slightly startled himself. "A stiff whisky, if the sawbones isn't there—"

"A cup of tea, George," his wife corrected him, as they began to pick their way back to the station wagon, while Len (with a muttered "S'right" of acknowledgement) hurried down towards Marsh Road in accordance with instructions. "Not whisky," said Lady Colveden firmly. "Miss Seeton will have a cup of strong, well-sugared tea, and then I'll pop her in the spare-room bed with a hot water bottle until Dr. Knight comes—and I'm sure," as Miss Seeton uttered a quavering squeak of protest, "that he'll say there's nothing to worry about—but it won't do any harm to make sure. Yoga," said her ladyship, with a laugh, "or no yoga. You can practise your deep breathing in bed, Miss Seeton. It will help you to sleep."

As they reached the car, Sir George, on the point of opening the passenger door, paused, his head to one side. "Thought so—sirens. Off you go, Meg—drive carefully—I'll stand guard here. Don't want Miss Seeton bothered with a lot of questions, do we? But . . ." He coughed, very gently, and Miss Seeton dragged her horrified gaze back from the wreck of the Haunted Oak to the plump, familiar figure of her friend. "Er—no idea how it happened, I suppose?"

With a gulp, Miss Seeton shook her head. "One minute I was walking towards the holly tree—the magpie was chattering, I remember watching as it flew away—and then somehow I tripped—oh yes, it was my umbrella, I remember now—and then there was, well, that enormous bang. Twigs and earth and mistletoe berries everywhere . . . For a moment, you know, except that there were very few trees in London, I thought I was back firewatching, in the Blitz . . ."

Sir George nodded gravely. "Not so far wrong at that, I'd say—right sort of vintage, I've little doubt. Lucky there's nothing here to catch fire, though. And nobody hurt—nothing to fuss about—no need to talk to anyone until you feel a bit more up to it. Meg'll take care of you—in you get, now."

The door of the station wagon was open, and Miss Seeton had been popped inside, almost before she realised what was going on. The sound of sirens, police and ambulance and fire engine, drew ever nearer. Sir George closed the door upon Miss Seeton with a firm hand, and watched his wife hurry to the driver's side.

"Off you go, Meg. Never mind me—I'll tell 'em they can't talk to her till the sawbones has seen her," he promised; and, as Lady Colveden nodded, her husband marched away from her across a field brown from ploughing, blackened with ash, littered with splinters from the ruined Haunted Oak.

chapter

~9~

Dr. Knight, when Lady Colveden telephoned the nursing home at the far end of the village, wasn't there.

"Heard that enormous bang, rang Potter, and was off like a rocket to see if he was wanted," the Howitzer advised her ladyship crisply. "Anythin' I can do for you? Over the phone, that is. Don't care to leave the patients without someone in charge unless it's a real emergency." Major Matilda Howett, Dr. Knight's second-in-command, took her responsibilities as seriously as might be expected from one who was Army trained.

Lady Colveden thought briefly of Miss Seeton, cosily ensconced in the most comfortable armchair before a blazing fire, a blanket round her knees, a full teapot at her side. "I can't say it's exactly an emergency, Major, but I would rather like him to take a look at Miss Seeton as soon as he can—she's just, er, had something of a shock, you see."

The Howitzer uttered a short, barking laugh. "Might have known she'd have somethin' to do with that bang," she said, with a chuckle. "Tryin' to start World War III single-handed, I suppose. How'd it happen?"

"I'm really not quite sure. Miss Seeton seems a little confused, and really it's hardly surprising, but from what she's told me I gather she went poking about with her umbrella in the Haunted Oak looking for mistletoe, and seems to have disturbed a hand grenade or an unexploded bomb or something that must have been lying there since—oh! Oh, how dreadful . . ."

"Lady Colveden?" There was urgency in the Major's tone as Meg Colveden's voice faded away into a series of horrified shudders. "Lady Colveden, you all right? Brace up, woman—it's Miss Seeton who was nearly blown to Kingdom Come, not you. Needs you to keep an eye on her until the doctor arrives—though I must say, knowin' Miss Seeton, if there's anyone I'd back to survive an explodin' bomb without more than a few bumps and bruises, she's the one. Sets us all an example . . . Lady Colveden?"

"I . . . I'm all right, thank you," came the faint reply, as the Major's words brought Lady Colveden out of her trance. "It was . . . was when I realised that the bomb, or whatever it was, had been there simply waiting to explode all the time the children were growing up . . ."

Despite her attempt at normal conversation, she could not continue. Major Howett said quickly: "But it didn't, thank the Lord, until now. Lucky escape for them, I grant you—but far luckier for Miss Seeton. Suggest you make yourselves a good strong cup of tea, with plenty of sugar, and try not to think about it. Soon as the doctor's back, I'll send him along."

Thus it transpired that, by the time Sir George returned home, he found his wife lying, a blanket across her knees, on the sofa in front of the fire. Miss Seeton—who, having been passed fit by an amused Dr. Knight, had refused to go to bed with a hot-water bottle—was in the kitchen, making another cup of tea, and wondering whether, in the circumstances—dear Lady Colveden seemed unable to stop shivering—a tot of whisky, for medicinal purposes, might not be a bad idea. If, that was to say, one could only remember where dear Sir George kept his spirits, and if it would not seem too much like prying into other people's affairs, to which they might rightly object, even when they were, as one hoped the Colvedens did not mind being considered, old friends . . .

Sir George quickly reassured Miss Seeton, produced the whisky, heard his wife's lament, and poured three generous tots. Miss Seeton's faint denial was ignored: after all, if his wife could be so upset just thinking about it, how much more upset must his guest, who'd actually been there at the time, be?

When Nigel, after a successful hunt for tractor spares, came in half an hour later expecting his lunch, he found a party atmosphere burgeoning in the sitting room, and reeled back under a barrage of wartime reminiscence.

"I wondered what all the rumpus was," he said, helping himself to a drink just to be sociable. "The fire engine came out of the station like one o'clock, and at least two police cars passed me in a matter of seconds. And all that racket with bells and sirens—modern ones," he added with a grin, "not yours."

"Moaning Minnie," supplied Lady Colveden, who had begun to perk up with the arrival of her husband, and on seeing her son felt her old self once more. "Goodness, how I hated the sound of that thing! Just like somebody trying to play a . . . a bassoon, or a trumpet, or something, and getting stuck on one note."

"An enchanting young woman," said Miss Seeton, sipping her scotch and water and feeling a warm glow inside. Lady Colveden, uncertain as to whether or not she was being complimented, blinked. "A great tragedy," sighed Miss Seeton. "At so early an age . . ."

Her ladyship rallied, and murmured that there had been only too many lives lost in the Blitz. Miss Seeton, she knew, had done her share of firewatching at the time. Some friend of hers, perhaps? How very sad . . .

"The trumpet," said Miss Seeton, who appeared to have heard none of this. "So very difficult to play, although she did, indeed, as I understand it, to have the fingering accurate, and was dubbed, if that is the right term, afterwards. When dear Nigel mentioned the police cars—chasing them along the road, except that as I recall they were motor cycles, and racing, of course, is entirely contrary to the spirit of the occasion. But so very amusing—the clock in the bedroom . . ."

There was a frozen silence while everyone racked their brains, and Miss Seeton sipped whisky and chuckled quietly at visions only she could see. Lady Colveden glanced at her husband, and signalled with discreet eyebrows. Perhaps she had been too shaken herself to realise that Dr. Knight might have over-estimated Miss Seeton's resilience—perhaps he should be summoned again, or—

"But then," said Miss Seeton, "that was last month, was it not? The London/Brighton Rally is always in November, of course. Like the Lord Mayor's Show. And Guy Fawkes . . ."

Three pairs of Colveden eyes met, and looked hastily away before their owners could commit the host's unforgivable sin and burst out laughing. The month of November did indeed herald Guy Fawkes Day—about which, of all the inhabitants of Plummergen, only Miss Seeton, in her habitual innocence, could speak with such calm after the disruption that had so recently occurred . . .

Nigel clapped a hand to his forehead. "*Genevieve!*" he cried, remembering a cancelled pantomime rehearsal, a long, empty evening, and a spate of television viewing. "Gosh, all those marvellous old cars—and what was her name—the one who played the trumpet?"

"Kay Kendall," supplied Miss Seeton, a minor movie buff. "And that enormous dog . . . to die so young. A tragedy."

"Lovely gel," agreed Sir George, with a nod. "Have to admit Dinah Sheridan's more my type, though—English Rose, and so on. Blonde, isn't she?"

"For myself," said Lady Colveden, whose thick, wavy hair was brown, "I've always had a soft spot for John Gregson. I remember he was in another film around that time, called— oh, dear—*The Holly and the Ivy* . . ."

"No getting away from it, is there?" Sir George poured himself another whisky, judged his audience was now sufficiently relaxed, and prepared to break the news. He turned, with a bow, to Miss Seeton. "Seems as if you may have, er, unearthed quite a find this morning. That crater—spreading roots, and so forth—one of the ambulance men fancies himself as an amateur archaeologist. Spotted some bits of pottery around, and took a closer look. Thinks he may have seen—well, Roman remains."

Everyone exclaimed. "Bones, you mean?" cried Nigel, enchanted, while Miss Seeton gasped, "Good gracious!" and Lady Colveden fell back on the sofa, stunned.

"Not bones, no." Sir George frowned. "Well, not yet, that is—but the feller asked if he could get a team of professional chaps to take a closer look. Had to tell him they were welcome, of course, though can't say it seemed much more than a hole full of stones, to me. But what's that stuff all little bits and pieces glued to the floor?"

"Mosaic," supplied Miss Seeton at once. Sir George nodded above the excited cries of his wife and son.

"That's the ticket—mosaic. Feller thinks it may be something special—unusual. Not many Roman remains in these parts, apparently."

"Plummergen," said Miss Seeton, who had read widely in local history books since coming to live in Kent, "was on the coast in Roman times, I believe—a low promontory, looking across an inland sea to higher ground at Stone—the Isle of Oxney. But not a port, as far as I recall, or of any particular significance."

"Which is why this ambulance feller's hopping up and down," Sir George informed her. "Seems the Romans built a temple to some god or other over the way at Stone. Told me the name, though I forget—thought I'd be interested. The soldiers' god, indeed. Heathen poppycock," said Sir George, huffing through his moustache. The squire's unwritten obligations included, among others, frequent readings of the lesson in church.

"Mithras," Miss Seeton told him, with a faint smile.

Sir George huffed again, but his disapproval was drowned out by demands from his family to be told more. A Roman mosaic, if indeed they had one on their land, was not to be lightly dismissed.

"Don't you remember, George, when I went on the Women's Institute outing to see the Orpheus Pavement at Woodchester?" Lady Colveden's eyes were bright. "You were with the school party, weren't you, Miss Seeton—wouldn't you say it was marvellous?"

"Oh, indeed, yes, and the children thought so too, which was most gratifying, after such a long journey, and all Mr. Jessyp's hard work in arranging it—as Mr. Stillman," said Miss Seeton, twinkling, "would bear witness, I feel sure. That they enjoyed it, I mean."

"Why?" enquired Nigel, who had been shuddering at the very idea of riding in a coach from Kent to Gloucestershire in the company of Plummergen Village School's fifty Junior Mixed Infants. "I never realised Mr. Stillman had gone with either of the parties."

"Oh, he didn't," Miss Seeton explained, twinkling again. "But on the day following the excursion, dear Miss Maynard was a little under the weather—she suffers badly from motion sickness, poor thing. Such a long journey—and Mr. Jessyp asked if I would mind taking her classes, which of course I could hardly refuse, with having been so kindly offered one of the spare seats on the school coach when, indeed, I would have been happy to pay to go with the others—and I found the children had been most impressed with the mosaic, or rather what remained of it, and for an Art Project I suggested they might like to design their own mosaics, or at least the nearest we could manage in the time. Dried peas and lentils, sunflower seeds and so on—being easier to obtain than pieces of genuine tile, and a more interesting texture than cutting coloured cardboard into squares. I believe," concluded Miss Seeton, with a chuckle, "that Mr. Stillman's stock of grains and pulses was almost sold out within a day, for he certainly told me that he had to re-order."

Indeed Mr. Stillman had. Plummergen's young (and not-so-young) inhabitants had been captivated by their visit to the little village, just outside Stroud, where the remains of a great Roman pavement had been discovered in the churchyard towards the end of the seventeenth century. Antiquarians studied it, sketched its wonders, and then agreed that it should be reburied, since it was, after all, in now consecrated ground; but, in deference to public interest, church authorities would, from time to time, allow the covering of soil to be removed, so that the wonders of this masterpiece—nearly fifty feet square—could be seen again.

The mosaic was not perfect: almost half was missing, or damaged beyond repair. Mediaeval vandals had broken through it to steal the lead pipes leading to the central fountain; holes had been dug for graves. But enough remained to show what glories had originally existed—and everyone who saw it was struck by the complexity and beauty of the pattern, depicting Orpheus, with his lyre, taming the beasts.

During the three-hour journey from Plummergen to Wood-chester, Mr. Jessyp, Miss Maynard, and Miss Seeton had taken it in turns to keep their youthful fellow-passengers occupied with the story of Orpheus and Eurydice, and other myths of the Ancient World, as well as selected tales from Roman history, concentrating on the occupation of Britain. These tales, vividly narrated, had wrought mightily upon the imaginations of the Junior Mixed Infants; and Miss Seeton's suggestion, the following day, that they should make their own mosaics had resulted in some truly original work. So captivated by the scheme were several of the children that they begged to take their handiwork home, to continue it in their free time.

Parents wondered what their children were doing, messing about with glue and dried vegetables. Mr. Stillman counted the minutes until he could next go to the cash-and-carry to stock up. Miss Nuttel and Mrs. Blaine, shopping for vegetarian necessities, demanded to know why supplies were suddenly so short, and, on learning the reason, became convinced that it was a deliberate slight on the part of Miss Seeton, who—as everyone knew—was not to be trusted. The Nuts were even more annoyed in that, as members of the Women's Institute, they had refused their chance to buy seats on the coach on the grounds that their nerves had never fully recovered from the shock of having been held up, earlier in the year, by highwaymen. To hear everyone else in raptures over what they had seen was almost too much for Miss Nuttel and Mrs. Blaine to bear . . .

"Harrumph," said Sir George, thoughtfully: he was remembering the raptures of his wife after her return from Gloucestershire—as busy farmers, neither he nor Nigel had been either willing, or able, to accompany her. They had listened, made the right noises, smothered chuckles as she later displayed the photographs she'd taken (Sir George, keen amateur cameraman, had suffered torments), and forgotten about the whole thing—until now. Nigel's first reaction to the news of what Miss Seeton's exploits might have uncovered suggested a greater interest than his father might have expected: no doubt the boy, like his mother, thought it would be no bad thing to have a Roman mosaic on the property.

But Sir George wasn't so sure . . .

And, stroking his moustache, he harrumphed again, listening to his wife and Miss Seeton as they reminisced happily together over their Woodchester experiences; and made a mental note to look into things, as soon as possible.

chapter

~10~

THE AMBULANCE MAN was as good as his word. Within three days—after Bomb Disposal experts had examined the site and pronounced it free (as far as they could tell) from further surprises—a small team of archaeologists from Brettenden Museum, headed by Dr. Euphemia Braxted, had excavated selected areas of the Rytham Hall site, and were mightily excited by what they discovered.

Dr. Braxted buttonholed Sir George when, late on the fourth afternoon, as the tired December sun glowed redly in the west, he trudged glumly down to the dig to find out what was going on. It was, after all, his farm they were filling with craters, never mind Miss Seeton's efforts . . .

"Splendid news, Sir George!" Dr. Braxted jumped from her knees, which emitted a thunderous crack, and hurried across to the brooding baronet as he hovered to one side of what, to him, resembled no more than an area of mud decorated with hundreds of holes and an equal number of molehills, separated by lengths of pegged-out string in squares.

"A most thrilling find," carolled Euphemia, shedding earth and assorted scraps from her clothing—heavy tweed—as she came. "You have already seen, of course, the various fragments of pottery, and the glass items which will need to be repaired before we can be sure what they are—but today, Sir George, we have struck true archaeological gold!"

"Good for you," came the gallant response, as Sir George prepared himself to force admiration for another bally chunk of earthenware with scratch marks on it, or a collection of tile

fragments which, Dr. Braxted had said, were an essential part
of the pattern.

"It's more than *good*, my dear man—it's splendiferous!" Dr.
Braxted's eyes gleamed with a hysterical light. "Absolutely the
only word, believe me—the finest haul of funerary silver I've
ever seen!"

Sir George blinked. "Thought you said it was gold."

"A figure of speech, nothing more." Euphemia dismissed
her hyperbolic flight with one wave of a tweedy arm. "Come
and take a look at what we've found so far . . ."

Particles of earth showered to the ground as she beckoned to
the baronet to follow her, leading the way to the tiny tent which
had been erected as the excavation office. She glanced over her
shoulder and lowered her voice, although there was nobody—
except the other archaeologists, who must already have known
what she was about to reveal—within earshot.

"Once the news breaks, they'll be down on us like a ton
of bricks—the papers, the museums, the auction houses, the
blasted gawpers. You deserve a private viewing, with it being
your land the stuff was found on . . ."

Sir George was unable to put accurate names to the
assortment of tarnished, earth-stained, faintly gleaming ves-
sels which stood, labelled, in rows on a rickety table.
He was enough of a strategist, however, to know that
Dr. Braxted expected praise and admiration for this display; and praise and admiration, within his capabilities, he
duly gave.

"Not bad at all, Dr. Braxted. Most impressive, in fact."
She seemed to be waiting for something more. "Er—how old,
would you say?"

"Second century A.D.—and that's not a guess," said
Euphemia, seizing him by the elbow and pushing him
towards a large, shallow, circular dish lying slightly apart
from the rest of the flagons, plates, and bowls. "Read that,"
commanded Dr. Braxted, pointing to the rim: around which,
Sir George could see, an inscription had been wrought in letters
he could just about make out, but in words which were utterly
beyond his comprehension.

"Er—harrumph. Yes, well . . . Latin, I suppose?"

Euphemia patted him on the shoulder. "Sorry, old chap, I forgot this isn't everyone's cup of tea. Latin, yes, and pretty detailed, too. This"—she waved her arm in another earth-spraying, all-encompassing gesture—"is the dinner service of one Siberius Gelidus Brumalix, a government official at the time of Hadrian. Heard of him?"

"Ah. Hadrian." Sir George stroked his military moustache, frowned, and then perceptibly brightened. "The wall, of course. Good strategy, no doubt, at the time."

"Yes. Hadrian's Wall—built between A.D. 122 and 128," Dr. Braxted threw in, for the ex-soldier's professional information. "Hadrian was the adopted son of the Emperor Trajan, and himself reigned as emperor from A.D. 117 to 138. A bit of a reformer, our Publius Aelius Hadrianus, you know. He tidied up provincial administration no end, among other things—and that's what our friend here"—she tapped the silver salver with an emphatic finger—"was doing in this neck of the woods. And he's still here," she added, as Sir George did his best to look intelligent. She directed his attention to a tall, stoppered jug with a fluted pattern and an elegant handle. Like the dish, the jug stood somewhat apart from its fellows; in front of it were several portions of flat pottery, or tile.

"In there," said Dr. Braxted cheerfully. "According to these, anyway," and she pointed to the pottery pieces, which had been assembled into a rectangular whole. "The inscription explains that this is the favourite dinner service of poor old Brumalix, who died after a banquet—for *banquet* try reading *orgy*—and was cremated. His wife, poor woman, decided it would be no more than his just deserts if his mortal remains ended up filling the wine jar he'd always had such fun emptying—and there, as far as we can tell, they still are. Amazing, isn't it?"

"Amazing," echoed Sir George, who wasn't used to having ladies bandying such words as *orgy* so freely in his presence—but Dr. Braxted, of course, was as good as a scientist. No telling what these boffin types would get up to . . .

" . . . temple, of some sort," Euphemia was explaining, her eyes bright. "Now, if only we could discover to what god or goddess it was built—but it's early days yet, Sir George. Give us time enough, and we'll find out, I'm sure—not that you need worry if we don't, straight away. The silver alone is enough, believe me, to make Rytham Hall the most famous place in England before much longer!"

Sir George shuddered. Major-general though he was, not even those exploits which had won him the Distinguished Service Order could, he felt, have been accompanied by as much horror as that suggested by Dr. Braxted's words . . .

And, listening in a gloomy silence to her enthusiastic plans, Sir George Colveden considered what exactly he ought to be doing about it all.

With dusk came the end of the day's work: and dusk comes not much later than four o'clock in England in December. As the sun disappeared behind the horizon, the archaeologists packed up their belongings and headed back to Brettenden, bearing with them—at the insistence of Sir George—the silver dinner service of Siberius Gelidus Brumalix. He wouldn't, he said, know a minute's peace with so much valuable stuff on the premises. Never mind that they were in the middle of nowhere, in the middle of winter—never mind the need to maintain the integrity of the site. Certainly, let Dr. Braxted give him a receipt—Polaroid photographs, if she insisted— he'd bring newspapers from the house, if she wanted them for wrapping things . . .

And, though it was four o'clock in the afternoon, Euphemia and her colleagues were not invited up to Rytham Hall for tea.

"George—whatever is it? You look dreadful." Thus her ladyship greeted her returning spouse as he trudged round to the kitchen door and kicked off his muddy boots. "George— you're ill. Don't say you've caught the flu—if you give it to Nigel, with the pantomime so close—"

"Worse than flu," said her husband, stamping chilly feet on the flagstone floor and peering hopefully in the direction of the kettle. "Fancy a tot in it, I think. Sun's well over the yardarm . . ."

Lady Colveden, who would normally have made some remark regarding the influence of her husband's hard-drinking naval friend Rear Admiral Bernard "Buzzard" Leighton, said nothing: it was only too obvious that Sir George was seriously upset about something; and she made haste to brew the tea, making it twice as strong as usual, and adding plenty of sugar, for shock.

Nigel's frequent boast that he needed no watch when working because of the accuracy of his inside clock proved true, for he appeared as she was loading the final few items on the tray, and enquired: "What's up with Dad? He's in the sitting room, muttering to himself. Have you two had a fight? Am I to be the product of a broken marriage?"

Lady Colveden frowned, and handed him the tray. "Now you're here, you may as well make yourself useful. I don't know what's wrong with your father—he came in a few minutes ago in a terrible state, and said he needed a whisky. At teatime! For goodness' sake don't tell any of your jokes while we're eating—and don't ask him. You know how he is—he'll tell us in his own good time."

The time came after Sir George's second cup of tea, once the scotch-enriched effects of his first had worked their way through his system. He harrumphed loudly, breaking into an animated discussion between his wife and son over that night's pantomime rehearsal, and said:

"That gang from Brettenden—had a feeling they'd stir things up more than we'd like. They've found heaven-knows-what down there today—say we'll be in all the papers, and people from heaven-knows-where will want to come staring at the place they found it. Wish she'd never gone looking for mistletoe—still, hardly the little woman's fault." An officer and gentleman will never lay the blame at a lady's door . . . "These things happen. Left over from the War, of course—could have gone off anytime. Just our bad luck it happened now."

"And *our* good luck—Julia and me—that we worked up so many grisly stories about that tree we never played there," Nigel pointed out, buttering a scone. "I can only say again how sorry I am that Miss Seeton was mistletoe hunting in that particular spot. If I hadn't sent her there—but I had no idea what would happen, of course. Though with Miss Seeton involved, I suppose I might have guessed it would be something—something out of the ordinary."

Sir George huffed through his moustache, and muttered, adding out loud that *something out of the ordinary* was the bally understatement of the century. "Some dead chap's ashes in his dinner service—silver, what's more—ghastly!"

In response to the clamorous demands of his family, he told them as much as he could remember of Euphemia's lecture, and poured another tot of whisky in his tea.

"Been looking into all this, while everyone else was saying how exciting it was," he said, glumly sipping. "Had a word— quite a few words—with a chap in Woodchester."

"Woodchester?" said Nigel, frowning. "Oh, yes, the mosaic Mother went to see and the Nuts didn't. That was Roman too, wasn't it?"

"*And* unique, the way Dr. Braxted thinks ours might be," said Sir George. "Woodchester—largest Orpheus pavement north of the Alps. Plummergen—funeral arrangements certainly unique, Dr. Braxted says . . . Wretched woman's thrilled. Can't wait to carry on digging. Going to write reports in journals, and put this place on the map, she says. Said I didn't want her to."

There was a startled silence. Nigel said, cautiously: "I don't really see how you can stop her. It's a free country—that's what you fought the War for, isn't it?—and then there's the freedom of the press, especially the, well, the scholastic papers. If we've got it, we've got it—we can hardly cover it up again and pretend it isn't there."

"Ah." Sir George sat forward, eyes bright. "Like Woodchester—quite agree with you, we can't. People would only hang around waiting for us to uncover it again. But if we leave it open—ugh. Woodchester's a small place—know how many visitors they had, in seven weeks?" He did not wait for a reply. "More than a hundred and forty-one thousand. Hardly bigger than Plummergen," he pointed out, as Nigel and his horrified mother exclaimed aloud. "Imagine the chaos—roads blocked, nowhere to park, fences broken, trespass, not enough toilets . . ."

In his rising emotion, Sir George was turning quite red in the face, his moustache bristling. "Only people who did well out of it were local shops—everyone else glad to see the back of it for another ten years, poor devils. Except," he added, as Lady Colveden murmured that, now he mentioned it, the experience had not been one of the most peaceful of her life, "that they aren't going to, ever again. Couldn't face it—can't blame them, either."

"I suppose," said Nigel, "you can't. I hadn't realised things had been quite so bad."

"Grim," said Sir George, as Lady Colveden shook her head and sighed. "Can't have that sort of thing happening here, and so I told Dr. Braxted. Wasn't too happy at first, until I'd, ah, explained my, ah, brain wave—had it up my sleeve in case of emergency," he said. "I was right, wasn't I?"

"Were you?" Nigel grinned at his father, who was preening himself, stroking his moustache with a pleased forefinger. "How do we know, unless you tell us what this brain wave was and let us judge for ourselves?"

"We're sure it was," interjected Lady Colveden, shooting a dagger-glance at her son, who winked. "We've no need to go judging your ideas, George, because we both know they're always sensible. Er—what was this particular idea?"

Sir George tipped a third tot of whisky into his tea, and a smile crept across his face: his mood had lightened in direct proportion to the amount of alcohol inside him. "Told you I'd talked to a chap from Woodchester," he said, raising his cup in a silent toast. "Talked to another chap, as well, that this first chap knew—chap called Woodward. The second chap, that is. Saved our bacon, if I'm not mistaken—dashed hard work, but it'll be worth it in the end—told La Braxted it was this way or nothing. Didn't like it, but had to agree— my land, after all. My mosaic, what's left of it—and this way, she'll have the whole blasted lot in her museum, and more, and then she can leave us in peace. No gogglers, no gawpers . . ."

"Pity," murmured Nigel, irrepressible as ever. "What a captive audience they would have made! It could have been instead of an admission charge: *You don't get to see the mosaic and the silver tea set unless you come to the pantomime as well.* We'd have topped up the Organ Fund within minutes, and made a profit for the church roof, too."

"Nigel, really," protested his mother, without too much conviction; she'd been thinking the same thing herself. "Do tell us, George, what this brain wave was, and how Mr. Woodward helped. We're simply longing to lavish praise and admiration on you—and how can we, if we don't know?"

Sir George stopped gazing into his half-empty cup of tea, and beamed on his inquisitive family. "Easy," he said, with a slight slurring of the word. "Dig the whole thing up—fill in the gaps—cart it off to Brettenden, and Bob's your uncle!"

chapter
~11~

SIR GEORGE CHUCKLED, in a rather hazy fashion. "Bob's your uncle," he repeated, as if he found the phrase highly amusing. "That's his name," he explained, intercepting surreptitious glances from his wife and son in the direction of the whisky bottle. "Bob—Bob Woodward. Knows what he's talking about, all right. He's a builder, just the sort of chap we need. And Woodchester, as well . . ."

He went on to explain that, at the most recent—indeed, the last ever—uncovering of the Great Pavement at Woodchester, Bob Woodward, a local man, had been so taken with the beauty of the mosaic, damaged though it was; and so overwhelmed with sympathy for the plight of the villagers whose lives, as custodians of the treasure, were so sadly disrupted every ten years, that he had determined to bring this rare beauty to the world without the world ever again having to invade the village to see it.

Accordingly, he had spent over a week taking more than three hundred close-up photographs of the site; had transferred these photographs to colour transparencies; and had projected the transparencies to the underside of a table made of armoured glass, on which rested a layer of strong plastic sheeting. Piece by painstaking pottery piece, he and his brother John were matching size and colour exactly to the image from below. As each section was finished, it was removed, to make way for another: in this way, the Woodwards intended that their replica would be portable when it was complete.

"But how," enquired Lady Colveden, "*can* they complete

it? I'm sure they're both every bit as clever as you say, but there's almost half of the original missing."

"Books," said Sir George, waving his empty teacup with a flourish. "Research—museums, other pavements. Woodchester's not the only one, y'know, just the biggest. Don't suppose ours'll turn out to be the only one, either," he added, in a hopeful tone. "Not once they've uncovered the blessed thing properly, I mean."

"But suppose," enquired Nigel, who was starting to feel intrigued by the problem thus presented, "they find ours *is* the only one? What do we do then?"

His mother shot him a warning look as his father's moustache bristled in an alarming manner. "I'm sure I don't see why it should be," she said firmly. "If even Woodchester isn't, then I imagine they'll have others similar to ours in Italy, or somewhere . . ."

"Ah, Italy," said Sir George, who had served for a time in Italy during the War. "Wouldn't mind another trip there m'self. Research, y'know—harrumph! Leave that side of it to the experts, of course. Something to keep 'em busy until the spring."

"What happens in the spring?" asked Lady Colveden, which elicited a gurgling reply from her son she pointedly chose not to hear. Her husband, flushed and excited, hurried on with his explanation.

The silver dinner service having been removed, it was unlikely anything else of obvious value remained on the temple site; preliminary excavations had already shown it to extend no more than twenty feet in any direction, including the walls. As the winter was upon them, with shortening days and worsening weather, little could be done until—a glare for Nigel—general conditions improved; and, having taken photographs and made notes, the archaeologists would cover the excavations with soil and sand, return to Brettenden, and wait for things to improve.

While they waited, Dr. Braxted and, er, anyone else—Sir George stroked his moustache again—who might come in handy would consult with the brothers Woodward to learn as much as possible of the art of mosaic replication. Come the spring, the site would be uncovered, and photographs would be taken—Sir George's moustache positively smirked—in the same way as had happened at Woodchester. Then the entire mosaic would be lifted—

"How?" demanded his audience, who had watched the level sink in the bottle of whisky and now feared that it had all been too much for him.

But Sir George merely chuckled for their lack of faith. "Ways," he said, airily. "Glue gauze to the upper surface, cut through the cement, pop a board underneath and slide it on in sections—or roll the thing up like a bally carpet, if you prefer. Have to leave all that to the experts, of course. But once it's safely lifted—take it to a museum, fill in the gaps à la Woodward, and hey presto! Need never see another tourist here in our lives."

It was not to be supposed that Miss Seeton's inadvertent discovery of a Roman temple and its accompanying treasure would pass unnoticed outside the village. Only the fact that the way to the former site of the Haunted Oak was so far from the road deterred more people from coming to stare at whatever might be going on; but the local newspaper ran the story on its front page, and a stringer for the national press, recognising Miss Seeton's name, alerted a wider audience to the fact that the famous Brolly was once more in the news.

But things, even Sir George had to acknowledge, could have been worse. Short days and bad weather, coupled with the promise that by Easter things would be better organised, held off much of the dreaded invasion. An old Plummergen hand, Amelita Forby of the *Daily Negative* (enchanted by a Seeton scoop in which her close personal rival Thrudd Banner, briefly abroad on a World Wide Press assignment, for once could not share) conspired with the rest of her Fleet Street colleagues to minimise the fuss. As Miss Seeton so often (even if unintentionally) made headlines, and thus sold papers, she must be regarded as being their bread and butter; and it made no sense to disrupt the food supply, especially so close to Christmas . . .

So, by and large, the crowds stayed away. Not all visitors,

however, were unwelcome. The Colvedens acknowledged that, the as yet unidentified temple having been discovered within the parish boundaries, Plummergen had a right to show some interest in the proceedings. Local sightseers prepared to brave the mud and the rain were therefore welcome to watch what was going on—among these sightseers being, in the interests of furthering their education, a party of children from the village school, escorted by Miss Alice Maynard, Mr. Martin Jessyp, and Miss Emily Dorothea Seeton.

Miss Seeton was amazed at the changes that had occurred in the field since her mistletoe expedition of the previous week. What was left of the Haunted Oak had gone, loaded on a tractor to be sawn up for firewood. Nigel's suggestion that it could be used as a Yule Log had been vetoed on practical grounds: Yule Logs (as his mother pointed out to him) were supposed to burn on the hearth for the full Twelve Days of Christmas, and there wasn't enough left of the Haunted Oak to keep a respectable Guy Fawkes bonfire alight for more than a couple of hours.

From that place in the hedge where the oak had stood to a distance of some thirty feet around, the ground was in turmoil. What remained of the hedge itself was probably living on borrowed time: Dr. Braxted had dropped copious hints about its presence to Sir George, who was fighting a strong rearguard action but feared he would succumb in the end. In the fields either side of the doomed boundary, mud, trenches, planks, pegs, and string disturbed the regular brown furrows, neatly ploughed by Nigel before anything untoward had happened. The archaeologists scrabbled in the mud with forks and trowels, their brushes and notebooks and pencils close to hand; and Dr. Braxted, beaming, welcomed the party almost with open arms.

"So this is Miss Seeton!" She wiped an earthy paw on her skirt, a convenient mud-coloured tweed, and shook Miss Seeton warmly by the hand. "Without you, Miss Seeton, none of this"—the familiar earth-spraying gesture—"would have been possible. You've simply no idea how grateful we— historians everywhere—are to you. No idea at all!"

Miss Seeton, blushing, looked at her toes, making modest and noncommittal noises. Dr. Braxted nodded a vague wel-

come to the rest of the party, linked her arm in that of her
honoured guest, found the inevitable umbrella in her way, and,
with a quick word to Miss Seeton, hooked it over her own arm
as she dragged her captive VIP off to inspect the progress of
the dig: on which (she said) she would value Miss Seeton's
opinion.

Miss Seeton's secret opinion was that it was as well she
had remembered to wear her gumboots, and that she had
reminded the children to wear theirs. This, however, she felt
was hardly the sort of opinion such an expert as Dr. Braxted
would value. She decided it would be safer to say nothing,
and to do nothing but go where she was taken, and look at
what she was shown. With fifty pairs of youthful feet, kept in
check by the stern boots of Miss Maynard and Mr. Jessyp, following, Miss Seeton's size-four Wellingtons trudged dutifully
along the duckboards between the trenches, while Dr. Braxted
pointed out places of interest.

"This would have been the temple entrance . . . altar over
there . . . *lares* and *penates* . . . oil lamps—those are still in the
tent—show you later . . . broken statue—no identification . . .
ashes interred just *here*."

Euphemia paused beside a wooden peg. "Just think," she
said, with a shudder, "if some barbarian with a metal detector
had come along and found it—the Brumalix dinner service, I
mean. He'd have dug it up and melted it down for the silver,
or sold it to some megalomaniac collector with no sense
of history—and that would have been that. Lost to us here
forever—but thanks to you, Miss Seeton, we've managed to
beat the blighter!"

Miss Seeton felt her arm squeezed in fervent gratitude,
and blinked about her as if looking for the unnamed blighter
with his metal detector. She saw instead only the familiar
faces of her pupils and colleagues, the bent heads of busy
archaeologists. She smiled vaguely, and made an attempt to
break free from Dr. Braxted's oppressive clutch. Euphemia,
misinterpreting her movement as a sign of boredom, apologised, and led her on, the others trailing in their wake.

One muddy hole looks, to the uninitiated, much like another. Even the remnants of mosaic, clearly visible from above,

could only hold the attention for a limited length of time before the various pieces of the pattern so far revealed blurred and blended into a multicoloured haze, despite the detail of Euphemia's explanations.

"The correct name for the small tiles used by the *musivarius,* or mosaicist, is *tesserae* . . . cut from larger blocks of stone—broken off with pincers—hammer and chisel . . . natural colours . . . white, cream—various forms of calcium carbonate . . . red, orange—brick, tile, sandstone . . . blue, black, grey—shale . . . assorted marbles . . . coloured glass highlights . . . repetitive geometric patterns—grids, polygons . . . complex realistic figures—birds, animals, mythological characters . . ."

The watchful eyes of Miss Maynard and Mr. Jessyp prevented any misbehaviour on the part of the children, tempting though so much mud might be. Miss Seeton, held close to Dr. Braxted's side as that earnest enthusiast continued to propound, found herself succumbing to temptation, and suppressed the yawn she was unable to stifle without being too obvious. One had hoped that so much artistic skill, lost for generations and so romantically—Miss Seeton felt herself blush—restored to the world, would have seemed less like, well, like a building site. It was hard to envisage the whole, without actually seeing it uncovered to one's gaze: but this, it seemed, would not be possible until the spring of next year.

" . . . a thorough excavation," said Euphemia, savouring the prospect. "Sir George, of course, was happy to give us his blessing . . ." This, Miss Seeton (who had heard Lady Colveden on the subject more than once) took silent leave to doubt. "Not too happy, though," went on Dr. Braxted, "about having to wait a little to sow his wheat or barley or sugarbeet, whatever it was"—she dismissed the preoccupations of the working farmer with a wave of her supportive arm. Miss Seeton took advantage of the moment, and moved away. Dr. Braxted moved after her, and grabbed her arm again—"But, as I told him, in the interests of historical research, what do a few acres of potatoes matter?"

Miss Seeton could well imagine that Sir George and Nigel would say they mattered a great deal, though she was too polite to say so. She emitted another of her noncommittal murmurs, and Euphemia, acknowledging it vaguely, leaned closer to continue with her lecture.

"Sir George's Woodchester suggestion will, of course, require considerable thought before it can be adapted to this particular site. The Woodwards estimate that it will take them *ten years* to complete their replica—which is, admittedly, far larger than the Rytham Hall mosaic . . ."

Dr. Braxted swung out her free arm in the familiar gesture, intended to encompass the entire dig. Earth fragments flew from her tweeded sleeve—and with them went Miss Seeton's umbrella, which the engrossed archaeologist had utterly forgotten.

"Good gracious," said Miss Seeton, blinking.

From behind her, above the cries of apology from Euphemia Braxted, a chorus of fifty treble voices piped up:

"Miss, Miss, yer brolly's gone into orbit . . . Fifth of November was *last* month . . . If you don't want it no more, can I keep it, Miss? . . . Fetch it for you, shall I?"

Before anyone could speak, a maiden whose threshold of boredom had been far lower than that of her fellows had leaped from the duckboard into its accompanying ditch; had scrambled across the stretch of mud on the other side; and had then arrived at the spot where, point downwards in the otherwise untroubled earth, Miss Seeton's umbrella quivered like an arrow fired straight from a bow to its target.

"Got it, Miss!" cried the energetic one, as adult voices expostulated. "Hang on a tick . . ."

"Rachel Truman," commanded Mr. Jessyp, "come back here this minute!"

But Rachel, busily tugging at the handle of the umbrella as it seemed determined to remain stuck in the mud, did not hear him. "Come on," she muttered. "Come on, you . . ."

There was a pause, during which a rhythmic squelching sound filled the air as Rachel rocked the brolly to and fro. Then a shout of triumph, and the little girl, still clutching the handle, fell backwards with her feet in the air, the freed umbrella in her grasp.

"*Rachel Truman!*" The chorus of horrified adult voices was

enough to deafen an adder. Rachel, grinning, clambered messily to her feet . . .

And was about to return to dry land with her prize when she paused, and looked down.

"Here, Miss—you want me to bring this bit of writing, as well?"

chapter

-12-

AT MISS SEETON'S side, Euphemia froze. "Little girl, come here at once! That is—No, keep still! Oh, crumbs . . ."

Encouraged by the cheers of her friends, Rachel, dripping mud, tramped back across the raw brown wasteland, Miss Seeton's umbrella in one hand, the *bit of writing* in the other. She ignored both Dr. Braxted's anguished moans and the reproaches of Miss Maynard and Mr. Jessyp, clearly regarding restoration of the lost property as paramount.

"Here, Miss—here's your brolly. Oh, and the writing, if you want it."

As Miss Seeton gulped, and thanked her, receiving the umbrella from her eager hands, Euphemia Braxted snatched the *writing*—a fragment of dark red tile—and began to peruse it. Rachel, beaming, proceeded to brush mud from her small person without any sign that her parents, or her teachers, might reasonably complain at the state of her clothing.

Euphemia uttered a strange, strangulated little shriek. Everyone turned towards her: even the ditch-digging archaeologists dropped their trowels to stare.

"This . . . this inscription," babbled Dr. Braxted, waving Rachel's find aloft in one excited hand. "The most amazing thing—you'll never believe what it says—it's absolutely unique in Romano-British history—all the others are on the southern side of the Alps . . ."

She ran out of steam, and bent her head once more to the piece of tile, her nose almost touching the surface. "Unique," she murmured, lovingly. "History has been made today—and

all," raising her head, "thanks to you and your umbrella yet
again, Miss Seeton! You'll never guess . . . but this inscription
says that the temple erected by the family of Siberius Gelidus
Brumalix is in honour of the goddess Glacia!"

To which astounding announcement there could be only one
reply: and it was left to Miss Seeton to make it.

"Good gracious," said Miss Emily Dorothea Seeton.

Mud, string, wooden pegs, and firewood; goddesses and fairy
godmothers . . . to those with a pantomime on their minds, the
revelations of Dr. Braxted, though no doubt interesting, must
pale beside the excitements of Plummergen's *Cinderella*.

In the woodland glade, poor Cinders, exhausted from her
labours, sat on a tree stump, bewailing her sad lot. How hard
she had to work! But she wouldn't really mind, if only her
sisters would show her some affection—if only her dear father
would show her the affection he'd been used to show! In the
happy days of old . . .

Emmy Putts sang a plaintive little ditty, and wept tears Lady
Colveden had decided would be greatly helped if a raw onion
or two from Mr. Jessyp's string were to be concealed in her
wood-gathering basket. Cinderella sniffed, and daintily wiped
her eyes, squared her shoulders, and resolved to Carry On as
Duty Decreed:

> "For wasting time is not what I must do—
> My sisters would be angry if they knew."

Enter Buttons Colveden, full of sympathy. He will help
Cinderella to gather firewood, though he cannot spare much
time, being busy organising the rest of the picnic in case the
Prince should pass that way. Cinders tells him she has no wish
to get her dear friend into trouble, and that he should leave her
to manage on her own; which Buttons, with a few backward
looks and sighs, does.

Enter Prince Charming, revelling in a few moments' freedom from the restrictions of the Court. Maureen's legs might
well be magnificent, but her histrionic abilities were limited,
and Lady Colveden had given up trying to coax any real acting

out of her. It would be enough that she did not erupt into a fit of the giggles at crucial moments in the plot—of which this was one.

The Prince, on first noticing Cinderella, sighed aloud, observing sadly that the royal life was hard beyond belief. How he longed to be alone! (Maureen's imitation of Greta Garbo was excruciating, but the audience, Lady Colveden hoped, would be in kindly mood.) Even here, in the middle of the greenwood, a poor Prince could never have any privacy. Look at that girl over there! On the other hand—the Prince edged round behind a convenient bush for a closer look—she was undoubtedly a pretty girl . . . Maureen slapped a thigh, and struck an appreciative pose, unnoticed by poor Cinderella. Yes, a very pretty girl—perhaps she might be interested in a position at Court? But did a Prince really need any more people about him, when there were already so very many? . . . And Maureen hid herself behind the bush while making up her mind whether or not to approach the stranger with an offer of work.

Enter an old woman, bent and weary. Mrs. Stillman, a bag of sticks over one shoulder, a tattered shawl hiding her face, limps slowly across the glade, gathering up the few slivers of kindling not worthy of Cinderella's attention. Cinderella, dismayed, leaps from her seat on the fallen log to offer the poor old lady the sticks in her own sack: she is, insists Cinderella, young and strong and not at all tired, really. It will take her just a few minutes to fill her sack again . . .

Mrs. Stillman, pulling herself with an effort to her full height, accepts the sticks with becoming gratitude.

> "My child, this is a kind and generous act.
> I'll add your sticks to those within my sack,
> And homeward wend at once my weary way.
> (*Aside*) Before too long, your kindness I'll repay!"

Exit Mrs. Stillman, with a meaningful gesture lost on Cinderella, but fully appreciated by the audience. Cinders wipes away an onion-tear, sighs, and sinks back on the log, trying to summon up the strength to go wood-gathering again.

From behind his bush, enter Prince Charming, full of admiration for Cinderella's noble deed. He offers to help the young lady make up her bundle of kindling in double-quick time, and Cinders, with a sweet smile, gratefully accepts. They sing a duet, dance together, and drift off arm-in-arm, clearly so smitten with each other that it is going to be a long time before the firewood basket is full—the humour of this situation not lost on the audience, who had often been frustrated beyond belief by Prince Maureen in her everyday persona as deputy waitress/receptionist of the George and Dragon Hotel.

Maureen flicked a languid duster around Reception as Doris, her colleague and superior, tended the enormous cheeseplant that was landlord Charley Mountfitchet's most cherished possession, feeding it with liquid fertiliser and wiping its leaves with a milk-and-water-mixture-soaked cloth kept especially for the purpose. There came a rattle at the door, followed by a strident ring on the bell.

Maureen put up a hand to stifle a yawn, and continued to dust the banisters. Doris, on her knees, stared over her shoulder, and snapped:

"Wake up, do!" Maureen blinked. "Answer that door, for heaven's sake!" enlarged Doris, still on her knees. "And I don't know why it's shut in the first place, this time of day—get on with you, girl!"

Maureen lowered her duster as the bell pealed out again, and ambled along the hall without troubling to remind Doris that the door had been locked in case of accident when the carpets were being vacuumed. She turned the key, twisted the handle, opened the door, and wandered back to her duster without waiting to see whether whoever had been outside on the step had bothered to follow her in.

Doris stifled a snort of exasperation—Plummergen might moan about Maureen, but when foreigners were within earshot it closed ranks—and began to rise, creaking, from her knees to greet the newcomer, who was bumping a large and unwieldy suitcase over the threshold.

"Good morning," said the suitcase bumper, before Doris was properly on her feet. "Have you a room in this hotel?"

Had this question been asked earlier in the week, when the identity of the Glacia temple, so dramatically disclosed by Miss Seeton's umbrella, had been announced to the world. Doris would have been forced to say that they hadn't: but news dates quickly. Almost everyone who wanted to see the dig had now seen it; and it was widely known that the archaeologists were to cover the mosaic within a matter of days, and that nothing more would happen until the spring.

"Yes, there's a room," said Doris. "You want one?"

The newcomer—a small, slight, smooth-skinned man with a surprisingly bushy moustache—nodded. "With a bath, of course," he said in a soft, high-pitched voice, as he abandoned his suitcase and made for the reception desk.

Doris grinned: the American accent had already told her to expect as much. She opened the flap and went behind the counter, sliding the hotel register round so that the moustached one could fill it in easily. "Name first," she said helpfully, as he fished in his pocket for a pen.

"Ah, the name," said the American, nodding. "The George and Dragon—very inneresting. An original, of course."

Doris bristled. Did he think this was some modern jumped-up place all plate glass and plastic? "There's bin a George in Plummergen for hundreds of years," she informed the foreigner crossly.

"Oh, sure—but not in this particular building." Rather than signing the register, the American paused to survey the entrance hall with an apparently expert eye. "Nineteen-thirties, I'd say—no later. I could tell even while I was outside, my dear girl—but who cares for that?" as Doris bristled even more. "It was the name I was so inneresting in—the George and Dragon." He pulled the register across, and continued speaking as he began to write. "So many of your lovely old George and Dragon inns changed their names, you know, to the Green Dragon when King George the First came to the throne in 1714—because he was a foreigner, and spoke no English. So nobody wanted to seem to show disrespect to the new king, for all he was so unpopular . . ."

"That right?" said Doris, as he finished signing the register, pushed it back to Doris, and screwed the top back on his fountain pen. Doris pursed her lips as she read the name inscribed in a fussy, ornate hand.

"*Professor Caernavon Carter, Boston, Massachussetts, U.S.A.* Well, Professor Carter, you're in the Blue Riband Suite, on the first floor—here's your key. There isn't a lift," she added, as Professor Carter opened his mouth.

The moustache quivered. "Pardon me?"

"No lift," repeated Doris, and waved across at the suitcase lurking by the door. "Mr. Mountfitchet—he's the landlord—he's not here right now—and me with my back, so *I* can't help . . ." Pointless to suppose, even for a minute, that Maureen might be induced to assist.

Doris jabbed a finger towards the stairs. "On the first floor," she said again, very slowly, as if to Maureen on one of the girl's even-less-active-than-usual days.

Light dawned in the eyes of Professor Carter. "You have no elevator!" he cried, his voice rising to a squeak. "With rooms on the *second* floor, as we know it—how quaint, how old-fashioned. Living history!"

Doris wasn't sure she cared for being considered historical, and scowled. Professor Carter, however, was oblivious to all her scowls and bristlings, turning his back on her to tread lightly across the hall to the suitcase, which seemed larger than ever as he bent to pick it up.

Then he straightened, and turned round again. "I may as well leave it for the moment, until Mr.—Mountfitchet, was it?—comes back. It's easier for me to unload my equipment down here, for one thing—and the case won't come to any harm while I'm away, will it?"

"While you're away?" Doris found herself gaping at the professor in a most Maureen-like manner. "But you've only just got here."

"And here, my dear girl, I intend to stay—to sleep, at any rate." Professor Carter bowed, one pale, plump hand on his waistcoated middle. "During the day, however, I shall be at work—the dig, you know. I doubt if I'll even have time to come back for meals—which reminds me, I must make suitable arrangements with your Catering Manager. If he's around now, I'd like a word with him."

Doris, unlike Maureen, lived in, and with landlord Charley made up the George's full complement of catering staff, except at the height of the season—or unless the place was crowded with reporters after another of Miss Seeton's little exploits had become News. December was hardly the height of the season; and, as far as Doris knew, Miss Seeton hadn't been up to anything for almost a week, which (by Miss Seeton's standards) was news with whiskers on. She was therefore so surprised by the professor's remark that she found herself volunteering some comments on the availability of sandwiches before coming to her senses.

"The dig?" she repeated, even more Maureen-like. "D'you mean that Roman ruin Rytham Hall way?"

"The Temple of the Goddess Glacia," Professor Carter corrected her, his eyes glittering. "Final resting place of Siberius Gelidus Brumalix! The brilliance of the *faber argentarius*— the *magnum opus* of the master *musivarius*—what else could I mean?"

Doris shrugged. "How should I know what you mean? I've never learned French, or whatever that was . . ." The Latin for *silversmith* and *masterpiece of the mosaicist* was hardly common currency in Plummergen, even after the discovery of the Roman remains. "But if it's the temple you want to see, well, you can't, not anymore. Sir George—"

"Can't?" The squeak was back in Professor Carter's voice, and the moustache looked as if it might leap from his face in his agitation. "*Can't?* My good girl, what manner of word is that?"

Doris, about to take umbrage at his tone, hesitated, and regarded him doubtfully. The man might say he was an American, but how could the likes of her be sure of that? Maybe he was really French, which would explain it. For a second time, she slowed her speech as she addressed him, even more slowly than before.

"You. Can't. See. The. Mosaic. Sir. George. Doesn't. Want. People. At. The. Hall. Again. Until. Next. Spring." She paused, and watched the professor turn white with—rage? disappointment? "It's on Sir George's land, see, so he's every right to say who goes there and who doesn't—"

"Rubbish!" squealed Professor Carter, stamping a neat, well-shod foot. "Who is this Sir George? What rights can such an obvious barbarian claim over a national—an innernational—treasure—part of the world's cultural heritage? There can be no prohibitions, no boundaries in the innerests of historical and archaeological research—the past should be free to the world for the greater unnerstanding of the present!"

"I don't know about that, I'm sure." Doris dismissed past and present alike with another baffled shrug. "What I do know is that Sir George don't want no more visitors traipsing all over the show to gawp while him and the rest is busy working on the farm—and anyway, even Dr. Braxted's agreed that's the best thing to be done. So—"

"Braxted?" broke in the professor, spitting the word in his fury. "Who is this man Braxted, doctor or otherwise, to presume to *agree* to such a . . . a ludicrous proposal?"

Doris, coasting comfortably into middle age, was normally (except with Maureen) an easygoing soul. Never, in her blackest nightmares, had she dreamed that she would one day find herself flying the flag of women's liberation in the entrance hall of the George and Dragon. "Dr. *Euphemia* Braxted," she said, pointedly, "is from the museum in Brettenden, and *she's* going to dig up Sir George's mosaic at Easter and take it to Brettenden to keep—and that's where everyone'll have to go if they want to see it again. So I'm sorry if you've come all the way from—from abroad," she amended, "but you can't see the mosaic, and that's all there is to it—they've had a bundle of folk trampling the place to pieces along to the Hall, and her ladyship's fairly fed up with it, believe me. There's plenty to see in these parts if it's old things you're wanting," she added helpfully, as the professor emitted a furious snort of disgust. "There's Ellen Terry's house—and Brettenden Church, with the tower they built instead of the seawall, so the sea come in and flooded everywhere, and the vicar's memorial with the eleven days lost because of changing the calendar way back before Queen Victoria—and Wittersham, where they found the dinosaur's skellington—millions of years old, that was—"

"Pah!" Professor Carter dismissed these offerings with an even more disgusted snort. Forgetting his suitcase, he strode to the hotel door and flung it open. "Whoever these people are—Sir George and this so-called Dr. Braxted—they can have no unnerstanding of the responsibility that is theirs. Rytham Hall can be no more than half a mile away, if my reading of your national press is correct." Doris, startled by the fiery gleam in his eye, nodded dumbly.

"Then," said Professor Caernavon Carter, in a tone that meant Business, "to Rytham Hall I shall go!"

And, without another word, he stormed out of the George and Dragon, slamming the door so hard behind him that the inside handle fell off.

chapter
-13-

MISS SEETON, HER umbrella over her arm and her handbag open as she rummaged for her key, was just about to unlock the front door when she heard the sound of nearby slamming, followed by hasty footsteps—footsteps heading, she soon realised, in the direction of Sweetbriars. Though a gentlewoman does not display undue curiosity, Miss Seeton considered it not unduly curious of herself to wonder if there might be something wrong across the road at the George and Dragon, from where the sounds had obviously come.

She turned, and took a few steps down her short, paved path to see if she could render any assistance in whatever emergency had just arisen: and was somewhat startled to observe a small, pink-faced man with an enormous moustache and wild, glittering eyes rushing towards her at a rate even she—fond of walking and, thanks to her yoga exercises, more than usually fit for her age as she was—did not believe she could maintain for long.

The angry-looking little man shot her a sideways glance as he neared the gate, narrowed his eyes, and rushed on. His feet, thought Miss Seeton, tapped in an almost—she felt her own cheeks turn pink, with the realisation that one was being overfanciful—machine-gun rhythm . . .

"Rytham Hall!" As Miss Seeton—startled on hearing her thoughts, as it seemed, read by this small stranger—jumped, dropping her umbrella, the man wheeled round and glared at her. "Is it down this road?"

"Rytham Hall?" Miss Seeton, bending to pick up her brolly, blinked. Really, one was so confused . . . "Yes, it is, I believe—that is . . ."

For all his hurry, the moustachioed man came to a halt, staring: at the key she still held in her hand, at the door it so obviously opened. "You live here, and you can't tell me who lives down this road besides you? I know you English are supposed to be insular, but that kind of talk is . . . is plain foolish! The whole village seems full of fools, to my mind— fools, and ignorant barbarians." He darted back several steps until he was standing right beside Miss Seeton's gate, which he slapped with an irritable hand.

"Tell me, ma'am, what manner of spelling do you call *that*? *Sweetbriars!* Check in any dictionary—I suppose no such thing as a Webster is obtainable in this godforsaken spot—and you'll find the word takes an *e*, not an *a*. Ignorant fools, the whole crowd of you in this village, and not deserving of your good fortune! It seems I arrived just in time . . ."

With a whirl of his coattails, the man spun on his heel and was gone, leaving Miss Seeton gazing after him. Really, it had all happened with such speed, it was no wonder . . . Just what was it this Mr. Webster had said? Something to do with her cottage—or had it been the gate? Really, if only one had been less preoccupied with recovering one's umbrella—it must certainly have seemed rude to address a gentleman from a half-stooped position, although the term *ignorant barbarian* was possibly—was surely, she felt, a little undeserved, in the circumstances. Except, of course, that Mr. Webster had clearly been in a great hurry to find the Colvedens, and even the least delay must have been vexatious . . .

Miss Seeton, with a sigh of regret for her unwitting lapse of courtesy, gathered up her belongings, unlocked her door, and went inside without once remembering that she had intended to find out whether all was well across the road at the George and Dragon.

Miss Seeton's memory is not so much faulty as selective. Like the sundial, she recalls only the golden hours; within minutes of her homecoming, she had forgotten the brief irruption of the angry little man into her quiet life, and was in the kitchen making herself a cup of tea—a most welcome reward after a day spent teaching children who, as the holidays approached, grew ever more excitable.

Not, of course, that any had misbehaved: in the presence of Miss Seeton, who is held in awe by every Plummergen child and not a few adults, no one misbehaves. Miss Seeton does not fully understand the great respect in which she is held: she accepts the invariable good conduct of her classes as no more than anyone with similar years in the profession would achieve—but she is wrong . . .

The children, however, even under Miss Seeton's watchful eye, were far from angelic; and, with Christmas coming, and the promise of presents, found their high spirits ever harder to curb. Miss Seeton, carrying her tray into the sitting room, chuckled as she thought of the results of this afternoon's session. The Flight into Egypt having been read aloud, and the Bible passed in turn along the neat rows of desks, the children had been told that they could paint or draw whichever scene from the story they chose.

Miss Seeton had come to the desk at which Katy Evans, her dark head bent over the paper, was putting the finishing touches to an undoubtedly vivid picture. A thin man in a flapping headdress and flowing robes held the reins of—a camel? No, a donkey—on which sat a woman, carrying a baby—all save the donkey with saucer like golden haloes round their heads—and, with semicircular dotted lines indicating its bouncing progress, behind the donkey a monstrous, long-legged, bug-eyed creature with green antennae.

"Nearly finished, Miss." Katy rubbed briskly with her forefinger at a line which displeased her, and added a quick green scribble of grass. "There—done!"

Beaming with pride, she held the masterpiece up for Miss Seeton's approval. Miss Seeton, puzzled, stared.

Katy's face fell. "Don't you think it'll do, Miss? You said we could draw what we liked, so I did . . ."

"It's very good," said Miss Seeton, without a qualm: the child's disappointment at her teacher's lack of initial enthusiasm was proof enough that the imaginative experience—whatever it was—must have been profound: and her attempts to portray it had, clearly, been equally profound. Which was, naturally, good, and deserving of praise: the purpose of art being to teach the children to see, and Katy having all too evidently seen *something* . . .

Whatever it was. "Katy," said Miss Seeton gently, "I may be very foolish, but I fear I cannot quite see . . . which particular part of the story you have chosen to illustrate. If you could give it a title, we will pin it up on the board with some of the others."

Little Miss Evans looked as puzzled as her teacher. "But it's the bit in the Bible, Miss, that I heard Helen say clear as anything. God said 'Take the young child and his mother and flea into Egypt'—and there they all are, see?"

Seldom had Miss Seeton found it so hard to keep her face straight, and seldom had she been so grateful to her yoga for giving her strength of mind as well as body. "Yes, my dear," she said, her voice imperceptibly shaking, as Katy pointed in turn to the thin man, the baby, the woman, and the monstrous, bouncing—no, as a flea it must surely be hopping—creature. "I shall give you," said Miss Seeton firmly, "a red star for this, Katy . . ."

And, as she outlined a six-pointed star in the bottom corner of the picture, Miss Seeton was pleased to note that even her hand did not shake.

It shook now, as Miss Seeton, pouring tea, gave herself up to kindly amusement. She saw again the bug-eyed hopper, the camel, the thin man with his eastern headdress . . . and found herself, as she wondered which biscuit she would eat first, starting to hum.

Yet it was not, as she might have expected, a Christmas carol which came from her tuneless lips as she chose a chocolate digestive. "Like Webster's Dictionary," warbled Miss Seeton, "we're Morocco bound—good gracious!"

Miss Seeton had seen, and enjoyed, all the *Road* movies; had laughed as Bob, Bing, and Dorothy Lamour changed voices in the middle of the mirage-making desert—as Bob had hurtled across the ocean in the runaway diver's outfit—as Bob, the desperado, had demanded lemonade in a dirty glass. Yes, these had been some of her favourite films—but why . . . ?

"*White Christmas,*" said Miss Seeton happily, the voice of Bing Crosby crooning in her imagination. "Of course . . ."

And she finished her tea without giving the matter another thought—another conscious thought, that is. But it is the *sub*conscious of Miss Emily Seeton which is the more interesting animal: and her subconscious was already going into overdrive as she tidied away the tea things, then carried them into the kitchen, and shook her head at the dishmop. Her hands (she argued) were still shaky from her burst of laughter; her fingers were twitchy, uncertain—she had no wish to risk breaking anything by washing-up too soon—one did, after all, live on one's own—there was little, if any, urgency . . .

But it was not the aftermath of mirth which made the fingers of Miss Seeton twitch and fidget. From deep within her subconscious, the urge to draw—to Draw, in that special way which she tries never to acknowledge, of which she is so ashamed, which the police value so highly—was growing ever more strong.

"Oh, well . . ." Miss Seeton found herself leaving the kitchen without a backward glance, drifting in the direction of the sitting-room bureau in which much of her artist's paraphernalia is stored. "Well, I suppose . . ."

Her fingers were dancing now, the ache as she tried to restrain them almost painful. Miss Seeton, reckless of all else save the need to release the pins-and-needles tension, hunted out a selection of pencils and her drawing block, and settled, with relief, to work at the sitting-room table.

Scotland Yard might view influenza as a problem in logistics: Miss Erica Nuttel saw it as a personal affront. Did she not embrace the healthiest of lifestyles? Did she not eschew tobacco, alcohol, and (where possible) Water Board plumbing? Did she not walk miles daily, and forswear the fume-making internal combustion engine except once, or in unusual circumstances twice, a week?

It could only have been (the Nuts had decided, as they sneezed and sniffled their slow way back to health) on the Brettenden bus that flu germs had lurked in sufficient concentration to overcome even their vegetarian invincibility.

"Perhaps," suggested Mrs. Blaine hopefully, as Miss Nuttel sat weakly watching her chop spinach-beet leaves for a poultice, "we could think about acquiring our own transport, Eric. Then we wouldn't be forced to travel with everyone else—too unhealthy, crammed together like . . . like that," she swiftly amended: she'd been about to say *like sardines in a tin,* which would, she knew, have infuriated her friend. She scraped the noxious-looking mess from the board to the waiting saucepan, and turned up the heat.

"We could at least *think* about it, Eric . . ."

Miss Nuttel nodded slowly, as a horse contemplates which blade of grass it will munch next. "Time enough to think, while I was ill," she said at last. "Been meaning to talk to you about it—could be a good idea, Bunny. Have to look into it thoroughly, of course, but . . ."

Mrs. Blaine's little blackcurrant eyes gleamed. "Surely we have enough in the bank to buy just a *secondhand* car, Eric—it needn't be too—"

Miss Nuttel, who had been slumped in a convalescent pose at the other end of the kitchen table, sat bolt upright as if someone had jerked her bridle. "A car? Certainly not!" She narrowed her eyes, and flared her nostrils. "Petrol and oil cost money, never mind the pollution. Thought we might check in the local paper—classified—bound to be a tandem going cheap, somewhere. Ground's flat enough around these parts, goodness knows."

"I suppose it is," said Mrs. Blaine, faintly; and attacked the next bunch of beets with so much force that the resultant poultice was as much made of splinters as spinach.

The Brettenden bus—Plummergen's only public transport—runs, as its name suggests, northwards to Brettenden, and back again. Passengers wishing to travel farther afield must change in Brettenden in order to do so. The bus stop in Plummergen stands almost exactly opposite Lilikot, home of Miss Nuttel and Mrs. Blaine: a convenient location for their self-appointed purpose of keeping a close eye on everything that happens at the northern end of the village, but highly inconvenient when, as now, they wish to travel in a southerly direction.

Since they scorned to ask anyone for a lift, and none of their car-owning cronies thought to offer one, it was not until Miss Nuttel was well past the cottonwool–legs stage of influenza that the Nuts decided the time had come to pay a visit to the Temple of Glacia at Rytham Hall, about which they had read in the newspapers, and heard so much on television and the wireless.

With the approach of Christmas, the days become not only shorter, but colder. Mrs. Blaine, still sulking for the secondhand car they'd so nearly had, sulked all the more when Miss Nuttel, having delayed the start of the excursion by her hunt for extra clothes, appeared at last with her thin frame wrapped in an extra cardigan and two woolly scarves underneath (to Mrs. Blaine's annoyance) Mrs. Blaine's second-best overcoat, appropriated by Miss Nuttel from its peg in the hall on the grounds that Bunny couldn't possibly wear two coats at once, and she (Eric) needed a larger one to accommodate so many additional layers.

Words were exchanged. The Nuts banged their way at last out of Lilikot and down the front path without either of them remembering to lock the door. This having been sorted out, it was a grim procession which made its way down The Street: in the lead, Miss Nuttel, pinch-faced and pale from long days immured in bed, striding out defiantly; pattering on her short legs irritably in the rear, Mrs. Blaine, trying not to let Eric hear her wheeze, and thinking that if she should suddenly drop down with a heart attack from Too Much Exercise, then it would Serve Some People Right.

The Nuts allowed their quarrel to lapse into abeyance, however, when they came to that southern end of The Street where it divides in two and either narrows, or turns right into Marsh Road. Sweetbriars is situated at this junction; and one could never be sure what spells Miss Seeton might choose to cast, with what evil eye she might choose to look, on the hapless traveller who passed her garden gate.

Once safely past the neatly lettered sign which had so disturbed Professor Carter, the Nuts resumed their schismatic progress for perhaps another hundred yards. It was then that Miss Nuttel, feeling she had proved her point, permitted her pace to slacken, her step to slow, and herself to slump against a convenient tree stump, moaning.

"Eric!" All other considerations now cast immediately aside, Mrs. Blaine panted up to Miss Nuttel and stood wringing her hands, while Miss Nuttel continued to moan. "Speak to me, Eric—don't say That Woman has bewitched you!" And she threw an anxious glance over her shoulder in the direction of Sweetbriars, and the chimney pots just visible above the trees. "Oh, Eric . . ."

Miss Nuttel, suppressing a smirk of satisfaction, gasped that she would be better soon, and that Bunny shouldn't fuss—but perhaps if she'd let her take her arm, they'd be able to move out of range rather than have to wait here . . .

Limping, weary, and worried, Mrs. Blaine supported Miss Nuttel's faltering form as far as the magnificent entrance to the Rytham Hall drive. Sir George (opined Mrs. Blaine), as a neighbour, a magistrate, and the one who was indirectly responsible for Miss Nuttel's misfortune, would of course be Only Too Glad to give them a lift home, once they'd seen the temple and the mosaic. If Eric felt strong enough just to make her way up the drive, they could ring at the front door and ask if there was anyone free to take them straight to the field where the digging was going on.

Eric felt strong enough, if only Bunny would continue to help her. Bunny would—what else were friends for? Peace having been restored, the two friends staggered together up the drive, rounding the last curve to see Sir George Colveden's car providentially, it seemed, at the ready; and, next to it, Sir George.

"What luck—" Mrs. Blaine was beginning, when Miss Nuttel dug her in the ribs with a bony elbow. Being taller, she could see more clearly what was going on.

"Talking to someone," she hissed, over Bunny's indignant squeak. "Looks as if they could be arguing—don't know who it is, though."

"Let's move closer—but quietly, of course," said Mrs. Blaine, in a glow of virtue. "We wouldn't want to interrupt them if it's obviously private business—too embarrassing, especially once we find out who the other person is—"

Miss Nuttel rounded on her with an exasperated snort. "Didn't say I couldn't *see,* Bunny—said I didn't *know* who it was. Man's a complete stranger. Never seen him before in my life."

"Oh," said Mrs. Blaine, as the two began to creep forward on silent-as-possible feet. "A complete stranger . . . you're always right, of course, Eric, but"—as the sound of raised voices reached them on the crisp winter air—"if he's such a stranger, how can Sir George know him well enough for them to be having such a terrible quarrel?"

chapter
-14-

THE TERRIBLE QUARREL between Injecta and Instructa came
at last to an end, as the Ugly Sisters completed—with the aid
of a weary Cinderella—their toilet and flounced away to the
Prince's ball, leaving Emmy Putts despondent and alone in
the scullery.

The evening's pantomime rehearsal was running rather late,
as it had taken Lady Colveden some time to calm her husband down after his altercation with Professor Carter. He
had brooded right through supper, and even Nigel had been
unable to jolly him out of it until he reminded his suffering
parent that the Show Must Go On, and Admiral Leighton
would be expecting him to help, as usual, with the sound
and lighting.

Nigel now made his entrance, pausing in the doorway to
watch Cinderella, dozing by the red-cellophane-and-lightbulb
fire, stretch, wake, and rub her eyes as she left her dream
behind.

"A kitchen-maid again—no more princess!" Emmy uttered
the best attempt at a sob she could manage, and sighed.

"I dreamed that I was decked in gorgeous dress
  With gems and jewels—oh! in such profusion!
  And midst a scene of glittering confusion,
  A handsome youth—whose looks contained no faults—
  Whirled me round wildly in the giddy waltz.
  I wake, alas! to life's far different round,
  In these, the dullest vaults that could be found."

106

Buttons, in an adoring aside:

"Alas! With all her *vaults*, I love her still!"

Nigel darted across to Emmy, and seized her hand in one of his own, placing the other against his heart.

> "Oh, make me happy, Miss—do say you will.
>   Love in a Buttons may appear a riddle:
>   I know I'm *but an* 'umble indiwiddle,
>   But still my heart's in the right place—I mean
>   That *you* have got it, as you must have seen."

Emmy pulled her hand from his, and turned away.

> "Oh—don't be deaf as *post*, Miss, I beseech you:
>   Let the memorial of this sad page reach you;
>   Don't stop its course by letting pride prevail
>   Or wrong *de-livery* of this *mourning mail*!"

Buttons struck a despairing attitude, and Cinderella was pleased to pat him kindly on one shoulder even as she sighed that her heart, she feared, was broken. She was so unhappy! She had so longed to go to the ball with her sisters—when the Prince's invitations had come, she had been so excited— and to have her dreams shattered was almost more than she could bear. Wouldn't Buttons please leave her to mourn her lost evening of delight in peace?

Buttons, determined to cheer poor Cinders even if he may not love her, promises that she *shall* go to the ball—to *a* ball, anyway, as he will show her if she'll only let him. Cinders, too tired to argue, allows herself to be gently bullied by Buttons. With the tablecloth for a train, the hearthrug for a cape, the frying pan for a fan, and Mr. Jessyp's string of onions as a necklace of outsized pearls, Cinderella is, says the besotted page, as beautiful a lady as any in the land.

But they both know it is only make-believe; and when the door has once more closed behind Buttons, Cinderella sobs into a tattered handkerchief that she had so wanted to go to the ball . . .

With a flash of golden light (courtesy of Admiral Leighton)

and a fanfare of fairyland bugles (Sir George, playing another extract from the tape of Naval signals recorded, one convivial evening, for this especial purpose by the Admiral) the star trap opened to allow Mrs. Stillman, her crone's costume looking rather bulky, to appear in the gloomy scullery and startle Emmy Putts into a muffled shriek.

Mrs. Stillman addressed poor Cinders in a soothing tone.

"Your wish shall be fulfilled, I tell you true—
As you helped me, so now will I help you.
You think that I am powerless, poor, and old—
I am your Fairy Godmother! Behold!"

Warily, the star trap opened again, just enough to allow those underneath to tug the crone's tatters from Mrs. Stillman's carefully positioned form, so that she was revealed in all her godmotherly glory. Cinderella gasped aloud; and the Fairy Godmother issued brisk instructions as to the collecting of a pumpkin, a lizard, some rats, and some mice—the last two species being demanded in large numbers, so that the intimates of the children concerned would be sure to buy plenty of tickets . . .

"We'll stop there," said Lady Colveden, firmly closing her script. "Most of the children have gone home, because it's so late—we'll carry on from this point at the next rehearsal. Thank you very much, everyone—and goodnight!"

A good night for some: for others, not so good. In her cosy bedroom at Sweetbriars, Miss Seeton, having carried out her customary yoga routine and cleaned her teeth, slept with the light of an almost-full moon gleaming in at her window, and did not stir until morning.

In his bedroom at the George and Dragon, Professor Caernavon Carter, having laid himself, fully clothed, under the counterpane, woke to the sound of his alarm clock, muffled beneath his pillow, and swung himself lightly to the floor. Without putting on the bedside lamp, he groped for his waiting boots; checked that his small canvas bag was ready packed with torch, notebook, pencils, and camera; swung the bag over his shoulder, seized the boots with his free hand, and opened the door of the Blue Riband Suite as quietly as he could. He tiptoed along the corridor, down the stairs, and across to the locked front door as midnight floorboards creaked, and he listened for sounds of discovery . . .

In her bedroom at Rytham Hall, Lady Colveden turned over in her sleep, stretched lazily, and stiffened. She opened her eyes, and lay still. She sat up, her head to one side; then nudged the sleeping form of her husband, and hissed:

"George—George! I think we've got burglars!"

The old war-horse was awake with the first call to arms. As his wife opened her mouth to say something else, he waved a frantic hand to silence her. "No sense in alerting the blighters," he cautioned, very low; and pushed back the bedclothes, groping with bare feet for his slippers.

"George! What are you going to do? Wait—let me come with you." Lady Colveden began to hurry after her husband as he headed for the door. "George, do be careful—"

"No, Meg." Sir George frowned. "Come with me, I mean. No show for a woman. Go back to bed. Call Potter, if you like," he added. "Better—wake Nigel first . . ."

"While you go downstairs by yourself, and someone hits you on the head? Nonsense, George." Meg Colveden, mindful of the proprieties even when an encounter with weapon-wielding desperadoes seemed imminent, slipped on her dressing gown and pattered purposefully in her husband's wake as he sighed, shook his head, and quietly turned the handle of the bed-room door.

In the moonlight, they had no need to turn on the light as they made for the head of the stairs, in the opposite direction from the bedroom of their son and heir: Sir George was a realist. Once his wife had made up her mind about something, he knew that even his powers of persuasion were of little practical value. He suppressed a smile as she seized one of the heavy brass dishes which adorned the carved blanket box his mother had given them for a wedding present, and waved a warning finger at her: as a magistrate, he knew to a nicety the limits of violence to which one should, or should not, go in order to protect one's property . . .

After more than a quarter of a century's residence, the Colvedens knew instinctively which of Rytham Hall's floorboards were more likely to betray them in their stealthy progress down the stairs. In this knowledge, they had the advantage of the burglar, who could be clearly heard moving about as the pair paused by the bottom newel post and listened again: whoever-it-was was rifling the sitting room, and Sir George nodded, pleased. In order to reach the sitting room, they must pass the hall stand with its collection of umbrellas and walking sticks . . .

Moonlight can be very deceptive. Sir George, reaching cautiously for the battered old knobkerrie brought back by his father from the Boer War, swore afterwards the dashed thing must have moved—or Meg must have bumped into him . . . either way, it was a bally nuisance. The blighter had been warned off, dammit . . .

The clatter of Sir George among the walking sticks was at once echoed by a louder clatter from the sitting room.

"Blast!" Sir George cast caution aside, snatched up his chosen weapon, and thundered down the hall, uttering the battle cry of his regiment as perfected when bayonetting the enemy. Lady Colveden, dropping the brass dish in favour of a more manageable weapon, grabbed her alpenstock and rushed after him. The dish, its wide, round, metal mouth open as it rolled and reverberated to and fro on the floor, sounded the tocsin to the heavens above . . .

Or rather, to the rooms. As Sir George threw open the sitting-room door and charged inside, roaring defiance, with Lady Colveden close behind him, the landing light was switched on, bare feet ran down the stairs, and Nigel flooded the entrance hall with more light as he called out, above sounds of battle from the garden, demanding to know what in heaven's name was going on.

He stubbed his toe on the brass dish, which had taken on a life of its own and sneaked into an ambuscade position on the edge of a patch of shadow. He swore loudly.

"Please, Nigel—language. You grow more like your father every day." Still clutching her alpenstock, his mother emerged from the sitting room, slightly breathless, and went to the telephone.

Nigel, his head on one side, stared at her as she began to dial. "Have you and Dad taken to moonlit revels?" he enquired, as the sound of distant vegetable blunderings and incoherent shouts came through the open sitting-room door. "Or is it better for a mere son not to enquire too closely as to what on earth his parents—who should be setting him a good example—are playing at?"

His mother ignored him. "Mr. Potter? Meg Colveden. I'm so sorry to bother you in the middle of the night like this, but we seem to have had burglars . . . I'm not really sure, but I think only one, as far as we could see. George chased him out of the sitting room through the French windows . . . I don't suppose so for a moment, or of course I'd have stayed out there chasing him too. But he did look several years younger and several stone lighter than poor George, so . . . Yes, please. That would be most kind of you."

She rang off, and turned to her son, who had been listening intently to the one-sided conversation, rubbing one bare foot against the other.

"Nigel, you look like a striped stork in those pyjamas. For goodness' sake, why didn't you put on your dressing-gown if you had to come downstairs? It's absolutely freezing in here with the French windows wide open, and if you catch flu just two days before opening night, I'll never forgive you."

She paused, laid the alpenstock gently in its rightful place, and as she checked the status of her dressing-gown belt gave Nigel the chance to speak.

"For goodness' sake," Plummergen's premier thespian mimicked her ladyship's tone exactly, "what did you expect me to do—don top hat, white tie, and tails before I even considered doing the full cavalry-to-the-rescue bit? Honestly, Mother, sometimes I wonder if—"

"Don't be rude, Nigel—and don't try to pretend you weren't going to be, because I know better. All I meant was that there's no need for you to run around the house practically nude when your father and I have the situation perfectly under control—well, almost," as there came a sound of panting footsteps, and

Sir George, his moustache no longer bristling with the spirit
of battle, appeared in the sitting-room doorway.

"Scoundrel's gone to earth," he said, as his wife and son
chorused a demand for information. "Got a few whacks at
him, though—find it hard to sit down for a few days, the
blighter. Won't be doing it in police custody, more's the
pity." He favoured his wife with an accusing glare. "Shame
you bumped into me just as I was arming m'self—gave the
show away before it'd even begun."

"And a very good thing too," returned her ladyship firmly.
"From what I saw of him, he was half your age and twice
your size—muscles, I mean—well, that's how he looked, in
the moonlight—and besides, I don't think he actually got away
with anything, did he?"

By unspoken agreement, all three Colvedens drifted back
to the sitting room and gazed about them. "You see?" said
her ladyship, surveying the scene with the eye of restrained
anguish. "What Martha will say if I haven't cleared up all
this mess before she sees it, I shudder to think—but at least
I don't believe he got away with anything much. At least, he
wasn't carrying anything bulky—nothing seems to be missing,
anyway. We must have disturbed him before he had time to
get properly started."

"No," said Sir George, surveying the scene with the eye of a
magistrate who has studied a wide range of police photographs
in his time. "No . . . must have been here quite a while, for
things to be so topsy-turvy—not an ordinary burglar, if you
ask me. Not breaking in on spec—or why," as his family
chorused again, "didn't he pocket a few of the smaller pieces?
Still there, all of 'em."

He nodded towards the corner cupboard with its curved
glass front and display of silver on inside shelves as well
as on the top. Nigel and Julia, when young, had spent many
a rainy afternoon polishing the salt and pepper pots, the egg
cups, the mustard bowl, and assorted small spoons: all of
which remained, as Sir George had pointed out, in clear and
easy view of anyone entering the room minded to indulge in
petty thievery. "Not a chance break-in," said Sir George again.
"Looking for something, I'll be bound . . ." And he muttered

darkly into his moustache until PC Potter arrived.

Potter, after a quick but thorough investigation, said that dusting for fingerprints might as well wait until morning, but he'd take preliminary statements now, while events were still fresh in everyone's mind. This he duly did, and agreed that there could well be something in Sir George's theory, given the state of the sitting room, but that it was going to be a little difficult to fill in his report unless he had more details. Did Sir George, or any of the family, have any idea what it was the burglar had been looking for?

Sir George frowned. His wife, divining his unease, kept quiet, and favoured PC Potter with her widest stare. Potter turned to the remaining Colveden and looked a question.

"Well, not the s-silver, it s-seems," said Nigel, who had refused to go in search of dressing gown and slippers in case he missed any of the fun, and was starting to wish he hadn't been quite so much the hardy son of the soil, inured to each and every change of temperature. "As Dad p-pointed out, he didn't p-pinch a s-single s-spoon, and they'd be by far the easiest things to s-steal—and to s-sell afterwards, I'd've thought."

"Nigel," began his mother, exasperated, "if you're going to sneeze, I shall—"

"No," said Sir George, so firmly that everyone turned to stare. "Nigel's wrong—the blighter was after silver, all right. Afraid this sort of thing might happen—why I asked 'em to take it away. Doesn't believe it's in Brettenden—thinks we've kept it here. Wouldn't listen when I tried to tell him," he added, once more muttering darkly.

"Ah," said PC Potter, as light dawned. "So you think the miscreant was looking for the Roman treasure, do you, Sir George? And you've got an idea as to who it might be as was looking for it? How about you give me the bloke's name, and I can take it from there?"

Sir George's mutterings grew louder, and mention was heard of the laws of slander, by Gad! PC Potter was as firm as ever Sir George, on the bench, could be.

"Privilege, now, Sir George. Just between these four walls— for purposes of elimination, you might say, nothing more . . ."

He opened his notebook, and stood with pencil poised, an expectant look on his face.

"Slander," protested Sir George again, weakly; whereupon Nigel, his teeth chattering, sneezed.

"Oh, really!" cried Lady Colveden. "We can't stand here all night catching our deaths—I'm sorry, George. He'll have to be told—if he doesn't know already, with the Nuts having a grandstand view, according to you . . ."

"Ah," said PC Potter again, as Sir George turned purple. "Ah, yes, Miss Nuttel and Mrs. Blaine—I'd heard something of the sort, and dismissed it as idle talk. But maybe there was just a grain of truth in it, hey, Sir George?"

And, with the beans so well and truly spilled, PC Potter persuaded Sir George to admit, at last, his deep suspicions of Professor Caernavon Carter.

chapter
-15-

IN THE PRIVACY of her bedroom Miss Seeton, having refreshed her memory from *Yoga and Younger Every Day*, sat on the travelling rug with her right leg straight out in front of her, and her left knee bent up. Her left foot was flat on the floor, the heel tucked in close to her body, the inside edge resting against her right thigh. As she breathed out slowly, she twisted her torso, just as slowly, through ninety degrees to the left, and with further gentle twisting succeeded in wrapping her right arm around her left knee to grasp her left hand behind her back.

Her limbs thus disposed, Miss Seeton breathed in, out, and in again, feeling pardonably pleased with herself for having thus achieved the *Marichyasana,* which the book said was so good for the spine and shoulder joints—not, fortunately, that one was particularly afflicted in that way, but it did no harm to take precautions. A certain amount of stiffness was only to be expected, she supposed; comparing herself to others of a similar age, she had to admit she enjoyed remarkably good health—was blessed, indeed, not only with good health, but in so many other ways, as well. She had a lovely home, friends, an adequate income—dear Mr. Delphick! kind Mr. Jessyp!— and so many fresh interests that one might almost say she was busier now than she was when she retired, seven years ago.

There was, for example, the pantomime. How flattered one had been when Lady Colveden and Miss Treeves had insisted that one's experience as a teacher of art made one the per- fect—Miss Seeton felt herself blush—choice to design the scenery for *Cinderella*. The diorama had particularly pleased them: and one was, perhaps, slightly justified in feeling a very little smidgin of pride (Miss Seeton blushed again) over the unusual effects which could be accomplished by painting the background on a long strip of canvas, wound across the rear of the stage from one outsized cotton reel (dear Nigel's amusing term for the apparatus) to another. When the Ugly Sisters, in their crinolines and plumes (how clever were dear Martha's fingers, and Miss Armitage's sewing machine!) were on their way to the ball, it really seemed, at first glance, that the coach in which they rode was moving through the night, rather than the night, as it were, moving behind the coach while it stayed still—apart, that was, from the rocking and lurching achieved (how clever of dear Sir George to think of it) by an assortment of farm workers and members of the Plummergen Tug of War Team.

The Colvedens—dear Martha, and Stan too, of course—one was fortunate indeed to—

Miss Seeton, still happily breathing in and out with her hands interlocked behind her back, awoke from her daydream to hear the telephone's tintinnabulation rising from the hall below. Should she (she wondered) respond to its call—or should she assume that, if the matter was of any great importance, whoever it was would ring back? True, one was not as physically convoluted as from time to time happened in some of the more advanced postures, but even so it took time to uncurl, and—

The telephone fell silent. Miss Seeton, with a sigh, allowed herself one more twist and handclasp, then relaxed into the *Shavasana*, or Dead Pose, and breathed deeply for a count of one hundred. She then stretched, opened her eyes, rolled over, and proceeded to dress herself properly before hurrying downstairs to breakfast rather later than usual. The rehearsal, at which one's prompting services were fully required, had gone on rather later last night than one had expected, and . . .

The doorbell rang. Miss Seeton, glancing at the clock, guessed it must be Bert with the morning post, which, with the approach of Christmas, arrived later every day. As she hurried down the hall to the door, she was waiting for the rattle of the letterbox, and the thump of laden envelopes falling to the floor . . .

"Why, Martha, what a surprise! That is—surely today is your morning for the Hall, isn't it? Oh, dear," said her employer, flustered. "When I haven't quite finished tidying just yet—indeed, I—"

"Now then, Miss Emily," Martha said quickly, "for goodness' sake don't you go fretting yourself into a state, now. As if I've never seen dishes not cleared away before this! Besides, you haven't got it wrong, not a bit of it. Today's my normal day for doing up at the Hall, yes, only—well, only just not today, seeing how things are, and her ladyship ringing to say they're all at sixes and sevens, poor souls, on account of burglars last night—"

"Burglars! Martha, dear, surely not—how dreadful!" Miss Seeton could hardly believe her ears. Such people as burglars—as criminals of any kind—did not, to Miss Seeton's way of thinking, belong in a peaceful place like Plummergen. "How dreadful—and how shocking. Oh, dear—and so distressing. Poor things . . ." It was unclear, from Miss Seeton's tone, whether those to be pitied were the Colvedens, for having had burglars, or the burglars, for having stooped to such a crime.

"Dreadful's the word, right enough," said Martha grimly. "Or blooming cheek, depending on how you look at it. Came in through the French windows, so he did, bold as brass, and dear knows what he took, with her ladyship in too much of a state to tell me proper—and with it being none of my business anyway," she added quickly, remembering that Rytham Hall was not the only place to have French windows, and that Miss Seeton lived alone. "And so—well, I thought, if you didn't mind, I'd do you today, instead of the Hall, and see to her ladyship tomorrow, after"—she sniffed—"after the place is put to rights."

Like her fruitcake and her sewing skills, Martha Bloomer's sniffs were renowned in Plummergen. They could be more expressive than words, when she chose. This particular monumental specimen expressed her considerable scepticism that anyone other than herself could be deemed capable of putting the Hall to rights—and expressed also a corresponding

intention not to stop anyone (whoever they might be) finding
out the hard way just how capable, not to say indispensable,
she was.

"Put to rights, indeed—as if I don't know what *that* means!
What with Potter there now with fingerprint powder and Lord-
knows-what, and her ladyship saying I'd have forty fits seeing
everywhere so messy—which I allow is more than likely right.
I mean to say, fingerprint powder! I've seen it on the telly too
often not to know the worst of it—the way they chuck that
stuff about's a regular scandal. Like a blooming snowdrift,
sometimes, brushing it all over the show when like as not
he wore gloves, so it's all a waste of time—and you can be
sure nobody'll know rightly how to dust after, and they'll
go treading it all over my carpets, when it's always such
a job to keep them clean anyway, with young Nigel never
remembering about his boots . . ." She frowned, brooding on
the future baronet's carelessness in the matter of footwear.

She sighed. "If it'd only been some tramp, now, taken those
boots—and maybe an old overcoat, with half of 'em hanging
on the peg fit for nothing but the rag bag, only you know
how Sir George hates to throw anything away, look at that
old hat of his, and Nigel taking after his dad in more ways
than one—and maybe a bite to eat, with her ladyship the last
person to go begrudging a square meal to a hungry man, this
weather—well, I'd not be complaining, believe me." Martha
frowned. Had it sounded as if she'd been making excuses for
the burglar? "That is, not so much, anyway—but whoever that
was it was no tramp trying to keep warm now the weather's
turned nippy, mark my words. He was after summat a bit
fancier—take it away and sell it in London, or something.
After Sir George's medals and the silver, if you think about
it, that's what he'll have been up to . . ."

Miss Seeton, feeling it hardly her place to ponder either
the dirt-harbouring qualities of the boots of the Colvedens'
son, the scruffiness of his attire, or the theftworthiness of
his father's possessions, felt a change of subject to be in
order. "Was that you, Martha dear, who rang a few minutes
ago? I'm so sorry not to have replied," as Martha indicated
that it had indeed been herself on the telephone, "but I was

twisting my spine, you see. These things take a little time, if
one wishes to avoid damage—untwisting, that is. But by all
means, come today, rather than tomorrow. Naturally, anything
I can do to assist Lady Colveden at such a time . . . Would it
be an impertinence, do you think, if I were to telephone and
say how very sorry I am, and ask if I can be of help in any
other capacity?"

Although Martha said that she thought it would not be, Miss
Seeton decided, in the end, not to telephone: the Colvedens—
or at least the lady of the house, her menfolk more likely to
be busy about the farm—would be far too preoccupied with
the aftermath of the burglary. What a sad state of affairs, in
her pleasant, peaceful Plummergen—and so near Christmas,
too: it quite took the edge off one's enjoyment of the cards
and letters which, with the expected rattle and thump, had just
tumbled through the metal flap to the mat below. Miss Seeton,
pleased to be remembered by so many of her acquaintance,
gathered up her correspondence and, forgetful of breakfast,
hurried into the sitting room . . .

Where she found herself quite unable to relax and enjoy
her letters and cards. She picked up the paper knife, and put
it down again; her fingers drummed on the topmost envelope
as she tried to decipher the postmark; she had no desire to play
her little private game of recognising the writing and recalling
who had written it . . .

Miss Seeton, in short, was twitchy. She blamed her fidgets
on Martha's news of the burglary. She hardly noticed as,
abandoning her unopened Christmas cards, she headed for
the bureau, and all her drawing gear.

"Go on, sir—it'll be the experience of a lifetime," begged
Detective Constable Foxon, waving two hand-printed tickets
under the nose of his superior. "Half the price of a West End
show—no problem with travel, or parking—"

"Half the price, yes—but is it," demanded Superintendent
Chris Brinton, "any good? You may *say* you expect packed
houses every night, but they could be so desperate for enter-
tainment down there they'd sit in rows to watch paint dry, if
someone told 'em it was for a worthy cause."

"The Organ Fund, sir." Foxon adopted an air of outraged virtue. "A *very* worthy cause—and me acting my socks off, all in the interests of good public relations . . ."

"*Plummergen* public relations," sighed Brinton. Anywhere else, and he would have booked seats for his wife and himself without a qualm. But Plummergen . . .

"Rehearsals going well, are they?" he enquired, as Foxon dropped into the visitors' chair and accidentally let fall his tickets on the superintendent's blotter. "No hiccups? No exploding footlights and the village hall in flames because someone shorted the circuits with her umbrella? No scenery crashing on people's heads because certain other people's brollies bumped into it? No bodies huddled at the bottom of the star trap because someone caught the handle with *her* blasted handle and opened the damn thing up?"

"No, sir." Foxon's tone was prim, though his eyes were dancing. "Miss Seeton—who, incidentally, designed all the scenery, though it was painted by a team of volunteers—has been sitting in the prompt corner every night doing no harm to a soul. What she *has* been doing," as Brinton muttered, "is a damn good job, sir. Years of teaching, I suppose," he went on, above Brinton's further mutterings of disbelief. "If anyone dries, her voice carries just far enough and no farther, and you can hear every syllable, sir. Not, mind you, that by this stage we really need prompting—word perfect, most of us, by now. As you'll see for yourself, sir, when you come . . ."

Brinton groaned. "Foxon, you're starting to sound like a nagging wife—but I suppose it *is* the season of blasted goodwill, and all that. You may convince me yet, though I must be stark, staring mad even to think of going to Plummergen of my own accord—"

He was spared the indignity of putting his hand in his pocket to pay for the tickets by a ring on the telephone. Shooting a triumphant look at Foxon, he picked up the receiver with one hand, and started to push the tickets back with the other.

"What?" The grin disappeared, to be replaced by a hard, weary look which Foxon knew well. He, too, lost his jocular

ir and sat upright, straining to hear the voice which was pour-
ng information from the earpiece of Superintendent Brinton's
elephone.

Brinton jerked his head towards the extension on Foxon's
esk, but before the young man had pushed back the chair and
eached it, the superintendent barked: "We're on our way!"
nd rang off. Foxon turned an enquiring face to him, even
s he carried on to his desk and began collecting notebook,
encil, tape measure, camera, and all the other paraphernalia
f investigation.

"Trouble, sir." It was not a question.

Brinton nodded. "Season of goodwill, indeed—as likely to
murder someone at Christmas as any other time . . ." He, like
Foxon, was gathering things together as he talked. "Here I was,
aying I'd never go there of my own accord—it was tempting
ate, laddie. I should have known better—"

"You mean we've been called to Plummergen?" Foxon went
ery still. "Not—not MissEss, sir!"

"Not MissEss, Foxon. Not anyone we know, as far as they
an tell—which isn't very far. Body of an unidentified male,
vith his head pretty badly bashed in—found," said Brinton
grimly, "in the middle of a muddy field at Rytham Hall.
Where last night, according to Potter, the Colvedens surprised
a burglar, and Sir George gave him the hiding of his life before
ae got away . . ."

chapter

~16~

THERE ARE BASICALLY two routes from Ashford, regiona
police headquarters, to Plummergen. The direct route, from
the north, runs along more or less main roads via Brettenden
The slower, meandering, southerly route passes through Har
Street and Brenzett before turning sharply back on itself an
creeping into the village via the bridge over the canal. Onc
over the canal, the road is constrained between high brick wall
in that narrow lane which widens into the familiar tree-line
Street only after it has passed Miss Seeton's cottage on th
corner . . .

The superintendent weighed up the alternatives as he issue
rapid instructions for an investigative team to be assembled
Any good detective takes a pride in knowing his patch; i
Brinton's case, however, such knowledge as he'd acquire
wasn't so much out of pride as sheer self-preservation, thoug
he could never hope to know the Plummergen area as wel
as PC Potter, the local man. Plummergen was where Mis
Seeton lived: as Brinton himself, when pressed, would poin
out, enough said! He barked his last set of orders into th
telephone, banged down the receiver, and scowled at the ma
on the opposite wall. The Brettenden route would mean thei
having to drive past the post office, which at this time o
day, Brinton knew only too well, would be full of gossipin
shoppers . . .

"We could turn off before we got right into the village
sir," suggested Foxon, "before they'd had time to spot us
and come in the back way—there are dozens of those littl

122

oads we could take without them seeing us."

"Oh, yes, dozens. Know all of 'em by heart without a map, do you? We're on our way to a murder, laddie, not some perishing picnic where it doesn't much matter if you're a few minutes late. We haven't time to stop at every blasted crossroads to check where the hell we are—and you know as well as I do they never put all the signposts back after the invasion scare."

Foxon, normally willing to risk a little cheerful insubordination, judged this to be a bad moment to remind his superior that at least thirty years had elapsed since 1940; besides, he was prepared to concede that it was no more than an even chance the signposts would in fact have been replaced. In outlying districts of the United Kingdom of Great Britain and Northern Ireland, the assumption of the natives all too often seemed to be that anyone who managed to make his way there ought to have known where he was going in the first place.

"We could ask for a guide, sir—Potter, or someone—"

"A guide?" Brinton paused in the act of slamming the office door, and glared. "Why not indent for a few glass beads while you're about it, for heaven's sake? And Potter's on guard at the site, anyhow. We're on our own, laddie—so come on!"

"The Brenzett road then, sir?"

"Have to be." Brinton shrugged as he strode down the corridor, Foxon close behind. "Takes longer, of course, in one way—but on the other hand, it gives us a little more breathing space before the rubberneckers come crowding us out. We won't be able to sit on this forever, especially in a place like Plummergen, but we don't want the blighters let loose until we're ready for 'em, which is why we're in a hurry, Foxon—although *if* you don't mind," as they arrived at the police car park, "we'll take it nice and slow and steady in the neighbourhood of a certain cottage owned by a certain party of our acquaintance. No bells, no sirens, no flashing blue lights. If Miss Seeton doesn't realise we're there, it'll be that much longer before she and her brolly come crashing into this case the way I know—never mind how hard we'll try to stop her—they both, heaven help us all, are bound to do."

Brinton flung open the car door. "So what are you waiting for, laddie? Get your skates on—move!"

Foxon moved.

The body was pronounced dead, photographed, measured, loaded on a stretcher, and taken to the mortuary for postmortem by Dr. Wyddial, the police surgeon who expressed herself with some force on the topic of blood, bones, and jigsaw puzzles before driving off in the wake of the ambulance with a resigned tootle of her horn. Brinton and Foxon waited until the rest of the forensic team was busy with pegs, string, trowels, and small plastic bags, then directed their attention to Sir George Colveden, who had hovered nearby in uncharacteristic silence as the methodical drama of detection unfolded before him.

"Perhaps," suggested Brinton, "we could go back to the house, if that's all right with you, Sir George? No sense in hanging about catching pneumonia. This lot'll survive with no bother because they're on the move, but standing around in the mud's no job for anyone." And he pointedly stamped a frozen foot or two.

"Ah. Sorry." Sir George roused himself from his trance and turned to lead the way. "Bad business, this. A bit of a shock, y'know, especially after . . . after last night." The major-general, mindful of the traditions which had won him the Distinguished Service Order, stopped, squared his shoulders, and looked Brinton straight in the face.

"Admit I gave the blighter a couple of good wallops with the old 'kerrie, but nothing along *those* lines." He nodded grimly in the direction taken by the ambulance. "Backside, mostly—making a run for it. Managed it, too, more's the pity. Really wish I'd collared him, then he'd never have ended up . . . like that. Nasty. No sight for a woman."

"You mean it was Lady Colveden who found the body?" The superintendent was surprised: he knew little of the habits of the gentry, but had always supposed that it was the male of the species who prowled the ancestral acres when the dawn was barely risen.

"No, no." Sir George, having made his confession, had continued on his way. Sturdy gumboots sucked at the mud as he walked, while Brinton and Foxon—particularly Foxon, who prided himself on the nattiness of his attire—commended the soles of their shoes to fortune, and trudged together by the baronet's side.

"Last day of the dig," Sir George went on. "Just Miss—I mean, Dr.—Braxted here—a few loose ends, photographs, that sort of thing. She arrived later than usual for some reason—car, I think. Found . . . him, and came screaming up to the Hall in hysterics. Never would have thought it of her, y'know. Always seemed such a capable creature—scientific. Shock, of course. Anyway, I told Meg to take care of her while Nigel and I did a recce—thought it better not to waste time waiting for Potter with his fingerprint gear. Said he'd be along after the burglary, you see. Saw what had happened, and sent the boy to telephone from the house while I stood guard."

He stopped again. "Looks bad, I know. Every chance to interfere with the evidence—but better me than the boy, I thought, in case of, ah, suspicion." The major-general's voice was gruff through the drooping bristles of his moustache, and his shoulders were once more very straight. "I'm not a fool—know you'll have me on your list, after last night. Nigel never even saw the chap. As for Meg, didn't leave the house—too cold, thank the Lord. Just me out in the garden . . . and him."

"If," said Brinton, "it's the same chap. Potter seems to think there's some doubt about that, from the descriptions you and your wife gave last night of your burglar being a tall, fit young man, when our corpse—begging your pardon, Sir George—is rather on the small side, for a man."

Sir George's eyes held a hopeful gleam, but he was not one to clutch at straws. "Moonlight's pretty deceptive," he said sadly. "Could tell you a few tales about the war—but there, nothing to do with all this. Afraid we may have led Potter astray, in all the excitement. Heat of battle—ah." He huffed through his moustache. "Unfortunate choice of words. Sorry." He resumed his gloomy progress towards the house, his shoulders more squared than ever.

"Yes, Meg was in a bit of a tizzy, bless her. Worried I wouldn't be able to take care of m'self—after him with her alpenstock, of all things. Cold light of day, she'll realise he wasn't a . . . a seven-foot muscle man after all . . ."

"I never," protested Lady Colveden, when asked her views on her husband's theory, "said anything of the sort! Seven feet tall, indeed. George must think I'm in my dotage, or hallucinating from drink, or something equally ridiculous. I *know* it was dark, and unexpected, and moonlight—but that burglar was certainly as tall as Nigel, if not taller. And Nigel," she added, before Brinton could even dream of asking whether the future baronet would allow himself to be measured for the record, "is six foot one."

Brinton nodded. He knew Nigel well, and indeed would have given him the benefit of an extra half inch. If the burglar surprised and knobkerried so vigorously by Nigel's father had been around Nigel's height, then it couldn't be his body which had been taken to Ashford for postmor—

He jumped to his feet. "Can I use your phone?"

"By all means." Lady Colveden was somewhat startled by Brinton's sudden eruption from his chair, but, ever the perfect hostess, said nothing, and proceeded to make polite conversation with Foxon—the pantomime rehearsals were a safely neutral topic—until, five minutes later, Jasper's superior clumped back into the sitting room with a look of cautious relief on his face.

"Lady Colveden, your husband's, er, little exchange with the burglar—you witnessed it?"

Even at such a tense moment, Meg Colveden couldn't help smiling. "Well, in part, yes. Until they ran out through the French windows, that is, and George started chasing him round the garden and—well, and then he gave him the slip."

Brinton grinned. "But not before he'd been on the receiving end of a few good wallops from Sir George's stick, is that right?"

Lady Colveden stifled a giggle. "I'd have walloped him myself, if I'd been near enough—oh dear, I suppose I really shouldn't say that, but he did make me so cross. And I suppose I was rather worried about George—he's not growing any younger, you know. He was quite out of breath when he came back."

"Back from the garden—where he'd given this blighter a good hiding?"

"Well, yes." All giggles forgotten, Lady Colveden opened her eyes in a wide, worried gaze. "But he was perfectly able to run away afterwards—I saw him. And George never touched him anywhere near . . . near his head," with a shudder she could not suppress. "Poor Dr. Braxted told me all about it—I suppose it was good for her to let it out of her system, but I do wish she hadn't. I expect I shall have nightmares about it—and I'll have even more," abandoning her helpless look, "if you arrest George for murder. He's the last person in the world—"

"I'm not going to arrest him, Lady Colveden—not for, murder, anyway." Brinton's smile was now as broad as his earlier frown had been severe. "Mind you, I won't promise not to run him in for assault and battery, if the burglar ever decides to press charges . . ."

"What? Oh," said Lady Colveden, as light dawned. "You mean the . . . the body *isn't* our burglar? Why, that's wonderful—oh dear, I didn't mean it quite like that, but—goodness, yes." Then she sat up. "You're really sure it isn't? How can you tell?"

"I've had a word with our Dr. Wyddial, who's doing the postmortem. I asked her if she'd found any signs that the deceased had recently undergone a . . . a beating round his rear end—and she said he hadn't. So, whoever he is, our body's not your burglar . . ."

"And George can stop worrying," cried Lady Colveden, in heartfelt delight. "And so can I—Mr. Brinton, you've no idea what a weight off our minds this will be. Except—oh dear. There's still someone—someone dead, isn't there? And on our property. And I've absolutely no idea what he can have been doing there . . ."

"We'll have a good idea once we find out who he is," Brinton said, with rather more confidence than he felt. If a murder happened in Plummergen, you could bet your boots it wasn't any run-of-the-mill affair according to safe, everyday rules. "You didn't see him, of course, so you wouldn't know if he was a local—not that it would have helped, come to think of it, considering the state—begging your pardon—he was in, poor devil. Still, whoever he was, once we do find out, it'll help us know why he might be prowling round a Roman ruin in the middle of the night, and why someone might, er, want to stop him doing it." No need to distress her further by saying that Dr. Wyddial was insistent the body hadn't been moved to the dig after death: there could be no doubt (the doctor said) that the murder had taken place in the exact spot where the corpse had been found. And Brinton refused to believe that anyone in his right mind would be walking casually across a muddy field in the moonlight and just happen to bump into a murderer with a bludgeon in his hand.

"Whether or not she's up to it," he went on thoughtfully, "I've got to have a talk with Dr. Braxted. She's an archaeologist—she'll know if there was anything left behind anyone'd want to pinch that'd be worth someone else braining him for . . ."

But Euphemia, on being questioned, was as firm in her opinions as ever Dr. Wyddial could be. Everything worth finding had been, well, found. Given the twin constraints of the time and the weather, they'd put together a crack team and pulled out all the stops so that it would be over, as Sir George had insisted, by Christmas.

"Which it was," she told the superintendent, no hint of uncertainty in her tone. "One of the most thorough—if the most hurried—excavations on which I have ever worked, in so short a time. Dashed *hard* work, as well! But everyone was absolutely splendid—no passengers on *this* ship. The only reason I came along today was . . ."

Her sallow cheeks flushed. "You'll think me a sentimental old fool, Mr. Brinton, but the Temple of Glacia was—is—special. I've put a lot of effort into this dig—and as for Siberius Brumalix, I've, well, taken rather a fancy to the chap. Quite a character, by all accounts. It sounds ridiculous to an outsider, I'm sure, but—I shall miss him. You've no idea how much I'm looking forward to the time when we can have his relics on display, with the completed mosaic—

a remarkable achievement. Or it will be, once we've achieved it. Which I'm sure we shall—eventually . . ."

"I suppose," said Dr. Braxted, with another blush, "I was just—well, saying *au revoir . . .*"

chapter
-17-

BRINTON HAD WARNED that it wouldn't be long before news
of the sensational discovery at Rytham Hall leaked out: and it
wasn't. Rumour, counter-rumour, and slanderous speculation
swiftly spread (by the customary, indefinable, osmotic process
of dissemination) from the houses nearest the Hall to those in
the rest of Plummergen; from Plummergen to Brettenden; and
from Brettenden, where an alert stringer for the *Beacon* saw
the titbit as an early Christmas present, to London—to Fleet
Street—and to Amelita Forby, demon crime reporter of the
Daily Negative.

Mel Forby always kept an overnight bag packed in case of
emergency. This bag was kept in the *Negative* office rather
than at home, since home was a flat with a door with a key
which was shared by her close personal friend and professional rival Thrudd Banner, star of World Wide Press. Mel,
naturally, possessed a reciprocal key to Mr. Banner's flat:
but Thrudd was far more devious than Mel, and much better
at keeping secrets from his intimate acquaintance, no matter
how intimate that acquaintance might be. Despite her every
endeavour, she hadn't managed to scoop him on one of his
own stories yet.

Three minutes after the alert was sounded by her editor, Mel
and her overnight bag were in a taxi heading for Charing Cross
railway station. Having bought her ticket, she judged she had
just enough time to scribble a quick note to Thrudd to say she'd
be out of Town for a few days; and she dropped that note into
the letterbox with a decided chuckle. Banner the Boy Wonder

could hardly blame her if the Christmas mail overload meant he didn't hear from her for a while—she'd done her best to keep him as posted as any competitive colleague had a right to be . . .

Mel was so busy congratulating herself on her cunning that she ended up having to sprint for the train, and jumped into the last carriage as the conductor's whistle blast was fading and the green flag was raised. Damn. She'd had no time to buy anything to eat—she'd take a bet there wasn't a buffet car on this service . . .

Desperate remedies were called for. She only hoped her friends—naming no names, but the initials TB came at once to mind—would never find out how low she'd let the banner (she stifled a giggle) of women's liberation slither down its flagstaff. She favoured the elderly gentleman sitting opposite with one of the Forby Specials, her beautiful eyes pleading, helpless, in need of protection. "Excuse me, but would there be such a thing as a dining car on this train, do you know?"

The elderly gentleman lifted his hat, bowed, and regretted very much having to disappoint a lady, but there was not. On the other hand, as one who was accustomed to travel the route at this time of day, he always brought sandwiches with him. If his charming young companion would care to share, when the appropriate hour arrived . . . ?

Elevenses for one, eaten by two, will stave off the most serious pangs, while leaving hollows yet to fill. When Mel had waved goodbye to her new friend at Ashford, she hunted out the station bookstall and enjoyed a few moments of quiet gloating before making up her mind which chocolate bar—or bars—to choose.

"For myself, I prefer peppermint cream," came a voice from over her shoulder. "Something with biscuit in would be more substantial, though. Do I take it you didn't get round to stocking up before you caught the train? Take a leaf out of a top newshound's notebook, and always keep a packet or two of crisps in your briefcase."

"Banner!" Mel, who had leaped as the voice first spoke in her ear, now groaned as she turned to face the speaker. "You louse. What are you doing here? And what's with this top newshound nonsense?"

"Same as you—what else?" Thrudd grinned wickedly as he instructed the startled stall-holder to supply one of every item along the top row, to begin with. "And I'll ignore the insult as it's Christmas. If you really need to ask, I'm on my way to Plummergen, scene of riot among the Roman ruins, murder and mayhem amid the mosaics. And I've already filed that," he added, as a calculating gleam shone in Mel's undoubtedly beautiful eyes.

After a moment, she laughed. "Guess your stringer must be more efficient than ours, for once. Just one of those things— but we start level from now on, okay?"

They walked together in an amicable silence to the platform for the Brettenden train. Mel laughed again. "And you were going to take old Mr. Baxter's taxi when you got there, I suppose?"

"You bet." Thrudd opened the carriage door, took Mel's bag, and swung it up into the rack. "*And* check in at the George to get all the gossip—*and* pop across to wish MissEss the compliments of the season, of course. Quite like old times, isn't it?"

Mel munched hungrily on her Chomper Bar (the Meal in a Mouthful), and brooded. "Fair shares, Banner," she warned. "You see Miss S—I see Miss S. No sneaking her sketch-book—no messing with my camera. Fair shares . . ."

"Share a room, too?" Thrudd turned the full force of his smile on her. It worked as well as Mel's Forby Special had upon the old gentleman with the sandwiches.

"Oh, shucks," said Mel, and laughed again, and blushed. "Oh, well, I guess—as it's Christmas . . ."

"It's Christmas," said Thrudd, as they stood at last in the entrance hall of the George and Dragon. "If this murder isn't sorted out pretty sharpish, we could be shortchanged on our holiday, unless we box clever. I don't mind pushing the boat out, if you don't—or rather if our respective editors don't. We'll have to see what can be arranged when we come to sign for our expenses—hey, yes. Where *is* Charley, for Pete's sake?"

For the second time, he banged the bell. In the silence of Reception, only he and Mel stirred.

Mel chuckled. "Seems the nearest you're going to get to Charley Mountfitchet today's this outsized lump of vegetable life he's so fond of." She stroked a polished leaf of the gigantic cheeseplant beside the desk, and smiled. "Remember the time that arsonist had a go at burning Sweetbriars down? Oh, no, of course, you weren't here then—so you missed the sight of Fire Fighter Forby in action. I won't say my technique wasn't effective, but I'm not so sure what Charley thought—I reckon if this precious plant of his'd come to any lasting harm after I dumped it on the floor to use the earth, he'd never have let me in the place again."

"Could be he saw us—you—coming," suggested Thrudd, "and vamoosed out of the back door to save having to pretend he hasn't a room free—ah! Signs of life!"

"A slight exaggeration, wouldn't you say?" murmured Mel, as the swing doors at the far end of the hall were pushed open, and Maureen, stifling a massive yawn, drifted into view. Whether or not her appearance had been prompted by Thrudd's thumping of the bell was impossible to say: there was no nod of acknowledgement, no attempt at hurrying. She drew slowly closer, allowed her eyes to focus vaguely on the newcomers, and wearily raised the counter flap to go behind the desk.

"Hello, there—Maureen, isn't it?" Thrudd switched on the Regular Clients personality. "We'd like your best room, please—the Blue Riband Suite, as I recall. Mr. Banner and Miss Forby . . ."

Maureen stared at him. Mel said sharply: "Miss Forby and Mr. Banner," then giggled. Thrudd sighed, and reached for the open hotel register. May as well fill it in while this halfwit girl got her brain into gear . . .

"The Blue Riband Suite?" Deep in the recesses of Maureen's mind, something stirred. "You can't have that."

Mel giggled again. "The Moral Majority speaks out," she said, as Thrudd demanded to know why not.

Maureen spoke but two words in reply—and those muffled behind her hand, as she yawned again. Thrudd raised an irritated eyebrow.

"Late night? Too late to suggest another room we could have instead?"

Maureen mumbled something that sounded like *Charming*. Mr. Banner, bristling, was about to unleash the full force of his sarcasm in response when Mel, who had (in her rival's absence abroad) covered the Glacia scoop without him, and was therefore more familiar with current Plummergen gossip, exclaimed:

"Hey, yes. You're a star, Maureen!" Thrudd looked at his ladylove as if she had gone off her head—then looked in amazement at Maureen as the girl actually smiled, and became animated.

"Dress rehearsal tomorrow, then three proper performances next week. You going to buy tickets?"

"To stay in the Blue Riband Suite?" exclaimed Thrudd, in some bewilderment. "But this is a hotel, dammit—ugh!"

Mel withdrew her foot from his ankle, and did not even pause to glare before smiling at Maureen. "Guess we might, if it's as good as I've heard. So how about that room?"

"You can't have it," repeated Maureen; then, prepared to expand a little for one who so obviously appreciated her, she added: "It's took."

Mel kicked Thrudd again before his snort of exasperation could jeopardise their chances of any room at all. "Maybe whoever it is won't stay long," she said hopefully. "We'll have another room until they've gone, and then swap, if that wouldn't be too much trouble. Er—they aren't reporters, by any chance?"

Maureen blinked at her. "He's a professor. From America. There's no reporters here yet."

"Only one," muttered Thrudd, rubbing his ankle.

Mel ignored the insult, and was honey-sweet, monumentally patient. "Well, how long is this professor staying?"

"Dunno. He didn't say." Maureen frowned. "Funny, now I come to think of it . . ." Cogs could almost be seen whirring as she came to think. "You've just got here from London, right? S'pose you must be hungry. Fancy a bite to eat? Only he's not had breakfast, and it's paid for in the price, and cooked, and put on the hotplate waiting. I got no time to run around with room service, not with Mr. Mountfitchet saying we'll be full up with reporters soon, and the beds to air and all . . ."

Honey turned to steel, Thrudd stiffened, as he and Mel realised what Maureen had perhaps just told them. "This, er, professor," began Thrudd, over Mel's excited "Not had breakfast?" They glanced at one another, and tacitly agreed that this, too, would be shared. Thrudd bowed slightly. Mel nodded, smiled, and spoke.

"Does he usually have breakfast, Maureen?"

Maureen shrugged. "It's paid for, though mind you, he's not bin here above a day or two, so I wouldn't care to say for sure, like. Still, I've no time to run around after him, if he don't want it in the dining room—"

"Of course you haven't," said Mel, honey soothing every syllable, although the idea of Maureen running anywhere was so ridiculous that she had to stifle a snigger. "Perhaps he, er, isn't well enough to come down to the dining room. Has anyone been to check?"

Maureen stared: this train of thought was clearly going too fast for her. Mel was about to apply verbal brakes and repeat her question in another form when Thrudd, losing patience, said:

"*I'll* go and check, shall I? Save you the bother, as you're so tired," and was away before Maureen could find the energy to reply.

While he was gone, Mel (with some difficulty, Maureen having lapsed into near-suspended animation as she digested the notion of the professor's possible prostration) probed further into the habits, manner, and origin of the (maybe) missing man, making mental notes, writing headlines on air. There could always (Mel doubtfully conceded) be a mundane, logical explanation—Maureen, the somnambulist, might have forgotten she'd seen him—it might have been Doris, head waitress, who served his breakfast . . . but her reporter's nose told her there was more to it than that. Unless this Professor Caernavon Carter was a diet freak, starving himself when the temperature outside was around freezing, she'd take odds on his being the mystery corpse down at Rytham Hall. And for all the rest of the Fleet Street gang seemed to have gone straight to badger the Colvedens and the police (and Mel knew her Brinton. He'd be as close as an oyster until he knew just what was what) she had a definite feeling she and Thrudd had scooped the lot of them by following their instincts and checking first into the hotel . . .

When Thrudd came down the stairs with a worried, yet somehow triumphant, look on his face, she knew the instinct had been right.

And after they'd run Charley Mountfitchet to earth, and he'd helped search the place—and after she and Thrudd had filed Stop Press flashes that the mystery man was believed to be a visiting American archaeologist—and after they had hurried with their brain wave to Rytham Hall and insisted, as they forced their way through an eager crowd of fellow journalists, on talking to the police . . . Superintendent Brinton knew it, too.

chapter

-18-

WHILE THE REST of Fleet Street pestered the police for more information, and rushed in search of telephones, Mel and Thrudd retired discreetly to their bedroom at the George and Dragon, from where they rang across the road to Sweetbriars. They had no wish to risk reminding their colleagues of Miss Seeton's invaluable services to the forces of law and order by being too noticeably knocking at her door if she wasn't going to be there to open it.

They need not have worried. Miss Seeton was there: and, when her telephone rang, picked up the receiver almost at once. "Why, Mel, my dear—and you say dear Mr. Banner is with you? What a pleasant surprise! I should so much like to see you both again. I wonder, if you have not made other plans, whether you would care to come . . ."

A quick pause, while she consulted the clock. "To come to tea this afternoon?" concluded Miss Seeton.

"We-ell," demurred Mel, herself checking the time; and Miss Seeton at once began to apologise for having been so forward in assuming that her friends had no better way of spending the first day of their holidays than to come to tea with—

"Steady on, Miss S! It isn't that way at all—we really want to see you, and *soon*. Sooner than that, even. We were kind of hoping you could make it, say, in five minutes time? And please don't worry," heroically, "about lunch, or anything—tea, I mean. I—we—had something on the train coming down."

Miss Seeton, a conscientious hostess, would never entertain the notion that any of her guests should run even the slightest risk of starvation. Had Martha not baked one of her celebrated fruitcakes? Were there not, in a borrowed tin, the remains of a batch of mince pies which dear Miss Wicks had insisted Miss Seeton should share, after the pantomime Refreshments Committee had somehow managed to overstock during rehearsals? And Miss Seeton had naturally not been so tactless as to let slip that the committee, of which she was ex officio a member, had taken particular care to ensure there was too much food for the simple needs of the cast, expense of energy after acting or not. Almost all of Plummergen was in a giant conspiracy to convince the aged and independent Miss Wicks that she could remain, despite her age, independent to the very end . . .

And so it came about that Mel Forby and Thrudd Banner settled themselves in Miss Seeton's sitting room and tucked into mince pies, plum cake, and other festive fare, while Miss Seeton poured tea and chattered happily about the progress of the pantomime, and the amount already raised for the Organ Fund from ticket sales. If (she twinkled) it happened that her friends were staying long enough in the village to attend a performance, she rather thought she had some tickets to spare . . .

"You drive a hard bargain, Miss S," said Mel, trying to imagine the cosmopolitan Thrudd enjoying the *Cinderella* experience. "But we really don't know how long we're going to be around—depends on how quickly the murder's solved, you see. Which is why—"

"Murder?" Miss Seeton set down the teapot. "Someone has been murdered—in Plummergen?" She sighed, and shook her head in disbelief. "In Plummergen, of all places—when one tends to think of life being so peaceful here—though I do realise, of course, that such things, regrettably, happen. But surely not in Plummergen . . ."

"Sorry, honey." Mel leaned over and patted Miss Seeton on the shoulder. "Guess we assumed you'd have heard by now. I mean, what with Martha doing for you as well as for the Colvedens—we thought she'd have been one of the first to know, and, well, the way she talks . . ."

Even from the depths of her evident distress, Miss Seeton managed a smile. "Dear Cousin Flora always said Martha's tongue must be fastened in the middle—but the most kindhearted soul in the world. I am so very fond—" She broke off, suddenly registering Mel's words in full.

"The Colvedens! But—how dreadful! Surely I must have misunderstood—you cannot mean—"

"It's okay, MissEss—take no notice of Forby." Thrudd shot a furious look in his lady's direction, and in his turn patted Miss Seeton on the shoulder. "The Colvedens are fine—we saw them ourselves, ten minutes or so ago, and apart from being a bit upset, as anyone would be, they're, well, fine. All of them."

A gentlewoman tries to maintain her self-control in every circumstance, no matter how startling any circumstance may be. Miss Seeton, finding herself reassured by Thrudd's firm words and Mel's apologetic nod, achieved a stiffening of the spine which would have impressed a sergeant major, lifted the teapot, and began pouring again with a hand which was almost steady . . .

Unlike her voice. She had to clear her throat twice before she could ask the next, obvious question.

Mel, anxious to make amends for having caused her friend such a fright, was quick to answer. "Some professor—an archaeologist from America. Name of Carter, staying over at the George." Miss Seeton gave a little start. Mel looked gratified, nodded, but hurried on without comment: "Seems he was interested in the Temple of Glacia and the Brumalix silver, and sneaked up there in the middle of the night for a . . . a private viewing, with the dig officially closed until the spring . . . and, well, someone disturbed him."

"Or he," said Thrudd, "disturbed them—nobody knows for sure, at this stage. But while Superintendent Brinton and the others are busy doing the official investigation, MissEss, I—we—wondered if you'd care to give us the benefit of your opinion of the case, in the, uh, usual manner."

"My—?"

"Your *exclusive* opinion," Mel cut in. A trusting little soul like Miss S, and the rest of Fleet Street gearing themselves up to descend on Sweetbriars once they'd sucked Brinton & Co. dry? It didn't bear thinking about.

"Exclusive." Miss Seeton, glancing from Mel to Thrudd, suddenly nodded and smiled. Of course—a newspaper term. They were such close friends, and such friendly rivals: no doubt it was the approach of Christmas which had made them decide to work, for once, together—even on so unpleasant a subject as . . .

"Murder," said Miss Seeton, slowly. "Really, although of course one would always prefer being able to help one's friends, I'm very much afraid that any opinion I could offer on that subject would be, for your purposes, not worth having. Someone like Mr. Brinton would be so much more useful, I'm sure—a professional, who understands these sad matters only too well—and as I gather you have already spoken to him, I really don't see how anything I might say could be less . . . than presumption on my part. I have," said Miss Seeton earnestly, "no experience of murder, you see."

Mel and Thrudd exchanged speaking looks, but dared say nothing, though the record of Miss Seeton's exploits over the past seven or eight years presented themselves before their inward eyes to contradict her innocent assertion. She herself, however, frowning, was oblivious to their mood, and went on thoughtfully:

"An American professor . . . yes, I believe there may have been something about the way he spoke . . . but it was for so very short a time—one has enjoyed watching the old black-and-white films on television, you see, and so many of them are American, which I suppose made me recognise . . ."

Mel nodded again, smiling, and murmured that she'd thought so. Thrudd, beside her, stiffened as together they watched Miss Seeton's hands begin to dance on her lap, her eyes focus vaguely on some incident in the past. Mel said, in a voice she strove to keep calm:

"So you've met Professor Carter, Miss S? And maybe, just maybe, you drew a picture of him?"

"Oh . . ." Blinking, Miss Seeton returned her attention firmly to the present. "Oh, dear, I do beg your pardon, but I was recalling . . . if indeed he was that particular visitor to the hotel . . . but he did ask me the way to Rytham Hall, so he probably was, though the Colvedens have many friends, and he might have been one of those—the professor, I mean, or rather the man I thought he was, outside my front gate—he was outside, I mean. I was inside," she explained earnestly, "having dropped my umbrella, when he addressed me"—Mel muttered something about *figures* which Miss Seeton failed to understand—"except that one would expect them to know the way there, of course, if they were." She took a deep breath. "Friends, that is, except that he was—well, rather abrupt in his manner, I thought—so he probably wasn't. Though it *is* probable, from my recollection, that he was staying at the George, because I heard it slam—the door, I mean—and he seemed to be walking very fast from that direction . . ."

"Sounds like our man," said Thrudd, leading her gently on without disturbing the daydream he could see was once more casting its spell: he, too, knew the meaning of the dancing hands, the blank stares, and uncomfortable blushing attempts to act like any other teatime hostess. "When was it you talked with him, MissEss? And what else did he say?"

"And what," said Mel, "did you draw? Come on, honey," as Miss Seeton blinked again, and blushed. "You can't fool me—I know the signs. You must have drawn *something*—and you know you can trust us. Don't you?"

Miss Seeton gazed at her in dismay. Oh, dear, had she somehow given the impression that she considered her friends—for such, after so many years, they surely were—to be untrustworthy? When they were guests in her house, too! It was . . . it was . . .

"Oh, dear—such bad manners," gasped Miss Seeton, pink with embarrassment, and lapsed into silence.

"I'll say it was," Mel promptly agreed, "if he was rude to you at your own front gate for no good reason—I can't believe you were rude to him first. But you aren't the only one. He certainly wasn't a friend of the Colvedens, from what we heard up at the Hall—he as good as gate-crashed the place, and tried to bully Sir George into letting him see the Temple site, when he'd been told it was closed until next year, on the grounds that he'd come all the way from America on purpose—which,

I admit, is a pretty valid sort of argument—and that if Sir George was angling for a handout before he'd let him see it, he was willing to offer way above the market rate—yes," as Miss Seeton drew in her breath, and winced with disapproval, "you can imagine how *that* argument went down! So don't worry anymore if you drew the man as a bad-tempered, ill-mannered lout, because by all accounts that's pretty much what he was."

"Oh, dear." Miss Seeton gazed down at her fingers, now interlaced in an attempt to still their dancing. "One hesitates to speak ill of the dead, but he did seem . . . although not so much rude, to me, as . . . well, as abrupt—impatient. The academic mind, you see, is often so far above that of the ordinary person . . ."

"Nobody, Miss Seeton," said Thrudd solemnly, as Mel had to look hurriedly away, "could ever regard you as an ordinary person. And nobody with your particular talent has the right even to think of herself as ordinary. So . . ."

Between them, he and Mel, as all along they'd known they eventually would, persuaded Miss Seeton to fetch her portfolio from the bureau drawer, and to retrieve the sketch she'd made just after talking to Professor Caernavon Carter. And they asked her—since she was clearly as unhappy about displaying her work as she ever was—if she'd be kind enough to take pity on two hardworking hacks, and make another pot of tea: which Miss Seeton, overcome, was only too happy to do, vanishing kitchenwards in a relieved domestic flurry, leaving them free to study the sketch at leisure.

They duly studied it: and, within seconds, were back to their customary sparring, for it was impossible to make out whether the scene showed an island, in a gently lapping sea— or a sandhill, in the foreground of a tide of rolling dunes. They wasted some moments arguing this point through (and coming to no acceptable conclusion) before agreeing to turn their attention to the rest of the picture.

Miss Seeton had sketched two human forms. The main one—tall, thin, with flowing hair and robes—stood with its back to them, gazing up at a huge, many-pointed star hanging low in a sky dotted with clouds: clouds from which flakes of snow floated in cool serenity to the earth (or sand, depending on one's point of view) below. In the foreground was a large volume which looked like a reference book, though the spine, with its identifying letters, was darkened by the shadow of a nearby building, and thus too hard for them to read. In the background, a row of small, spiky-branched trees marched along the crest of a hill (or island). In the middle distance, a beast of burden, species indeterminate, trudged its weary way with a mangy dog loping by its side.

The second human figure, his face half towards the outside observer, lurked just outside the building, which was of decayed, though vaguely classical, aspect, supported by broken pillars, decorated with headless statues.

"Ozymandias," murmured Mel: and Thrudd had to admit he'd thought of something similar himself, even if those carved birds on the roof looked more like eagles—which were hardly desert birds—than vultures, which were. Eagles were Roman, weren't they? The legions . . .

Ozymandias was a man with an unkempt beard and bristling moustache, above which narrowed eyes glittered with the light of the fanatic beneath a metal helmet, military style. In his hands, a machine gun pointed directly at the back of the stargazer, though his body, complete with dancing feet, was twisted to face the same outside observer: who longed—so powerful was the image conjured by Miss Seeton—to shout a warning to the figure in the flowing robes.

Mel and Thrudd looked at each other. Neither seemed too keen to rush into speech. Thrudd rubbed the tip of his nose thoughtfully; Mel coughed, and cleared her throat.

"Ah," said Thrudd, turning hopefully to his lady. "You wanted to say something?"

Mel raised an eyebrow. "Suddenly, you're mindful of the courtesies, Banner? That I should live to see the day! Why can't you admit it like a man—you've no more idea what all this," with a sweeping gesture at the desert island/desert wasteland sketch, "means than *I* have, have you?"

"No," admitted Thrudd, with a rueful grin. "And that's our mutual brain wave down the drain . . . so what do we do now, Forby?"

But Mel was far from despondent. She cocked her head to one side, and listened to the approaching chink of china.

"Easy," she said. "What do we do now? We ask the one person who's going to know for sure, that's what!"

And, as she spoke, Miss Seeton pushed open the sitting-room door, a tea tray in her hands.

chapter
-19-

TWO PAIRS OF eyes fastened accusingly upon her.

"MissEss."

"Miss S."

Together: "What does it mean?"

Miss Seeton blinked. The teatray tilted. Thrudd leaped to his feet to mind more of the courtesies, giving Mel a chance to enlarge on the question.

"It's a very interesting sketch, Miss S, but kind of on the confusing side. I mean, here's this woman on an island, peering up at the sky while a man tries to shoot her—"

"Here's this man," corrected Thrudd, setting the tray on the table as Miss Seeton once more took her seat, "lost in the middle of the desert and trying to find his way from the stars—"

"But at least," supplied Mel, "we're agreed about the temple ruins—except we can't tell if those birds are Roman eagles, or vultures. And as for the dog, and the camel—"

"Horse," said Thrudd. "But I grant you it's a dog, even if—with all due respect, MissEss—it's rather a dismal-looking specimen. Those ribs—it can't have had a square meal for weeks, and you can tell it's got fleas." He shrugged, and grinned. "We've both tried to make sense of everything, but . . ."

As Mel sighed her agreement, Miss Seeton suddenly chuckled, and turned pink. "Oh dear, I hadn't realised—and I'm so sorry to have misled you, but—it was the children, you see. Our Bible reading, in class, and little Katy Evans and

Bing Crosby—because of what he said about the spelling, of course, although I checked it afterwards in the dictionary and it *is* optional. Rather like artefact, which nowadays is so often spelled with no thought of its Latin origin. With an *i*, that is. Really, the language can be so very confusing, can't it?"

The same unspoken thought crossed the minds of the two reporters, but neither Mel nor Thrudd dared say aloud that of all the confusions around, Miss Seeton's seemed the most confusing. What had crooner Bing Crosby to do with lessons, whether Bible-reading or spelling, at Plummergen Village School? The Latin, or rather Roman, connection they could accept—just—but the rest of what she'd said . . .

"And of course," she told Thrudd, who could only stare, "you were quite right to say that the poor dog has fleas, because they do—pariah, isn't that the word? Or pye. I'm not exactly sure, though dear Jack Crabbe, of course, would know. So very clever, the crossword puzzles he writes—or rather *composes*, as I understand the correct term to be."

She lifted the lid of the teapot. "No leaves floating on the surface, so it must be properly brewed—Mr. Banner, if I could trouble you to pass dear Mel's cup?"

Mr. Banner passed Mel's cup, and then his own; and as Miss Seeton chattered on they drank, and listened, and began to make some sense of her drawing, after all. *White Christmas*—falling snow, fir trees—*The Road to Morocco*—the camel—eastern costume, with its flowing headdress (Thrudd and Mel exchanged looks)—Katy's red Achievement star—the machine-gun rhythm of the stranger's footsteps as he hurried from the George—Bing Crosby, and his singing the song for which he was best loved and known in front of the troops in the movie—the devastation of war, the ruined buildings—the machine gun, although perhaps, since Bing Crosby was an American, one should rather say *tommy gun,* which one understood to be the correct American expression . . .

Perhaps conscious that she had begun to repeat herself, Miss Seeton stuttered, and blushed. "I rather fear—that is," she said, hesitantly, "none of this can be of any real interest to you, surely? After all, my drawing is . . . is just a . . . an assortment of ideas . . ."

"The machine gun, twice," muttered Thrudd. "Tommy gun—Tommy Gunn?" He shook his head. "Never heard of him."

"Hey!" cried Mel, in sudden excitement. "Not Tommy, but—of course, *Treasure Island*—I *knew* those weren't sand dunes—Miss S, you're a marvel!"

Miss Seeton stared at her: so did Thrudd. "*Treasure Island*?" said Mr. Banner, frowning. "I've read it, sure, but that was when I was a kid. I don't see . . ."

Miss Seeton smiled, and nodded. "Toasted cheese," she said, happily. "Poor fellow. And Long John Silver, and Jim Hawkins, and the *Hispaniola* . . ."

"Silver again," said Mel, throwing Thrudd a triumphant glance. "Shows what a dedicated life of crime can do, don't you think? You foreign correspondents, never settling down to anything for long enough to know—but never mind." With an apologetic look for Miss Seeton, she jumped up.

"Thanks for the tea, Miss S, and I'm sorry if you think we're being rude, but we have to be off now. Banner, you can't sit there like a stuffed dummy all afternoon. You can either help Miss Seeton with the washing up—though if she takes my advice she won't let you near one solitary saucer—or you can come with me to enjoy the fun when I give Superintendent Brinton Miss S's clue to the killer's identity. *After* I've rung the *Negative* and told them to hold the front page . . ."

Superintendent Brinton, meanwhile, had been far from idle in the investigation of the Rytham Hall murder. Once he had, thanks to Mel and Thrudd, a lead as to the likely identity of the corpse, he sent PC Potter along to the George to ask if anyone (although he had a sneaking suspicion who it would be) might be either willing or able to go to the Brettenden mortuary in order to confirm that the body was that of Professor Caernavon Carter.

Potter, like his superior, suspected that it would be landlord Charley Mountfitchet who took the burden of identification upon himself: and so it happened. "No use asking that Maureen," he said (which Potter knew only too well). "Doris, now, she's busy seeing to all these reporters we've got wanting rooms—and it's not a woman's work anyhow, having to look at corpuses. Besides, even if it *was* Doris as signed the man in, I reckon I saw as much of him as anyone—and I've my licence to be thinking of, haven't I?" He favoured PC Potter with a long, slow wink. "Always best to keep on the right side of the law, that's what I say!"

Which, translated, meant that Charley—who sometimes found life in Plummergen (even living, as he did, just over the road from Miss Seeton) rather dull—looked forward to his few minutes of excitement. Whenever a serious crime was committed, whenever the men from the Yard came down, Charley Mountfitchet followed the ins and outs of the case with more enthusiasm than anyone else in Plummergen, which was saying a great deal. He had been known to brood if not required to give a statement, and would ply the detectives with quantities of after-hours whisky, dropping hints about the Duty of the Citizen to Aid the Forces of the Law, and talking wistfully about the Good Old Days of the Amateur Sleuth.

Potter was pleased now to be able to humour his friend in an undoubtedly worthy cause. "Yes, best it should be you, Charley—in the circumstances." And he returned Charley's wink with one of his own.

Pausing only to scribble a note for Doris, Charley hurried outside with Potter before the policeman could change his mind. A blast of icy air swept from the Marsh across the roof of the waiting Panda, rattling the wooden "George and Dragon" sign over which Professor Carter had enthused ever while eating his dinner: Plummergen should be proud (he had said) of having maintained its traditions rather than kowtowing to the Hanoverian who'd succeeded Queen Anne . . .

Charley shivered. Potter glanced at him. "Reckon you'd have done better to wear your overcoat, Charley. Want to slip back in and fetch it, do you?"

"It's not such a long walk the other end, is it? Don't think I'll bother—mustn't keep 'em waiting, must we!"

Potter gave an exasperated laugh. "Get on with you, Charley Mountfitchet, no sense in freezing to death—could be snowing by the time we get there. You pop indoors—and don't worry," he called, as Charley, with some reluctance, started to take his advice. "I won't run away!"

Some seven years earlier, when Miss Seeton, still teaching full-time, had owned her cottage for no more than a few months, and came down from her London flat only in the holidays, Plummergen had managed to embroil itself in the War of the Roses. The War was a notable landmark in village history: partly because of the strongly divisive emotions it engendered, but mostly because it heralded virtually the final episode of such history for which nobody, no matter how they might try, could possibly blame Miss Seeton.

War had been declared on Christmas Eve. Miss Nuttel, Mrs. Blaine, and three of their cronies had spent the summer drying flowers, foliage, and grasses to decorate the church for the festive season: and this they had, to their own satisfaction, accomplished at the appointed time. It was not, however, to be supposed that such accomplishment would satisfy those—among them Lady Colveden—who preferred honest fresh flowers to dessicated vegetation of indeterminate origin and vintage. Her ladyship, on finding the church, as she believed, full of dead flowers, had emptied the vases, thrown the lot out, and burned them. Plummergen church was adorned with Lenten roses that Christmas . . .

The War raged until February, when a sharply worded letter in the parish magazine, above the signature of the Reverend Arthur Treeves (but emanating, as everyone knew, from his sister Molly) demanded a cessation of hostilities.

The flower rota is a perpetual thorn in Plummergen's female flesh—as Mrs. Henderson and Mrs. Skinner, not to mention the Nuts, will readily bear witness. One or other of the various aggrieved parties may often be observed prowling about the church, which stands at the southern end of The Street close by the George and Dragon, to check up on what their opponents may have achieved in the way of floral beautification . . .

And it was after Charley Mountfitchet had vanished indoors for his overcoat that Miss Nuttel and Mrs. Blaine, having enjoyed a few minutes' highly successful prowl, were walking through the lych-gate back into The Street.

"Eric! Did you hear that?" Mrs. Blaine clutched Miss Nuttel
by the arm. "PC Potter is trying to arrest someone, and he's
running away!"

Miss Nuttel quickened her step, nostrils a-quiver with the
scent of brewing scandal. Mrs. Blaine clutched her by the arm
again. "Eric—suppose whoever it is comes this way? Suppose
he's armed? What shall we do?"

"Our duty," said Miss Nuttel, the intrepid. Being so much
the taller, Miss Nuttel had already spotted PC Potter standing
beside the Panda car, and recognised unworried reinforcements. Mrs. Blaine, however, was not party to this recognition,
and slackened her pace accordingly.

"Oh, Eric, you're so brave! You'll take care, won't you?"
as Miss Nuttel strode staunchly onwards. "Eric . . ."

"All right, Charley?" The masculine voice was borne towards
Mrs. Blaine on the clear winter air. Mrs. Blaine gave a little
shriek.

"Oh, Eric, it must be an escaped lunatic! Calling himself *a
right charlie*—too dangerous . . . Eric!"

But Miss Nuttel, rapidly deducing that Charley Mountfitchet must be the object of PC Potter's arrest, and knowing
him to be unaccustomed to firearms, put on another burst of
speed, and arrived on the forecourt of the George and Dragon
in time to see the landlord hurry down the hotel steps and
into the Panda with no more than a glance in her direction.
PC Potter gunned the engine, and the Panda drove away.

"Said he'd come quietly," Miss Nuttel gleefully informed
Mrs. Blaine, as Bunny panted up, her fear on her friend's
behalf being even greater than for herself—unless it was her
curiosity that was greater than either. What Charley had in
fact said was that it didn't matter how long this all took,
because he'd left everything nice and quiet behind him. But
Miss Nuttel heard only what she wanted to hear . . .

"Brought his overcoat with him, what's more." This made
Mrs. Blaine blink. Miss Nuttel snorted. "Disguise, at the other
end. Photographers," she explained. "Put it over his head, and
who's to know?"

Mrs. Blaine's blackcurrant eyes widened in amazement.
"Charley Mountfitchet, arrested? But . . . but the professor was

a guest in his hotel!" That this was no Lady Macbeth–like protestation of "What! In our house?" her next words proved. "And now—he won't get paid!"

"Not by the professor," said Miss Nuttel, with a peculiar emphasis on the words. "Someone else may, though—hush money. Or services rendered . . ."

"Eric! You don't—you can't mean . . ."

Miss Nuttel nodded slowly. "A hit man—paid to kill. Only obeying orders, that'll be his defence—and who's most used to giving orders? And who did we see quarrelling with the professor just the other day?"

"Oh, Eric, no!" Mrs. Blaine cast a furtive glance over one plump shoulder, her cheeks pale and quivering, anxious hands clasped in fright. "Not—not Sir George!"

"Body found there," Miss Nuttel pointed out. "First on the scene's the most obvious suspect. Everyone knows that."

"But you said Charley Mount—"

"Too obvious," interposed Miss Nuttel smoothly. "Camouflage—double bluff. Military intelligence during the war, of course. Easy enough."

"And the Hall was used for something secret, wasn't it?" Mrs. Blaine was warming to the theory, building her own elaborations. "The professor must have been some kind of spy, and Sir George spotted him and he had to be silenced—but, Eric, it's too suspicious. If Sir George is mixed up in all this, why hasn't he been arrested as well?"

Miss Nuttel assumed an air of lofty outrage. "Pressure, influence—corruption, that's why. Obvious."

"That's too dreadful!" Mrs. Blaine's squeak was indignant. "When the man's won medals—supposed to have won them, I suppose I should say, because I'm sure I've never seen them on display at the Hall, have you? And one is never allowed close enough on Armistice Day to see whether the ones he's wearing are *genuine*, which of course they wouldn't be, if he was a spy—but if they *are* genuine, by any chance, then he really ought to know better! A fine example to set the rest of the village! Eric, what should we do about it, do you think?"

Miss Nuttel, who had already thought, drew herself up to her full height. "Our duty," she said again: noble, resigned, a pattern of all the virtues. "Inform the police. At once."

Mrs. Blaine's startled eyes flew to the telephone box on the other side of The Street, just outside the bakery. Miss Nuttel knew what her friend was thinking. "Have to pay," she pointed out.

"Unless it's nine-nine-nine. Oh, Eric, I really think we—you—should . . . and at once, as you said before. And it might," said Mrs. Blaine, as Miss Nuttel hesitated, "be so much better not to give your name, and to hang up quickly—in case, you know, anyone else is trying to dial the emergency services. It would be too dreadful to block the line when someone's house was burning down . . ."

Which argument appealing greatly to Miss Nuttel, at Mrs. Blaine's continued urging she crossed to the telephone box, picked up the receiver with shaking hands, and began to dial those ominous three digits.

chapter
~20~

UPERINTENDENT BRINTON WAS back in Ashford police sta-
on, talking on the telephone to Scotland Yard while DC
oxon, at the extension, listened in.

"Oracle? Thank heavens I caught you—I was afraid you
nd your young giant might've been off somewhere—"

"We were," Chief Superintendent Delphick informed his
riend. "Just off, that is. Another five seconds, and you would
ave missed us. There's been another Shotgun robbery—a
illing, this time—and the ground force is screaming for our
elp. I can spare you no more than three minutes, Chris, and
at's more than I'd really like. Unless it's something you are
ositive you can't cope wi— Oh." Before Brinton could say
nything, Delphick spoke again, his tone now one of amused
esignation.

"All right, Chris, let me hear the worst. What's she been up
o now? Don't tell me you've had to run her in on suspicion
f the murder at Rytham Hall—naturally, the news has filtered
hrough—"

"No," broke in Brinton, "but I near as dammit had to run
ir George Colveden in—yes," above startled exclamations
rom the Yard, "and if it hadn't been for a bit of nifty—and
ighly unorthodox, let me add—sleuthing on the part of those
recious reporter friends of yours, I think I might've risked it,
hough it goes against the grain for a copper to use anonymous
hone calls as evidence. But when I asked him about it, he
idn't deny he'd been on bad terms with the deceased—our
nonymous pal said they'd had a blazing row, though I took

that with a pinch of salt, of course—and as far as I could see ▮
was the only one with anything like a proper motive. The dea▮
man's American, for heaven's sake. Never been in the count▮
before, according to his passport—found it at the Georg▮
where he was staying. The landlord identified him for us."

"Charley Mountfitchet?" The amusement had returned ▮
Delphick's tone. "Yes, he's a great one for cooperating wi▮
the forces of law and order. But I trust you don't suspe▮
Charley of making anonymous telephone calls—he's one ▮
the most straightforward and open characters one could ev▮
wish to meet, I'd have said."

Brinton grunted. "Potter says so too—*and* Foxon, who▮
acting in this blasted pantomime with the chap and thinks th▮
proves he's trustworthy—which to be fair," as Foxon bega▮
to expostulate, "I'd agree, from what I know of him, he ▮
Besides, the switchboard said it was a female voice that ran▮
in—gruff, but female. Or else a man trying to be a bit clever▮
he added.

Foxon made another attempt at expostulation, but Delphic▮
was before him. "I can hardly suppose you to suspect Mi▮
Seeton of making anonymous telephone calls, Chris, fema▮
though she undoubtedly is. Mentioning no names, however, ▮
believe all of us have some acquaintance with a gruff-voice▮
woman from Plummergen who's likely to know, or to thin▮
she knows, everything that's happened in the village in rece▮
days . . ."

"She's had flu," said Foxon, as Brinton groaned, and mu▮
tered a weak *of course*. "She's only just come back int▮
circulation—sorry, sir," as Brinton glared at him.

"Making up for lost time, no doubt," said Delphick, from th▮
safety of fifty distant miles, visualising the scene in Brinton▮
small office and trying not to chuckle. "Still, since you'v▮
made it very clear that you acted as a result of the, er, sleuthin▮
activities of certain persons as yet unnamed, but at whose ide▮
tity I am (if asked) prepared to make an educated guess, rath▮
than on the anonymous call—why have you now called me▮
If we have eliminated Miss Seeton from the proceedings—'

"We haven't," Brinton told him. "Well, not exactly." H▮
heard Foxon start to splutter, and sighed. "Oh, all right. Yo▮

girlfriend, Oracle, is right in the thick of things, as usual—
what else would you expect? That perishing Forby woman
and her World Wide pal have been taking a look at the
same artist's latest masterpiece, and—well . . . They borrowed
it and brought it along to me, of all crazy things—and now I'm
worried they've got me crazy, too. Because she may—just—
have something, only before I do anything about it and risk
making myself look the biggest fool in the county, I thought—
well, I thought I'd better talk to you . . ."

"You wish, you mean, to use me as a safety net." It was
hard to tell whether Delphick was smiling or sighing as he said
this. "Working with Miss Seeton does indeed have something
of the trapeze element in it—on which side will the unwary
copper fall? Or will he maintain his balance until the end?"

"Or will he take the plunge and end up breaking his neck
over the whole damn business?" Brinton's tone was resigned.
"I suppose I'll have to risk it, knowing how things've gone
on other occasions she's mixed herself up in murders—just
give me time to stock up on my blood pressure pills, and
then . . . Look, Oracle, you're in a hurry, I know. Just tell me
the name of that Art Squad bloke who's had dealings with
MissEss before, and then you can be off to your Shotguns. If
I'm on a wild goose chase, I don't see why it's always got
to be you who's dragged with me—even if Miss Seeton *is*
more your pigeon than anyone else's at the Yard . . ."

"The, er, bird you want," said Delphick at once, unable to
resist the chance for a gentle leg-pull at his friend's expense,
"is Inspector Terling: I'll put you through." And the connection was broken before Brinton could find any adequate reply,
though Foxon on the extension chortled briefly before turning
it into a cough.

Fortunately for Brinton's blood pressure, Inspector Terling
was in his office when the phone rang on his desk. He was
cautiously happy to be of assistance—caution entering the
equation as soon as he realised the exact identity and location
of his colleague.

"Brinton . . . Ashford? Ah, yes, that'll be Kent, of course.
Not Ashford in Middlesex, or Ashford in Devon, or Ashford in
Derbyshire—in view of this morning's late headlines, I mean.

An unidentified body at Rytham Hall in, er, Plummergen . . .'

Brinton groaned. Terling laughed: it sounded a little forced.
"My instinct tells me our friend Miss Seeton is on the loose
again, and you'd like me, for some reason, to help pull the
chestnuts out of the fire, rather than Chief Superintendent
Delphick. I won't ask why the Oracle can't—or won't—help:
ignorance is bliss, and all that. And I can't promise anything,
but I'll do my best. At least my life assurance is up to date.
So what's the problem?"

"*Nuts* is about right," muttered Brinton; then, in desperation: "Who d'you know who wouldn't be too bothered about
bashing someone's head to a pulp if they got in the way of
him trying to pinch a . . . a load of Roman artefacts?" There
it was out. He went on:

"It'd have to be someone who'd know the right market for
the stuff once he'd got it—someone who really didn't mind
using violence to get it—I know most of the chummies'll
have a bash if they think their rotten little skins are in danger, because bashing's all too easy, God help us. But it's
the specialist knowledge—the contact with the end-of-the-line
buyer—that'd be the big clue . . ."

Terling was silent. Brinton, having put his question purely
on the say-so of a couple of press reporters and an old lady's
scribble, could have kicked himself. He waited, gloomily wondering whether he should hang up before Terling told him there
was no such animal.

"You're not," said Inspector Terling at last, "suggesting
this basher was after the Temple of Glacia mosaic, are you?
Because that's one hell of a lot of old stone carpet squares to
pop in your haversack and flog to some bloke with more cash
than honesty . . ." The Inspector took great care to cultivate
the Perpetual Philistine pose. He insisted it was the only way
he could work in the Art Squad and still keep a sense of
proportion and, thus, his sanity.

"Not the mosaic, then—so you must mean the silver," he
went on, as Brinton could only grunt a vague acknowledgement. "And that'd be portable, all right. Bulky, mind you, but
from similar services in museums and so on I'd judge one man
could lift it easily, crate it up, and bung it on a plane to take out

of the country before anyone was on to him—except, I gather, that this time they were."

"No, they weren't." Brinton took courage from Terling's tone: if the inspector didn't think it far-fetched—and *how* far, with Miss Seeton in on it, heaven only knew—then perhaps it wasn't, after all. "Not if they'd been reading the newspapers, they weren't—at least, they should have known they hadn't any need to be, because the stuff wasn't there. The owners of the Hall didn't want the responsibility of a load of valuable tin-plate crockery, or whatever you care to call it, lying around the place inadequately guarded, so they insisted the old girl from the museum who'd been in charge of the dig took it under her wing—dammit," he added, the avian motif accidentally flapping yet another conversational feather.

"H'm. From what I've read, the Glacia site contained the usual odd broken pots and chunks of glass, but no bones or coffins with jewellery and so on . . . If he was after anything, it'll have been the silver, I'd take a bet. He just won't have read the papers properly—or else he didn't believe 'em. He's careless like that, if he's the chummie I'm thinking of—though he's one of three possibles," he warned the superintendent hastily. "The other two're more on the sceptical side than him—and it might not be any of 'em, anyway. Specialists with violence aren't such rare birds as you might expect . . ."

"Give me all three names," prompted Brinton, as Terling paused. He took a silent bet with himself that, given those statues in Miss Seeton's sketch, at least one of the possibles would be called—well, not Eagle, but something along those lines: Hawke, Falcon, Kite . . .

"Sparrow," said Inspector Terling. "Bob Sparrow—he's one of the wouldn't-believe-the-papers pair who'd think it was always worth checking out for himself. The other's a bloke called Jones, Archibald Jones—and don't anybody call him Archie, because he hates it. So I always do," he added, "when I book him—drives him mad. You'd be surprised what effect that has on the quality of his statement—talk about condemned out of his own mouth, the silly clot."

"Sparrow—Jones. Got addresses for these blighters?" Brin ton nodded to Foxon, who had already written down the names and was waiting for the next instalment.

"For all I know off-hand, it could be care of Her Majesty— I'll have to run a check in Records. Hang on while I call down on the other phone—"

"But what about the third man? Dammit," muttered Brinton, with a horrid feeling the name would turn out to be Welles, or Greene, or Lime.

"Sounds daft," said Terling, with an embarrassed cough, "but it really is his name—we've checked. Benjamin Algernon Gunnersbury-ffitch, two effs. Quite the black baa-baa of the family. They disowned him years ago. Calls himself, for professional purposes, Ben Gunn. What?"

"Sorry," gasped Brinton, who had uttered an astonished yelp which then went down backwards. "Sorry, Terling—hay fever." It was an excuse which always served him well, no matter what the season of the year. "Look, forget about the addresses for the first two—if he's at liberty right now, Ben Gunn's our man. According to a . . . a witness statement," he said, casting caution to the winds. "A . . . a pretty reliable witness statement . . ."

"Aha," said Terling, recognising embarrassment in another. "For *reliable witness* read *Miss Seeton*, I suppose? No wonder you didn't need the Oracle in on this, if she's giftwrapped the blighter for you already—just the right time of year for it, too. How exactly did she do it, or would you rather I didn't ask?"

"Don't ask," groaned Brinton. "And don't say anything!" he snarled in Foxon's direction, as that effervescent young man emitted a chortle. "Sorry, Terling. I've a case of rebellion in the ranks, as you probably noticed."

"That what it was?" Terling chuckled. "She has a funny effect on people, does Miss Emily Dorothea Seeton. But if she says it's only the one address you want . . ."

After he'd supplied it, and received Brinton's grateful thanks, Inspector Terling relaxed, conscious that, for once, whatever chaos Miss Seeton might be about to cause was highly unlikely to come his way. He waxed expansive.

"You've never told me about the corpse," he said. "Lots about possible villains, and a smattering about MissEss, but nothing else. Particular secret, is it?"

Brinton cursed. "Forget my own name next—that was another thing I meant to ask, with you being more up in the arty world than me. Name Caernavon Carter mean anything?"

Another pause, while Terling evidently scanned mental records. At last: "American," he said. "A high-up academic earth-grubber along the lines of—hey! If you're trying to tell me *he's* your victim, I can hardly believe it!"

"Too eminent in his field for anyone to want to bump him off, you mean? But I always thought these boffin types were the worst cutthroats of the lot."

"Well, there's something in that, as a general rule, but they'd have to go a long way to bump off Carter, and I mean that literally. By all accounts the man's a recluse—has been for, oh, two, three years. Started off quite normal, though—born in Boston, I think. Used to be an Egyptologist. Expert on pyramids and pharaohs' relics, which is how come I've heard of him. A few years ago he got caught by the sun, or something—maybe it was a fever—anyway, it sent him bonkers, whatever it was. Flown home from Egypt in goodness-knows-what kind of state. The shrinks and quacks said they'd sorted him out in the end, but he went to ground in Alaska once they let him out of the loony bin—a sort of reaction against the sun, I suppose, and perhaps you can't blame him. Anyway, nobody's seen him since."

"Maybe our chap's a phony, then. The real one might be dead, for all anyone knows, and—"

"I'm not saying yours *isn't* a phony—we'd need to see a photo or two before we could say for sure—but whoever's the real one's still in the land of the living, all right—if you can call it living in a place where the temperature never goes much above freezing. The poor bloke seems to spend all his time writing long and argumentative articles for top-notch magazines you can't even take out a subscription to unless you've got a string of letters after your monicker. And—hang on, yes, you could be right—that your body's Carter, I mean. I've just remembered—these articles. The reason they're so controversial is that they aren't about Egypt and pyramids anymore. Probably because of our lousy English weather, but—for some reason or other, he's switched to being an expert on Roman Britain . . ."

chapter
-21-

"TALK ABOUT GIFT-WRAPPED," gloated Brinton, who had dropped into Scotland Yard to report on how things had gone when he, Foxon, and PC Buckland (just in case) arrived at the south London home of the unsuspecting Benjamin Algernon Gunnersbury-ffitch, and (after cautioning) had arrested him under the name (Brinton's concession to Mel and Miss Seeton) of Ben Gunn. "Christmas's come early this year, all right—with a bit of help," he said, grinning in the direction of Inspector Terling, "from a few friends."

"Miss Seeton, for one?" Delphick—the preliminaries of the shotgun killing having been dealt with, and the details passed on to the flu-recovered team who'd been dealing with the original outbreak—had returned, with Bob, to his office: where, with Terling, the pair formed a fascinated triumvirate audience to the superintendent's statement.

"Miss Seeton," agreed Brinton, stretching luxuriously in the most comfortable of Delphick's visitors' chairs with another gloating smile. "That woman's a ruddy marvel, Oracle—a perishing nuisance sometimes, enough to drive a man to a nervous breakdown with that blasted brolly of hers—but they're fifty miles away, both of 'em, and our chummie's booked and on his way to Ashford nick without anything going wrong at all. Gift-wrapped, like I said. Christmas coming early . . . and not just for us. That Forby woman and her bloke—they put us on to it, and they'll get the story. I've told Foxon to see to that, so they'll be happy, too."

161

"I wouldn't bet on it," murmured Delphick, who had a so
spot for Amelita Forby, and gained perennial amusement from
the competitive companionship she shared with Thrudd Ban
ner. "I should rather say that one of them will be happy, and th
other—whichever is beaten to the headline story—will broo
on revenge . . . but pay no attention to my nonsense, Chris
I agree, you've done an excellent job—thanks to Mel, an
Thrudd, and Miss Seeton, as well as Terling here. Christma
gifts all round, I fancy—"

"And well deserved, too," said Brinton, who was becom
ing euphoric. "He came like a ruddy lamb, Oracle. Almos
anyway. Soon as we said we'd got proof it was a left-hande
bloke bashed the prof over the head, and there was Gun
trying to dial his solicitor with his left hand—and we sort o
suggested there were a few prints around the Hall, and Si
George and Lady Colveden might just've had time to mak
out a bit more in the dark than they'd remembered at first—
well, he came like a lamb. Pleaded self-defence, though."

"What!" exclaimed Terling, who alone of the triumvirat
had actually seen the guilty party. "But Gunn must be six foo
if he's an inch, and built like a navvy—"

"Which is how come he did all that damage to the poo
old prof's head." For a moment, Brinton lost his cheerfu
look, and shuddered. "A nasty piece of work, Ben Gunn
and bonkers with it, what's more. Says the professor starte
it—and him a little chap barely five-and-a-half feet tall! Bu
Gunn's pleading self-defence, which to my mind just goes t
prove he's bonkers. Dr. Wyddial says there's six or seven
pretty heavy blows to the head—which of course explain
why the poor bloke was in such a state nobody recognised him
until she'd had the chance to tidy him up—and it doesn't sa
much for the self-defence bit. Doc says the first blow woul
have knocked him out—the second, at best. I can't see he's a
leg to stand on."

"I should imagine," said Terling, "he'll've been a bit peeve
to find your tame archaeologist really had carted the silver of
to the museum, after he couldn't find it in the house. No
noted for keeping his temper, our Ben. Easily frustrated, an
greedy with it. That'll be why he lashed out, at a guess—

annoyed he'd most likely lost a profitable market. I'm sure
he wouldn't have wanted the silver just to melt it down. He'll
have had some millionaire with an easy conscience ready and
waiting . . ."

"Ah," said Delphick, thoughtfully. Bob Ranger, until now
a silent observer of the scene, was moved to murmur; but
Delphick quenched him with a look, and said:

"So all's well that ends well, Chris—when it comes to
the Mosaic Murder, anyway. If only we could be so lucky
with the Shotgun Gang. Give me the peaceful, underhand
type of crime with an element of wit about it any day—
the Night Safe trick, for instance . . . You know, I'm sorely
tempted, since she appears to be on top form at present,
to pop down to Plummergen and ask Miss Seeton for her
advice. Particularly since it would be on your recommenda-
tion . . ."

"Why not?" said Brinton, still euphoric. "Your sergeant's
more than likely to spend Christmas with his in-laws anyway,
I'd've said, with Dr. Knight being an Ugly Sister and all.
And Foxon—if he survives the trip back to Ashford, but
with Buckland riding shotgun I'm sure I don't see why he
shouldn't—does the Broker's Man to a tee, so he says . . ."

Scotland Yard might still have its collective hands full in
the run-up to Christmas, but Kent and other more rural areas
were inclined to relax a little. Crooks, like honest folk, enjoy
a holiday from work now and again; and Brinton raised no
objection when Foxon disappeared Plummergen-wards on the
opening night of the Padders' *Cinderella*—indeed, he hinted
that he might well take up the earlier offer of tickets for one
or other performance, if Foxon still had them.

Foxon, the perpetual optimist, still did: but other members
of the cast and production team, who had spent the past few
weeks trying to persuade people to buy, found themselves
with none left when last-minute hopefuls decided to attend
the theatrical experience of the year.

"I'm so sorry," said Miss Seeton, for the third time, as Mel
glared at Thrudd and muttered that it was all his fault. "I agree
that I had some earlier, but when dear Miss Treeves telephoned

and explained that she had been approached, and had no mor
to offer, I'm afraid I would have found it rather, well, diffi
cult to refuse. It is, after all, for the Organ Fund—and mos
gratifying that so many people wish to see the performance
The dear vicar, I'm sure, will be delighted . . ."

The Reverend Arthur Treeves had wondered, in his vagu
way, why there suddenly seemed to be so many more stranger
around than he would have expected in December, for it is i
high summer that Plummergen—particularly since its second
prize win in the Best Kept Village Competition—sees th
greatest influx of tourists. But these were no ordinary tourists
they might, in ordinary circumstances, have been prepared t
wait until spring before visiting the Temple of Glacia, as th
newspapers had advised—but that was before a body had beei
found there. With any luck, there might be blood, or signs o
the desperate struggle, remaining. Mr. Stillman's post-office
cum-general-stores did a regrettably roaring trade in flash
bulbs (the grey December skies requiring these) and film
although he salved his conscience by dropping heavy hint
about Emmy's unsold pantomime tickets—and the punter
paid up promptly.

"I'm so sorry," said Miss Seeton, yet again; then she bright
ened. "Miss Treeves did, as I recall, say something about th
response having been so good that she and dear Lady Colveder
are considering an extra performance—not on Christmas Eve
naturally, when everyone is always so very busy, but the day
before. Perhaps, if you are willing, I could make enquirie
about that evening on your behalf? If, I mean, they have one
Two, I suppose," with a twinkle. "Seats, that is. An extr
performance."

"You're on," said Mel, "and thanks—one performance, tw
seats. Banner, stop pulling faces. You'll enjoy it. Don't you
want to see Miss S's brilliant scenery?"

Miss Seeton smiled, and shook her head, murmuring tha
it had been such a pleasure, and the very least she could d
for the village where she had been made to feel so much a
home—and that anyway, all the hard work had been done by
others. She'd only had to design the sets—rough out a few
sketches . . .

"Well, if we can't be sure of seeing the genuine article onstage," said Mel, "at least we'll get the private view. Come on, Miss S—show!"

It is usual for Miss Seeton, when urged to display her artistic prowess, to be blushing and reluctant, even embarrassed: the reason being that such urgings are usually for her to display her most recent "instinctive" Drawings, for which her services are so valued by the police. Miss Seeton, whose firm opinion is that one should only draw what one sees, is made more than uncomfortable by the knowledge that, all too often, she draws what only she could have seen, with the inward eye of her unique imagination: and this makes her feel guilty.

She had, she knew, no need to feel guilty now. Were not the results of the sketches Mel and Mr. Banner were asking to see readily visible to all, scaled up in size and with far more flamboyant colours, onstage in Plummergen's village hall? It would be ridiculously false modesty to make a fuss about fetching her portfolio and letting her friends take a peep at her preliminary ideas . . .

But perhaps they would like a cup of tea while they took their peep? Not, of course, that she minded their looking—not at all—but it was, well, thirsty work . . .

"Now that," said Thrudd, indicating the first drawing, "even I recognise, though it's some years since my childish self revelled in visits to the pantomime. The kitchen at Hardup Hall, right?"

"The scullery at Stoneybroke Hall," Mel corrected him, she having taken time to read Miss Seeton's accompanying list of set headings, compiled with the best interests of the scene painters at heart. "She doesn't seem to have done them in any particular order," she went on, as Thrudd turned to the next sketch, which was, inarguably, the Palace Ballroom. "Wonder what they made the chandelier out of."

Miss Seeton, popping back while the tea brewed to ask if plain digestive biscuits and Battenberg cake would do, since she hadn't been out to the shops yet, explained that Mabel Potter and the Admiral had achieved quite remarkable effects out of crumpled aluminium foil, electric light bulbs, and a selection of old glass beads.

"Fortunately," she went on, "as I should regret its loss— dear Cousin Flora—not, of course, that I should worry abou lending my possessions in normal circumstances, but one can not help, after so many stage productions at school, but view these matters differently. Although normally, I am only too happy to help where I can—but in the necklace she left me the beads, although undoubtedly glass, are yellow. And a yellow chandelier would hardly have the same effect, would it? A crystal, that is. Dear Miss Maynard—she has spent so much time with the children, you know . . ."

Since neither Mel nor Thrudd could be expected to know that Alice Maynard was playing the part of Fairy Crystal, this remark made little sense to them; but they were, after so many years, accustomed to Miss Seeton's sometimes erratic mode of speech, and were able to make the right noncommittal noises before she popped back to her tea making and they turned to the next sketch.

As soon as they saw it, they looked at each other. This was no neatly limned set design with careful notes, scale markings for the position of curtains and flats, and recommen- dations for the lighting plan. This was one of Miss Seeton's cartoon-type drawings—one of her Drawings, they realised, even if, at first glance, it showed no more than any scene they might have expected a production of *Cinderella* to con- tain.

"But at second glance," mused Mel, "there's rather more to it than that. She's altered things in a way I'm not sure I understand—and that, Banner, means she knows something. Without knowing she knows it, of course."

"Of course," returned Thrudd, quirking an eyebrow. When he'd first encountered Miss Seeton, on the loose in Switzerland mixed up in a case of international currency fraud, art theft, forgery, and murder, he'd found it impossible to believe she was really the innocent catalyst of crime she didn't even try insisting she was, which marked her down (in the cynical view of the World Wide Press reporter) as a true profes- sional. Having seen her in action on home ground—and having been favoured with the views of Mel Forby, who'd known her longer—he'd tended to find himself revising his original opinion . . . but he still harboured doubts, which occasionally came to the surface.

And this was one of the occasions: except that, with the Mosaic Murderer apparently apprehended, what was there left for Miss Seeton to detect? "Of course," Thrudd said again, puzzled, picking up the sketch and frowning.

"Hey," cried Mel, "what's that on the back?" She leaned forward to peer. "Looks like a page of the script, to me. I wonder if she realises she's mislaid it?"

Thrudd turned the sheet of paper over, and scanned the lines on the back before consulting Miss Seeton's sketch on the front again. "False alarm, I think," he said, with a grin. "It may have looked as if it, uh, meant something, but I'd say she's just illustrated this particular scene in a . . . a less detailed way than you'd normally expect. Or else it's her first rough attempt at the Woodland Glade, when the Broker's Men are rushing about serving writs . . ."

"Oh." Mel squinted at the paper, then said: "Well, put it down and let's take another look . . . Banner, how long is it since you went to a panto, for heaven's sake?"

"Years," said Thrudd, staring at his lady as her tone betokened scorn. "I know I'm a bit hazy on the details—"

"Hazy? Down to zero visibility, I should say. Examine this picture—this doodle—carefully, Banner. Granted, it shows a picnic in a wood—that's the basket, I agree, and the plates and cups and so on. And this is poor old Buttons—who looks remarkably like Nigel Colveden—who's obviously had to cart everything by himself from Stoneybroke Hall, and no thanks to the Ugly Sisters, who're standing around watching other people do all the work, as usual."

"I can see that perf—"

"No, you can't. Plummergen may be only an amateur crowd putting on a panto, but I refuse to believe they'd let the Ugly Sisters appear onstage in flounced and ruffled dresses *with beards and moustaches*, never mind that behind all the whiskers they look exactly like Dr. Knight and Mr. Jessyp, who are both clean-shaven—or who were when I last saw them a month or so back, and even in Plummergen things don't happen that fast."

"Oh," said Thrudd, peering in his turn at the paper. "Then I guess I must've missed the fuzzy features—but you can't say I'm wrong about the rest of it, Forby, so stop trying to score over me after just one little, uh, lapse."

Mel snorted, but refrained from speech as Miss Seeton reappeared with the tea tray. As Thrudd jumped up to offer assistance, Mel studied the sketch again. Apart from the excessively masculine appearance of the Ugly Sisters, it seemed to be, as Thrudd had said, a first attempt at the traditional scene in which Baron Stoneybroke (or Hardup) is served with a writ by the Broker's Men just after having an argument with Buttons. The Baron had evidently been trying to belabour Buttons with a—

"A shotgun, Miss S?" Mel pointed to the strange-shaped stick carried in the picture by Baron Mountfitchet. "This would be a modern setting of the story, right?"

Miss Seeton stared, and blushed. "Really, I don't know what came over me. Fortunately, it's the Prompt copy, and nobody sees it except myself—but I had to copy out that page again last week, just in case I should fall ill and anyone else have to use it during a performance—having the stress of the words, and the moves and, ah, business"—she brought out the stage term with some diffidence—"noted on it, you see. And dear Nigel is so amusing in that scene—acrobatics, and so forth—and dear Mr. Mountfitchet—but it isn't supposed to be a shotgun. Dear me. Nigel breaks off a branch, and pretends it's a pitchfork—although quite why anyone should be making hay in the middle of a wood . . ."

Thrudd snickered, and Mel shot him an awful look. Fortunately, Miss Seeton hadn't noticed, and carried on:

"But I suppose it was the way he held it—with being my umbrella that night, as I recall, on account of the Props people having not yet completed the fallen tree trunk, you see. No doubt he held it in this way because it was, after all, borrowed—Mr. Mountfitchet, I mean. From me. And he very properly wished to take particular care of something belonging to someone else, when normally that scene is conducted with a great deal of high spirits and—one has to say it—perhaps some risk of carelessness, if they were to become carried away—not, of course, that they do, but they might, I suppose. Pantomime, you see, is a very *active* form of theatre," explained Miss Seeton earnestly.

"So it is," said Mel. "So it is. Are these two meant to be PC Potter and our friend Foxon? The Broker's Men?" Miss Seeton confirmed that they were. "And these," said Mel, "must be the writs. Big, aren't they?"

"Parchment," Miss Seeton told her, with a twinkle. "Or rather, wallpaper of suitable colour and texture, which Mrs. Potter has so cleverly made since I drew this—and very realistic they look, as well. One feels extremely sorry for the Baron when he is served with such documents—which is, of course, the intention."

"Signed, sealed, and duly delivered," agreed Mel. "But those are certainly some seals you've drawn here, Miss S. The size of dinner plates—well," in deference to the picnic basket, "saucers, anyhow. They look more like a . . . a row of medals hanging along the bottom there . . ."

She gave Thrudd a pointed stare, but Mr. Banner had not forgotten that Ben Gunn (as the burglar had turned out to be) had at first been suspected of burgling Rytham Hall in search of Sir George's medals and the family silver, until the discovery of Professor Carter's body. What was bothering Thrudd now, though, was how Miss Seeton had known. From what she'd said, she'd drawn this sketch several days before there was any hint of Gunn around the place.

"Medals," muttered Mel, subsiding. "That's what they're like, no two ways about it—so I guess Banner was right, after all. It hurts me to admit it, but this is more likely than anything to be either something we already know about, or just an ordinary sketch for a scene from *Cinderella* . . ."

chapter

~22~

FAIRY GODMOTHER ELSIE Stillman cleared her throat, ready to deliver some of the most important lines in the script.

> "Though at the Ball you'll dance on dainty feet,
> To walk there on those dainties is not meet.
> Within a gold and crystal coach you'll ride,
> Escorted by a page on either side,
> And pulled by two white horses—conjured all
> By my magic powers, to take you to the Ball."

She produced her spell book, and adopted a necromantic attitude in front of the assorted small animals (courtesy of Props) and the pumpkin (which her husband had been induced to lend from the post office's greengrocery department).

> "These rats into your pages I will turn—
> Turning the page is a trick we all can learn."

She turned the page, looked at the audience, and winked.

> "Aha! *This* spell of mice will horses make;
> This next, a coachman of your walking snake—
> I should say, *lizard*, but it's harder verse—
> Though crocodile or crab would be far worse.
> Imagine *crab* a coachman—gracious, no!
> I'll turn the lizard, rather—turn him—so!"

With a wave of the Fairy Godmother's wand and a flash of blue light (Admiral Leighton), up through the star trap popped, to tremendous applause from the Plummergen contingent— the sensation-seeking outsiders in the audience remained baffled—Jack Crabbe, in coachman's livery, and flourishing a whip. Jack, whose family owned the local garage, drove the twice-weekly bus into Brettenden, and, while he waited for the Plummergen shoppers to shop, composed cryptic crossword puzzles. These he submitted, under the name of "Coronet" (claiming that he had a very kind heart, really), with great success to various high-brow periodicals: but he was still a true son of the village, and entered into the pantomime spirit with considerable aplomb.

He scratched his head with the end of his whip, and registered utter bewilderment.

> "It's a puzzle to me what has happened
> When I find myself dressed in this rig—
> And compared to my size just a moment ago,
> I'm enormous—tremendously big.
> The Godmother says I must do as she tells
> Me—no doubt in my mind she's the boss—heard
> Her changing the rats and the mice with her spells,
> So I dare not say even one *cross word*."

Plummergen rocked with mirth, then switched to fond oohs and aahs of doting delight as assorted children, wearing white fake fur or grey, but all with whiskers and swishing tails, bounded onstage as high-stepping horses, outriders, and pages. Lady Colveden and Miss Treeves exchanged looks of deep satisfaction: this scene alone had been worth fifty tickets sold.

> "Your carriage from this pumpkin will appear . . ."

Admiral Leighton, busy with the Lighting as Sir George coped with Sound, had taken time to instruct the stage crew on the finer points of sea shanties. His lessons now bore spectacular fruit. With a yo-heave-ho and a skilful nudge from Jack

Crabbe's booted foot, the pumpkin rolled in a stately fashion into the star trap at exactly the same speed the Crystal Coach rolled on from the wings, pulled with ropes by the Tug of War team hidden behind the tormentor curtains on the opposite side of the set.

Fairy Stillman bestowed a gracious smile on Cinderella.

> " . . . And your conveyance is complete, my dear!
> But your *appearance* will not do at all—
> In rags and tatters to attend the Ball?
> A haute couture creation, nothing less,
> Will serve, to make you look like a princess!"

Seizing Emmy Putts by the hand, Mrs. Stillman led her, in her bulky rags, to stand just over the half-open star trap. Those same hands which had caught the pumpkin as it fell now reached carefully up, and tugged at the rags until, with another wave of Elsie Stillman's wand and some more of the Admiral's special effects, the press-studs gave way, revealing Cinderella in all her glory—apart from her bare feet, ostentatiously displayed. The Fairy Godmother ducked behind a convenient coal scuttle, and produced . . .

> "Oh! Crystal slippers! I'm afraid to take them,
> For should I dance in them, I'm sure to break them."
> "Fear not, sweet maid, what e'er may come to pass—
> They look like crystal, but they're toughened glass!"

Emmy gave the audience a twirl, tossed her blonde head, and simpered as she climbed into the coach. The Fairy Godmother shut the door (the handle rattled, and fell off, but Mrs. Stillman kicked it swiftly out of sight), and announced:

> "A guard of honour you must have, as well.
> We'll seek the dancers in the fairy dell . . ."

Lady Colveden winked at Miss Treeves. Miss Treeves winked back.

" . . . Who to the palace will escort you straight,
Because, my child, already it is late.
But, even so, mark closely what I say—
Only till twelve are you allowed to stay.
For, Cinderella, though my magic power
Is great, it will not last beyond that hour.
So, once the palace clock begins to chime,
Be warned that you are near the fatal time
When royal splendours fade right speedily,
And a humble kitchen maid once more you'll be!"

Whereupon Emmy, waving and smiling to the enchanted audience, made her exit en route to the ball.

"Went very well, I thought, Padre," said Major Howett, as everyone rushed round afterwards comparing notes. The Major (Front of House, Publicity, and Treasurer) nodded cheerfully to the Reverend Arthur Treeves, who stood vaguely beaming on the departing audience, doing sums in his head. "We'll soon have that organ as good as new!"

"Oh, Arthur, there you are," said Miss Molly Treeves, who'd been afraid her brother might have wandered off before she could rope him into helping. "They need someone to check how many programmes are left, in case we have to jelly any more. All these extra people . . ."

The Reverend Arthur drifted amiably away in the direction of the programmes, and his sister was about to follow to make sure he did as he'd been told when Major Howett caught her by the sleeve.

"Rather a lot of extra people," she said, lowering her voice and leaning close. "Strangers, the whole crew—and who's to say who they are, or where they've come from."

"So long as they pay," said Molly, who had a decidedly practical streak, "I don't see that it matters—oh."

"That's right." Matilda Howett nodded in a meaningful way. "They've paid, all right, the whole kit and caboodle of 'em . . . whatever sort of people they might be. Can't say, I'm too happy havin' so much cash floatin' around—it's a big responsibility."

"I know the nursing home doesn't have a safe, exactly," said Miss Treeves, frowning, "but isn't there a . . . a locked drugs cupboard, or something of the sort?"

"Hardly ethical, is it," returned the Major, in a tone of some reproach. "Well, maybe that's overstatin' the case, but we're puttin' on this panto every night, remember, and sellin' quite a few more tickets than we'd bargained for at the last minute. The doctor needs that cupboard for drugs, not for bundles of notes and bags of coin. I'd like your agreement—and Lady Colveden's, if she's around—to my bankin' it in Brettenden every mornin', for safety."

Miss Treeves, who privately thought—as did most of the village—that any sneak-thief who tangled with the Howitzer would come off a very poor second, could nevertheless sympathise with her friend's position. Should, by some ghastly chance, anything happen—should a dope-crazed thug smash the doors of the nursing home drugs cupboard, a burglar make his way unnoticed to the dispensary and there run amok—the Major would feel morally obliged to make good any loss that was sustained.

"No need to talk to Meg Colveden," said Miss Treeves. "She'll say you're right, I'm sure—banking it every day's the best thing for it. Unless you're too busy, of course, in which case one of us—"

"My job," said the Major firmly. "My responsibility. And I'm sure Dr. Knight won't mind my takin' the car, as the bus doesn't run every day . . ."

Even without the hazards of occasionally all-too-seasonal weather, the postal delays caused by the Christmas buildup meant that red-haired Bert, Plummergen's popular cockney mailman, brought the letters later and later every morning, and that much of one day's delivery was made up of items left from the day before—or even the day before that.

Miss Seeton looked rather anxious as she read the letter from the bank. "I'm afraid I don't quite understand," she told Martha Bloomer, who had brought in the bundle of envelopes from the mat, "what I should do about this. A new manager—well, I know he is, because I saw him some days ago, when I was cashing a cheque, and Mr. Jestin—such a helpful young man, and to be chief cashier at so early an age—but to introduce himself . . . should one," mused Miss Seeton, "write back and introduce oneself in return? It seems a little odd, in the circumstances—a professional relationship . . . but the courtesies, of course, should be maintained. Particularly as he writes," she said, consulting the letter, "that he looks forward to being of service to me in the future. Which could, of course, mean . . ."

Was he trying to say he believed her to be in need of such service? Miss Seeton had always thought she had her financial affairs in good order. The previous manager had advised her on the opening of a deposit account, into which she paid half her income—the police retainer, most gratifying—and with the interest from which she was accustomed to supplement her pension when any need arose. Bank managers were, she had understood from childhood, experts: and, as such, must know more about money than a retired teacher of art could ever do—as it seemed, indeed, that he had. She was happy, she felt, with the way her investments had been handled: but perhaps a younger man—for so, despite the handsome moustache which was all she'd really noticed about him at the time, she had judged the newcomer to be—would, being more recently trained, have fresh, possibly wiser, ideas. One had to remember that new brooms . . .

"The vault," murmured Miss Seeton. "Not that one would seriously suppose the new manager to have wielded the broom himself, but—had it not been for his insistence on tidying the vault, Martha, I understand that the medal chest would have remained undiscovered, which would have been a serious historical loss."

Martha, domestic paragon, sniffed. The morning's rain and wind had driven damp leaves deep into the house in the few seconds it had taken her to slip in through the front door, and her day's routine, as a result, was at sixes and sevens. "Wouldn't do no harm if there were a few more tidy people in the world, is what I say, Miss Emily. And if you could just move your feet so I can sweep under—and please don't go right back in there and start fidgeting when I've only set the place to rights five minutes ago . . ."

"Oh, Martha, I'm so sorry." Miss Seeton, who had been on

the point of heading for the sitting room and her sketching equipment—problems, large or small, financial or otherwise, could always be put in perspective once she had set them down on paper—blushed. Her hands danced unhappily, crumpling the bank manager's letter between them.

"Look, dear." Martha leaned her broom against the wall, and shook a reproving finger at her employer. "If you're not careful, you'll be worrying yourself into an early grave—and for no good reason that I can see, because there's the telephone, if you want to talk to the bank—which, where there's money concerned, I don't suppose it would do no harm just to check, if that's what this letter of yours says, and set your mind at rest so's not to spoil your Christmas."

"Oh." Miss Seeton looked at the telephone for a moment. "Oh, dear—I really don't believe I can, Martha. A letter, you see, hardly constitutes a . . . a formal introduction—and then, it may be that I am worrying about nothing. Christmas—a busy time of year—one hesitates to disturb him for no good reason—if only," she lamented, "I knew for certain whether it was. Or wasn't."

Martha snatched up her broom again as she spied a stray leaf. "No use asking me, dear, investments being something neither me nor Stan's ever had the ready for, and not wanting to poke my nose into your affairs anyway. Why not try asking someone like Sir George? Now all that nasty business is over—"

She broke off. There had been no need to disturb Miss Emily's peace of mind earlier by telling her a body had been found up at the Hall, bodies—although Miss Emily did seem to encounter a fair number, one way and another—not being what Martha thought acceptable matter for conversation, unlike burglars, which were plain common sense and locking doors, which Miss Emily wouldn't always remember without a jog or two for her memory.

"Well, anyway," concluded Martha briskly, "he'll have time to spare to explain, I'm sure, so why not give him a ring and ask?"

"Of course, a gentleman would know—perhaps, in normal circumstances—but I doubt if he has now, Martha dear, for I hardly think these are." Miss Seeton smiled faintly. "If you recall, during last night's performance, there were a few problems with the sound effects, and the lighting. Normal, I mean. And I distinctly remember hearing the Admiral arrange to meet dear Sir George at the village hall this morning to sort them out—a blown fuse when the tape recorder was working, or some such difficulty they wish to overcome before tonight— although the opinion of a gentleman, as I have said, would be reassuring . . ."

"Then why not go into the bank and have a word?" insisted Mrs. Bloomer, who longed to carry on with her cleaning but knew that, with Miss Seeton underfoot, she'd never get it done. "You don't have to talk to the manager if you don't want— there's that young Jestin, the chief cashier. You know *him* all right, don't you?"

Relief dawned in Miss Seeton's eyes, to be replaced by slow regret. "Martha, that is an excellent suggestion, but— on so unpleasant a day—would it be advisable, do you think, for me to bicycle to Brettenden in such a wind? When it is not a matter of great urgency—I hope. And the bus, you see, does not run today—"

"Major Howett," said Martha, who'd heard other things at last night's performance besides the Admiral's arrangements with Sir George. "She's taking the doctor's car into Brettenden for some business at the bank, so if she's not gone already— which knowing how she runs the Nursing Home to a timetable and not liking to overset it she won't have done—she'd give you a lift, I'm sure. If you make haste and call her now, you'll be bound to catch her . . ."

chapter

~23~

Major Howett was more accustomed to driving sturdy mili-tary trucks than the Nursing Home's small runabout, and stood no nonsense from anyone or anything she might encounter in the course of her daily round. Miss Seeton held her breath on more than one occasion during the six-mile journey from Plummergen to Brettenden, and heaved a sigh of quiet relief as, with a crash of gears and a few muttered curses, the Major succeeded, despite the Christmas crowds, in finding somewhere convenient to park.

Convenience, however, is a relative term. "Pity they haven't a customer car park," said the Major, as she locked the doors and hurried round to join Miss Seeton on the pavement. "Too much to hope for, I suppose—too expensive. No developer worth his salt's goin' to let a prime site like that go to waste for parkin' cars when he can squeeze in a few shops, and rent 'em out at a profit . . ."

The site in question was certainly prime, being on the corner of the town's main crossroads. Both of these crossing roads were busy at any time of year, but now, with only a few days to go until the official holiday, they were busier than ever. Passing vehicles threw up waves of spray as they drove through puddles, and Miss Seeton, her umbrella tilted to one side to stave off the worst of the onslaught, mourned the damage done to her now unprotected hat as the rain continued to fall sideways as well as from above.

The Major considered umbrellas on a windy day worse than useless. To keep her head acceptably dry, she wore a wide-brimmed tweed hat pulled down over her brow; her feet were kept dry with galoshes; and the area in between was protected by a flowing, waterproof, ex-army cape—an outfit admirably suited to the occasion, for, beneath that flowing cape, the canvas bag of pantomime cash was invisible to the casual gaze of the passerby . . .

Miss Seeton stopped in the entrance lobby to the bank, lowered her umbrella, and shook it briskly. Major Howett tucked the canvas bag into the belt of her skirt, and with both hands wrung a small cascade out of her hat to the tiled marble floor.

"Better warn 'em it's a bit slippery out here once we go inside," said the Major, pushing open the swing doors and ushering Miss Seeton before her. "Mind you, with everyone else as wet as we are, they probably know already. Haven't seen it so busy for ages. Which do you suppose is the shortest queue?"

Miss Seeton hesitated. "I had intended," she said, "to speak to Mr. Jestin, no matter how many others were waiting ahead of me—not, of course, that on such a day I had expected there to be more than a few—if I had thought about it, that is, which I confess I had not. But Mr. Jestin has always been so helpful . . ."

Miss Seeton never realised exactly how "helpful" he had been. On the occasion of her abduction by the absconding bank cashier, it was Percy Jestin who raised the alarm: but, since he had been too modest ever to mention the fact to her face, she had continued in that blissful ignorance of matters criminal which was her customary mental condition.

Major Howett looked across to the illuminated nameplate above Mr. Jestin's counter, and frowned. The queue to see the chief cashier was the longest of all: and she had become suddenly conscious, among the crowd, of the responsibility of the cash she carried.

"Think I'll try the next one," she said, with a nod. "See who finishes first, shall we?"

Miss Seeton nodded, and smiled, and watched the Major hurry to join what was undoubtedly—Miss Seeton sighed— a far shorter queue than that waiting to see Mr. Jestin: but

it would be so much better, she felt, to have her mind set at
rest—if, indeed, that was what was to happen—by someone
with whom she was more closely acquainted than by the other
clerks, with whom she, well, wasn't. And if it wasn't—set at
rest, that was to say—she would rather have bad news broken
by someone she knew . . .

Mr. Jestin waved goodbye and wished his departing customer the compliments of the season. Everyone shuffled forward a
few more steps, then settled to wait once more.

Near the head of the Major's queue, a shrivelled man in a
navy-blue suit decided it wasn't worth waiting, and marched
off to the swing doors with a scowl. The next in line moved
up, produced a chequebook and a bundle of paying-in slips,
and settled down to a long explanation.

Major Howett rolled her eyes, glanced at the clock, and
began tapping her foot. She looked across to Miss Seeton
and shrugged, miming frustration. Miss Seeton gestured back
sympathy, and dropped her umbrella, which sprayed water on
the legs of the woman in front. Miss Seeton, bending to pick up
her brolly, was profuse in apology. The woman said, well, she
supposed it couldn't be helped, and she expected Miss Seeton
had her mind on her Christmas shopping, which would explain
it because that was what she herself was in a hurry to do. Miss
Seeton explained she was most fortunate in having completed
nearly all her shopping last week—

The swing doors burst open. Heads turned to stare. Had the
shrivelled scowler in the navy-blue suit changed his mind, and
come back? Well, he could take his place at the end of the
queue behind everyone else, then . . .

"Hands up!" The three men who had entered through the
swing doors were neither shrivelled, nor wearing navy-blue
suits: but what could be seen of their masked faces, above the
sawn-off shotguns two of them carried, was certainly scowling.
"Hands up!"

The third man, who carried a haversack in either hand, made
for the door marked "Private" as his colleagues covered the
startled bank clientele with their weapons. People gasped, and
cried out. Most raised their hands . . .

Miss Seeton, recognising the scene from a hundred films,

obediently raised hers. Her umbrella, which she hadn't had time to slip securely over her arm, fell again to the floor. The masked faces swung towards her, the sawn-off muzzles likewise. Blushing, automatically, Miss Seeton bent to pick up her umbrella.

"Leave it!" A barked command.

"Heads!" Another, but louder. People ducked as, with an exploding whirl of her arm, Major Howett hurled the heavy bag of cash across the room, and caught the haversack man in the midriff. Winded, he fell.

"Get away!" Shotguns gestured as the crowd, seeing the possibilities of a hostage, moved in.

Major Howett moved faster. She leaped from her queue to Miss Seeton's, snatched up the fallen umbrella, and, uttering the war cry of her old regiment, opened it, fixed the point, bayonetlike, on the two by the door, and charged.

Blinded by spray as the Major twirled the brolly, their field of vision thus unexpectedly blurred, the Shotgunners were unable to focus in time to fire. With a whoop and a bloodcurdling yell, the Major was upon them . . .

And so, following her dauntless example, were reinforcements, though some stayed at the rear to subdue any signs of fight in the man with the winded midriff. The shotgunners, unnerved by the onslaught of a dozen furious shoppers, waved their guns frantically as the brolly spokes caught them in sensitive places. The Major twirled, poked, and prodded. Shotguns flew from hands governed by the laws of the simple reflex action, and skidded across the tiled floor . . .

Miss Seeton bent automatically to pick up her umbrella again—except that it wasn't. How dangerous. And it would never do to allow it to fall again into the wrong hands . . . Should she, perhaps, point it, and utter the traditional words? Except that she remembered dear Nigel once quoting her a little verse he said all country children learned:

> "Never, ever, let your gun
> Pointed be at anyone.
> That it should unloaded be
> Matters not the least to me."

Miss Seeton looked about her. Everywhere, it seemed, people were running to and fro—impossible to avoid pointing at one of them, at least.

She gave a little gasp. With a cry of: "I'll phone the police!" someone was slipping straight towards her over the damp, tiled floor . . .

Miss Seeton jerked the shotgun upwards.

With a deafening roar, it discharged both barrels. And, like early, indoor, Christmas snow, flakes—and chunks—of plaster fell from the ceiling to the astonished crowd below.

Within minutes, the Shotgun Gang were handcuffed, loaded into police cars, and taken to Ashford by a squad of Superintendent Brinton's men. Brinton himself, with Foxon, was interviewing selected witnesses in the bank manager's office while a second team interviewed others in the chief cashier's room.

"Jestin deserves a medal," said Brinton, nodding amiably to that young man, who was drinking hot, sweet tea as forcibly prescribed by his manager, Cole Green. Mr. Green—a plump, sleek, moustachioed man with a watch chain stretched across his corporation—had been alerted to the impending robbery at his new branch by the pressing of his hidden alarm button by young Mr. Jestin; Mr. Green had peeped through his office spy-hole, seen what was going on, and at once telephoned the police.

"But if Mr. Jestin," fluted Mr. Green, urging more tea on any who wished it, "hadn't pressed the button, I would never have known—never—not until it was too late!"

Brinton grinned. "I'm not so sure about that, Mr. Green. Even if Mr. Jestin hadn't sounded the alarm, I think you'd've noticed it all right when Miss Seeton, er, did her bit with the shotgun . . ."

Miss Seeton, sipping tea far stronger and sweeter than she normally liked it, blushed, and began trying to explain. Brinton laughed, and brushed her explanations aside.

" . . . and, thanks to her, the chummies were too surprised to put up much more of a fight. A fight providentially, I gather

er, started by you—with, er, Miss Seeton's umbrella, Major
Howett . . ."

Major Howett, who had backed Mr. Green's tea prescription
one hundred percent, turned pink with pleasure, buried her
nose in her cup, and said it was no more than an officer's
duty, by Gad, begging Mr. Brinton's pardon, to support the
forces of law and order, even in their absence.

"Which, thanks to Mr. Jestin here," Brinton reminded them
all, "wasn't a long one. *Three* medals, indeed—although I have
to point out that the police don't generally approve of ordinary
citizens rushing headlong into—"

A sudden choking sound erupted from the corner where
sat DC Foxon with his head in his hands, trying to think
of anyone's being so foolish as to regard Miss Seeton as
an ordinary citizen. The superintendent, divining his thought,
shot him a quelling look, spluttered a little himself, coughed,
and went on:

"Well, never mind that. It may interest you to know, Mr.
Green, talking of medals, that it was medals seems to have
been behind this particular robbery, from what we managed
to get out of the chummies before they came to their senses"—
he nodded to Miss Seeton, and winked—"and started yelling
for their solicitors. Seems they'd never even heard of the
Brettenden branch of the City and Suburban Bank until there
was all that in the papers recently about the chest you dug out
of the vault—but don't worry," as Mr. Green looked as if he
might burst into tears. "You weren't to know, and it certainly
isn't your fault if chummies act true to form. If I know the
Yard, they'll be so grateful to you for having baited the trap, as
you might say, they'll recommend *you* for a medal, too . . ."

Now it was Mr. Green's turn to blush. He lowered his gaze,
twiddled his fingers, and hastened to pour more tea. Brinton
chuckled, then became serious.

"I've rung Chief Superintendent Delphick, and he's on his
way—and he's asked me to pass on a warning—well," as Mr.
Green trembled behind his moustache, "a spot of advice, if
you'd rather. Today's effort's going to mean your branch has
made the front pages twice in as many weeks, near enough—
and these Shotgun people aren't the only crooks around who

might read the papers and have a . . . an unusual interest i
banks. It could just be you'll be paid a visit by the Night Saf
Gang, the Oracle says . . ."

Mr. Green uttered a startled yelp, and almost dropped hi
teacup in his fright. Brinton chuckled kindly.

"A friendly warning, that's all it is, sir—but he'd be grateful
if you'd keep your eyes open. It'd be rather foolish, he says
and I agree, to believe that nonsense about lightning neve
striking twice in the same place—you've had two strikes o
it recently, and they do say the third time pays for all . . ."

The sentiments may have been those of Chief Superinten
dent Delphick: the words, emphatically, were not. Censored
his original remarks had been to the effect that, now Mis
Seeton and her brolly were on the loose, no one could hav
any idea of how it was all going to end, and that everyon
within the fallout area should be warned to batten down th
hatches and fasten their seat belts. When—if—it came, it wa
likely to be a very bumpy night.

chapter
-24-

SUPERINTENDANT BRINTON TOOK Miss Seeton's umbrella with him, promising to have it repaired as soon as possible, but saying that, with the holidays so close, it was unlikely she would see it again until some time after Boxing Day. Miss Seeton assured him that it did not matter, as she had several others at home. The superintendent then asked her how she planned on returning to that home.

"Major Howett has been so kind as to give me a lift, Mr. Brinton, and, as we both still have unfinished business to complete—although one can readily appreciate, of course, that it was necessary to close the bank while the . . . the gang were arrested . . . but if Mr. Green, or Mr. Jestin, would be so kind as to spare the time . . ."

There was almost nothing that Cole Green and Percy Jestin wouldn't have done to oblige Miss Seeton and the Major. As soon as the door closed behind Brinton and Foxon, the two bank officials were falling over themselves to assist the heroines of the recent hour. To Mr. Jestin, chief cashier, now fell the task of accepting the canvas bag of silver and copper coins which, not so long ago, had played so stalwart a role in the fight against crime. (Brinton, with a grin, had threatened to impound the bag as either evidence or an illegal weapon. One look from Major Howett, and he hurried outside to fetch it himself, rather than sending Foxon.)

Manager Green was horrified to learn that Miss Seeton had been disturbed by his letter. It was no more than the latest bank policy (he explained, twirling his moustache in an

embarrassed manner) for incoming managers to write to the
branch's most valued customers (he bowed, and coughed) to
introduce themselves, and to assure them of their best service
at all times. Really, Miss Seeton had no need to worry—he
would find the official circular just to prove that he was telling
the truth . . . And Miss Seeton, horrified in her turn, could
almost have said she saw tears in the bank manager's eyes as
he flustered his way through the explanation, and thankfully
buried his head in his filing cabinet.

In an agony of embarrassment as great as that being suffered
by Mr. Green, she begged him not to bother—she would be
only too happy to take his word for it—she was sure she could
trust him to take the very best care of her investment portfolio,
if that was the correct word . . .

Portfolio made Miss Seeton think with longing of her artist's
equipment, back in her own dear cottage. Her fingers danced
unhappily, and she cast an anguished look towards Major
Howett—and was relieved to see that she and Mr. Jestin had
completed their transaction, and were now passing the time
of day.

"Ready to go, Miss Seeton? Splendid!" Major Howett was
never slow to take command when the situation clearly war-
ranted such action. "I'll be in again tomorrow, Mr. Jestin, with
tonight's takin's—quite a tidy sum, I shouldn't wonder. And
all for a good cause," she added, as inspiration struck. "I don't
suppose that you, and Mr. Green . . ."

What else could the bank officials reasonably do but say
they would attend a performance of Plummergen's pantomime
as soon as possible? Nobody could have called it blackmail, in
so good a cause as the Organ Fund, and when—if the Major
hadn't been banking the *Cinderella* takings at that particular
time—they would have lost a considerably greater sum than
that to be expended on two tickets.

"Four?" enquired the Major, with a hopeful look. Percy
Jestin blushed, and said he'd only buy one, thanks very much.
Mr. Green also blushed, but with more discretion, and mur-
mured that he was a widower.

Major Howett apologised briskly, and then said that, as
tonight's performance (officially the last) was sold out, they

vould have to wait until the next day's extra: she'd reserve
wo seats on their behalf, and telephone tomorrow morning
o let them know. Mr. Green and Mr. Jestin thanked her;
nd thanked her again, with Miss Seeton, for having come so
ortunately to the rescue—and escorted the pair out through
he bank's rear entrance, which would cut off the crossroads
:orner and be a shorter route to the place where the Major had
eft the car. With a cry of dismay, Mr. Green saw that it was
till raining: and sent Mr. Jestin to beg, borrow, or steal an
imbrella for Miss Seeton's especial use, as the Major made
t plain she had no need of one . . .

And thus the two ladies made their way home to Plummergen,
nd to well-deserved peace and quiet.

But peace and quiet, no matter how well deserved, could
only last until the early evening, when Miss Seeton had to
ake her place in the wings as Prompt, and Major Howett hers
s Front of House.

The house was, as expected, sold out: there was a buzz of
excitement in the air, which Miss Seeton put down to the
excellence of the anticipated performance, but which most
other Padders blamed on that evening's six o'clock television
news. It had never occurred to Miss Seeton that her earlier
activities would make headlines: she had, after all, only been
n the bank at all through the kindness of the Major and
her own foolishness in misunderstanding that letter from Mr.
Green. Nobody could possibly be interested in her affairs—
indeed, it would be rather impertinent to display such interest
(she would have said, had anyone asked her opinion).

But Plummergen knows Miss Seeton, and understands that
she—whether or not with justification even her friends, let
alone those who mistrust her, cannot decide—firmly believes
herself to lead the uneventful life of a retired gentlewoman in a
pleasant, peaceful village; the very idea that anyone might wish
to know more would never have entered her head; and nobody
would have dreamed of mentioning anything about what had
happened earlier that day . . .

Except the Major, who might be excused for having greeted
her fellow heroine with "Work's the best thing to take your

mind off it all, eh? Jolly good show!" A remark which puzzle
Miss Seeton deeply, although she had little time to ponde
it before the curtain went up, and Fairy Crystal spoke he
opening lines—after which, it went right out of her mind.

It was brought back next morning when Thrudd Banner an
Mel Forby turned up on her doorstep when she'd barely fin
ished breakfast, demanding the full story. Miss Seeton had t
think twice about what they meant, and then spent a great dea
of time trying to convince them that really, she'd done nothin
at all—it was dear Major Howett they should speak to, if the
wanted a . . . a story, or scoop, or whatever they called it.

"Come off it, MissEss," said Thrudd, fingering the strap o
his camera and wishing he could pluck up enough courage t
snap the lady in her own front parlour.

"Honestly, Miss S, you're one in a million," said Mel, he
beautiful eyes darkening in a frown as she observed what he
swain was about. "Don't you realise everyone wants to know
how you did it? Remote control yet—if what we've heard i
anything to go by. Seems you just threw your umbrella a
Major Howett, and it went into action pretty much under it
own steam—the scientists'll be beating a path to your doo
not to mention," with a chuckle, "the Honourable Company o
Plasterers, or whatever they call themselves. Banner snappe
one or two rather choice shots of what was left of the ceilin
after you'd done your party-piece . . ."

It then took some time to persuade Miss Seeton—who wa
possibly rather more shocked, despite the benefits of yoga
from yesterday's adventure than she realised—that Mel ha
only been joking, and the City and Suburban Bank was highl
unlikely to insist on her paying for repairs to the ceiling of it
Brettenden branch. In the end, she was coaxed into recallin
that the manager and chief cashier had perhaps not seeme
too annoyed about it: indeed, they were to attend tonight'
performance of *Cinderella*, which could well mean—

"Hey, that's not fair!" Mel's lovely eyes flashed. "If ther
are spare tickets going, why didn't you tell us first? Yo
promised, you know."

Miss Seeton, blushing, agreed that indeed she had. She wa
so sorry to have forgotten. She would telephone Miss Treeve

this instant, and ask how many spare seats still remained for tonight . . .

And when Chief Superintendent Delphick (who with Sergeant Bob Ranger had spent a sleepless night at Ashford Police Station, interviewing the Shotgun Gang) arrived in Miss Seeton's sitting room to ask what she'd been doing recently, it had become almost automatic for her to offer to supply tickets for *Cinderella* that night, if dear Mr. Delphick intended to stay in the village so long.

"Indeed I do," Delphick assured her cheerfully. "As far as I can make out, from what Bob says Anne says her father says, I wouldn't miss it for the world. I'm told your scenery and set designs are first rate, and the audience loves the whole thing, I gather . . ."

Love it or loathe it, the audience for that evening's performance was rather smaller than on the previous night. The day's papers had been full of the Shotgun Gang's attempted robbery of the Brettenden bank: the voyeuristic masses had decided that Brettenden, not Plummergen, was now the place to be. The fact that the Brettenden Amateur Dramatic Society had elected to present *Ali Baba and the Forty Thieves* every night that week was seen as no more than fitting, in the circumstances, and there had been a decided rush on tickets.

Plummergen village hall was, therefore, on this occasion comfortably full without bursting at the seams; and Major Howett shook her head over the reduced takings, and began to wonder whether she should institute a No Refund system, or charge extra for last-minute bookings . . .

The audience enjoyed itself quite as much as any previous audience had done. Since there were fewer outsiders—or those (such as Mel, Thrudd, Bob, and Delphick) who qualified as outsiders were sufficiently conversant with Plummergen ways that they could appreciate the humour—the laughs came loud and often. When the Broker's Men spoke of the safety of banks, people pointed out Mr. Green and Mr. Jestin, side by side in the middle of the centre row, and guffawed. The reference to the George and Dragon's cuisine brought the house down. Jack Crabbe's appearance as Cinderella's coachman had people waving their programmes and cheering. In the interval, cups of tea and homemade cakes sold as well as ice cream at any cinema, and Major Howett began to look more hopeful.

The First Footman (Trevor Newport) had sounded a blast on his trumpet, the Second Footman (Kevin Scillicough) had read the proclamation. Whichever lady in the land had a foot to fit the crystal slipper, she was to be the Prince's bride: every house, every hovel was to be visited in turn, and each must try her fortune.

Enter Dandini, played by postman Bert, his hair as red as the velvet cushion on which the glass slipper lay in solitary state. Prince Maureen was too dejected even to slap a thigh. If only she could find the girl whose foot fitted this slipper— but she feared it was a vain hope. How many houses had they so far tried? Useless!

Dandini reminded the Prince that there were plenty more houses yet to go. Why, just round the corner was Stoneybroke Hall. And didn't His Highness Prince Charming recall the Baron's two daughters he'd met at the ball? Maybe one of them . . .

Injecta and Instructa were discovered, greatly excited, at their toilette. Each being determined that she should be the one to whom the proclamation referred, they both nagged poor Cinderella shamelessly to bring them beauty aids, lovelier clothes, and whatever jewellery their father hadn't got around to pawning since the Ball . . .

Injecta tore off her Red Cross hat, and hurled it to the floor. "As there's only one tiara left, then I must be the one who wears it. I am older than you, after all."

"*Much* older," returned Instructa, pouting. "Ow!" as her sister slapped her face. "You big bully—it's too unfair!"

Injecta snatched the tiara from the patient Cinderella, cramming it on her corkscrew curls. "There! Don't I look gorgeous?" Dr. Knight preened himself before the hand mirror Cinderella, without waiting to be asked, held up for him. "Oh, what a princess I'll make!"

"Taking your bulk into consideration, and applying pure mathematics, I should estimate that you'd be far more likely to make *two* princesses of normal size," retorted Instructa, meanly gesturing towards her sister's over-generous curves.

"Don't be so rude. When I'm a princess, you'll have to treat me with much more respect, you know—and don't make faces like that!" as Instructa stuck out her tongue, thumbed her nose, and turned away in a huff. "You're so childish—why on earth don't you grow up, stupid?"

"I *have* grown up stupid," snapped Instructa, whirling to glare at her sister. Plummergen noted, with unholy glee, that her eyes behind the pince-nez somehow seemed to have a strange, dark, almost blackcurrant glow about them. Sideways glances at Mrs. Blaine, sitting beside Miss Nuttel, showed that neither Nut had recognised the all-too-accurate acting of Dr. Knight and Mr. Jessyp, for both were laughing as heartily at the antics of the Ugly Sisters as anyone else in the audience.

The squabble over the tiara settled to her satisfaction, Injecta began to lumber about the stage in a series of swooping motions. "I'm practising my dance for my wedding day," she told her sister, who had posed a sulky question. "Oh, how wonderful it will be, to marry the Prince—I wish he'd hurry up and choose me, so that I can go to the palace! I'm so excited—I feel so effervescent—"

"I never knew you when you effer wasn't." Instructa's waspish comment drew the expected laugh, and Mr. Jessyp tossed his tumultuous red locks. "Perhaps you should lie down and take a rest, for a *night* or two . . ."

More laughter, as Dr. Knight swooped and pranced blithely on. "Rest? Why should I? When the prince is due any minute—I'm going down to the hall to wait for him."

"Then so am I." Instructa wagged a finger in the direction of her stepsister. "You, Cinderella, can tidy up our things while we're gone."

"And then you can pack up all my best clothes," added Injecta. "I'm sure to want to take them with me when I go to the palace . . ."

The lights went down. Various creaks and groans as certain flats were removed heralded the transformation of the Bedroom of the Ugly Sisters into the Main Hall of Stoneybroke Hall. The lights went up again on an empty stage.

There was a pause. People shuffled their feet.

Miss Seeton's prompting voice was heard from the wings:
"Enter the Prince's herald, Mr. Scillicough!"

"Blimey!" A frantic scuffle, and Trevor Newport rushed
onstage. He raised the muted trumpet to his lips, and blew.
Out of sight, Sir George switched the tape recorder to the naval
fanfares kindly provided by Admiral Leighton. As the bugle
call died away, Kevin Scillicough stalked on and unrolled
his wallpaper scroll, reading the proclamation aloud. Button
Colveden appeared, and held open the main door.

In came the Baron, the Sisters, the Prince, and Dandini, with
the slipper on its cushion. There was much squabbling over
which Sister should try the slipper first.

Injecta won. Flouncing and preening, she settled herself in
a convenient chair, and hitched up her petticoats. "I will now,"
she announced, "get my foot in the crystal slipper!"

"Huh!" Instructa, who had drifted to the back of the stage,
turned round to snap: "You couldn't get your foot in the
Crystal Palace!"

And she was right: her sister failed to make her foot fit: it
was far too fat.

Instructa, emerging from behind a curtain, beamed, and
made her way in slow triumph to the seat her sister had
just left. Sitting daintily down, she extended for Dandini's
inspection a foot surely smaller than any foot had a right to
be. With a start of surprise, Dandini took the slipper from its
cushion, and handed it to Instructa . . .

The slipper fitted perfectly.

Gasps of amazement all round. Instructa smirked, and threw
her sister a triumphant glance. The Prince, dismayed, summoned up all his courage to stick to the absolute letter of his
promise and pronounce this lady his bride . . .

"Stop!" Buttons rushed to the rescue. "It's a trick, your
highness—look!" And, before the infuriated Instructa could
slap him away or lower her skirts, he had knelt at her slippered
foot, and seized it.

And pulled.

And pulled.

And pulled, tumbling backwards, as several yards of black
and-white striped stocking showed that Instructa had fitted a

false foot to ensure the slipper's suitability.

She squealed with rage.

"Stop! Oh, dear—stop!"

This was unscripted. People stared.

Miss Seeton, her promptbook cast aside, rushed from the wings to the centre of the stage. Blinking in the dazzle of the footlights, she addressed that part of the hall where she knew Delphick and Brinton to sit.

"Oh, dear—I've only just this minute realised, but—she isn't a man, he's a woman!"

chapter
~25~

"I MEAN—OH, dear," babbled Miss Seeton, as people began to murmur. "I mean—not a man, a woman . . ."

Nigel scrambled up from the floor and ran across to Miss Seeton as Mr. Jessyp and Dr. Knight gazed helplessly at each other. They'd always known they could put on a good show, but such confusion as this was ridiculous.

"It's all right, Miss Seeton," said Nigel gently, as he took her by the arm and tried to steer her offstage. "You know it's only Dr. Knight and Mr. Jessyp—not a woman, I mean not two—but men. Two men—the Pantomime Dames . . ."

The murmuring from the body of the hall grew louder, and several voices were heard to remark that they'd always known as Miss Seeton were more'n a bit queer, and didn't this just prove it?

"Delayed shock," suggested Dr. Knight, coming to his senses and hastening to Nigel's assistance. "I must say, I'd never have expected this, knowing her as I do, but it seems yesterday's little, ah, skirmish at the bank has proved too much for—"

"Oh, no," cried Miss Seeton, frantically brushing aside every attempt to escort her from the stage. "No, I didn't mean—I simply felt I had to tell him, the very instant I realised—Mr. Delphick, that is, or Mr. Brinton—the shocking affair at the bank . . ."

Among all the coughs and shufflings around the hall, there were signs of more than murmuring from the middle, where Mr. Green and Mr. Jestin were known to be sitting together. In the half-light, it was hard to make out what was causing this

194

ew commotion—not that anyone was too bothered, really.
What was happening onstage was far more interesting . . .

More interesting to most of the spectators, perhaps; but
not to all. Chief Superintendent Delphick, who had been as
astounded as anyone by Miss Seeton's interruption of the
pantomime's most critical scene, had stopped staring at the
stage and, rising to his feet, now scanned the audience with
his shrewd grey eyes.

"Could we have the houselights up, please?" he called,
making it more a command than a request. After a star-
led pause, Major Howett clicked switches by the door, and
light shone full on the audience. In his official box, Admiral
Leighton dimmed floods, spots, and lanterns onstage.

"You seem in something of a hurry to leave, Mr. Green,"
Delphick said, addressing the middle of the floor. "Wouldn't
you prefer to wait until the end, and get your money's worth?"

Mr. Green mumbled into his corporation, and continued to
push his way past those sitting in the same row.

"You don't feel well? Dear me," said Delphick mildly.
"I'm sure, you know, that—even though we have professional
medical advice available"—he indicated Dr. Knight on stage,
and bowed to Major Howett, still beside the switches at the
door—"standard police first aid training would more than
suffice for your particular problem. And there are plenty of
policemen here tonight, believe me."

"I . . . I need fresh air!" cried Cole Green, fanning himself
with a desperate programme. "I must get out of here—I feel
as if I'm stifling!"

"Oh, no, we couldn't possibly let you go without someone
to . . . take care of you," said Delphick, as Mr. Green reached
the end of the row and headed, stumbling, for the door. "Major
Howett, I wonder if you'd be so good—"

"Never mind!" burst out the bank manager, wiping his
forehead with a polka-dotted silk handkerchief. "Fresh air—
that's all I need—let me get away . . ."

"I beg leave to doubt," said Delphick, "whether that would
really—from our point of view—be such a wise idea. Foxon"—
to the Broker's Man, who from backstage had heard all the
disturbance and come hurrying round to the body of the hall—

"hold back, if you don't mind—if you'll excuse my issuin
orders to a member of your force, Superintendent Brinton. B
it would be far more . . . seemly, I believe, if Major Howe
could attend Mr. Green in his predicament . . .

"Or should I say, rather, in *hers*?"

It had all (thought Miss Seeton next day, as she stood co
templating the contents of her wardrobe) been really most . .
embarrassing; even in the privacy of her bedroom, she blushe
Embarrassing . . . and—if only one had kept one's head—s
very unnecessary, what was more. A quiet word or two wit
Mr. Delphick after the performance—or (she blushed again
perhaps, although one was never entirely confident that on
understood the correct professional courtesies, a word wit
Mr. Brinton, under whose command—if that was the righ
word, which she wasn't at all sure—the Brettenden Bank, an
thus its manager, surely came . . .

Miss Seeton frowned. "Responsibility?" she hazarded, a
she unhooked from its quilted hanger her best cocktail dress—
grey, with purple, pearl, and black embroidery, the gift of kin
Mr. Stemkos and his wife, who had—Miss Seeton smiled—
been so . . . so enthusiastic, on that whirlwind shopping tri
in Paris a few years ago. Miss Seeton closed the wardrob
door, and held the dress up against her petticoated shoulders
turning to admire herself in the full-length mirror.

She smiled again, shaking her head. Her very best dress—
quite lovely, but so wickedly extravagant. So much money
when one had so few opportunities to—

Money. Wickedness. Banks . . .

"Oh, dear," sighed Miss Seeton, who'd been doing he
best all day to forget last night's embarrassment, and wa
sufficiently honest to realise that her best simply hadn't bee
good enough. "But at least," she murmured, slipping the coo
silk-and-chiffon folds over her head, "one was, at least, doin
one's duty, even if . . ."

She'd lost count, over the seven years she had been a prac
titioner, of the number of blessings she had bestowed on tha
invaluable tome, *Yoga and Younger Every Day*. With nimbl
writhings and convolutions of hand and arm, she zipped an

hooked herself into the Parisian creation, smoothed the fabric free of wrinkles, and slipped on low-heeled, though smart, shoes. One would, of course, have been perfectly happy to walk the short distance along Marsh Road to Rytham Hall in the dark; but everybody had been so insistent that one's stout walking shoes would have been out of place at a party, and an inconvenience to change, as well as to carry, with a flashlight in the other hand and one's umbrella over one's arm—to which one was, after so many years of living in the country, quite accustomed, although it was kind of one's friends to be concerned. Not to mention, of course, one's bag. One's black court shoes, that was to say. An inconvenience. But when dear Mel, who with Mr. Banner had also been invited to the Colvedens' Christmas Eve party, had said that the car would be outside one's front door at—

"Oh, dear!" Miss Seeton caught sight of her bedside clock, blushed once more, and hurriedly seized her evening bag from the dressing table. She ignored the flicker of her reflection in the mirror and trotted straight out of her bedroom to the stairs. Halfway down, she had an uncomfortable few moments over her hat, then recalled having made her choice (the red felt, with its brown ribbon cockscomb, dark green trim, and miniature oranges) and brought it downstairs earlier, placing it carefully on the hall table beside the umbrellas: from which, of course, there would be no difficulty whatsoever in making a selection.

Miss Seeton buttoned herself quickly into the red plaid overcoat—for this time of year, and with her hat, such a suitable colour, if perhaps a little . . . overpowering for every-day wear—one normally wore it with the fawn-grey gaberdine reversed to the outside—and was fixing her hatpin in front of the hall mirror when the doorbell rang.

"Ready, Miss S?" Mel Forby's beautiful eyes, brighter than ever, scanned her prospective passenger with approval and amusement. "You look great—and that hat is really some-thing." Which was not (Mel comforted herself) untrue—just so long as she wasn't asked to say what kind of *something* it really was. Miss Seeton's hats, which she trimmed herself, were notorious for their idiosyncrasies, and the red felt with its miniature oranges was no exception . . .

"The taxi's here." Mel waved a cheerful hand towards the car, its engine idling, which waited beyond the gate, sending little dragon puffs of steamy breath into the chill winter air.

"Taxi? Oh dear, how dreadfully expensive—when I could so easily have walked—"

"Relax, honey!" Mel began to laugh. "I don't mean Jack Crabbe's car—well, not exactly. It isn't that I'd have minded putting a little business his way, season of goodwill and all, but he seems to be otherwise engaged tonight. He said he couldn't possibly drive anyone anywhere on Christmas Eve—sounded almost scandalised we even suggested it—so you'll have to put up with Banner the Boy Wonder and one of Jack's hire cars—on expenses," she added, as Miss Seeton uttered further sounds of startled protest, "so don't worry about a thing. Grab your brolly, and let's go!"

She gave Miss Seeton no time to think up anything else to worry about, but herself seized the gold-handled umbrella—could there have been any other choice?—from its clip, took Miss Seeton's bag from the table, and waited while her friend, blinking, fumbled for her keys and, hustled out to the front step, carefully locked her door. Under the clear, starlit sky, the wreath of twined evergreens, ribbons, and fir cones fastened to the knocker glittered with a faint powdering of frost; by the time Miss Seeton came home again, it would all be ice and silver beneath the rising moon.

"Going to be a nippy one tonight, Miss S!" Mel took a quick look at her friend's neatly gloved hands, and nodded. "Path not too slippery for you?"

Miss Seeton assured her that it wasn't, and uttered further assurances to Thrudd Banner, once she reached the car, that she wasn't in the least cold, that she was most grateful for the lift, that she hated to be a nuisance, that she could easily have walked—

"On Christmas Eve?" Thrudd snorted as he let in the clutch, and the car moved off. "Forget it, MissEss—think of it as your present from us come a day early, if it bothers you at all, though I don't see why it should. Can you seriously imagine Forby in her glad rags hiking half a mile down a road like this in the middle of winter in the dark?"

Above Miss Seeton's embarrassed babbles of regret that she had bought presents for neither Mel nor Thrudd, the voice of Amelita Forby rose in great scorn. "And can you, Miss S, seriously imagine Banner hiking half a mile down *any* sort of road, never mind what time of day it is? It'd have to be a dandy sort of story for him even to think of making the effort!"

"Talking of dandy stories"—Thrudd, reminding himself that it was Christmas Eve, was determined not to allow Mel to needle him—"don't forget, Forby, that if the Oracle's there tonight he's as good as promised us the inside dope on what he's been doing all day, so I hope you've brought your notebook with you. Season of goodwill or not, you aren't borrowing mine."

"Listen, you feeble excuse for a Fleet Street legend—"

Mel broke off with a yelp as Thrudd, braking for the turn into the Rytham Hall gateway, skidded with his back wheels, and threw her sideways. Miss Seeton, buckled into her safety belt, uttered a little squeak of surprise.

"Sorry, folks." Thrudd straightened the car and drove cautiously up the gravel drive. "Patch of ice—can't have melted from yesterday, to be as bad as that. Could be a sign that we're in for a hard winter. Isn't there some saying about the shortest day?"

"As the day lengthens," recited Miss Seeton obligingly, "the cold strengthens—which of course it has. Lengthened, I mean, though by only three days, which one would not have supposed to make so much of a difference. The equinox . . ."

They swept round the final curve in the approach to the house, and Miss Seeton's discourse on weather lore was forgotten in her sudden pleasure at the sight of Rytham Hall *en fête*. There were open curtains at every downstairs window, through which the warm red-and-golden glow of the festive season gleamed on grass and gravel and flower beds with a mellow, welcoming light. Miss Seeton's keen eyes did not miss the wreath of beribboned evergreens—so much bigger than her own—on the open front door, or the distant view of a tall tree, draped with glittering tinsel, festooned with streamers, at the far end of a hallway hung from wall to wall with paper chains. She thought back to Christmases long ago, and smiled to herself, and nodded.

"There's Nigel!" Mel stopped in the act of opening the car door. "Why's he waving at us like that?"

Thrudd cocked his head to one side, listening. "Sounds as if he doesn't want us to park just here—fair enough; we don't know how many other people have been invited. You two hop out, and I'll check where he'd like me to go."

Mel, still brooding on recent insults, was minded to mutter something, then remembered it was Christmas, and said nothing at all. She directed a fond look towards the back of her beloved's head, waited for Miss Seeton to join her in the open air, and then made her way across to greet the son of the manor with a quizzical upward lift of her beautiful eyes to the lintel above his head.

"What? No mistletoe? I was kind of hoping to wish you the compliments of the season in style, Nigel."

Nigel, who had finished gesticulating at Thrudd to move the car, winked now at Thrudd's lady. "There's a kissing-bough indoors, Mel, and if you're willing to risk it, I certainly am— not that it wouldn't be worth the risk anyway," he added, with hasty gallantry. "Still, it's Christmas. It wouldn't exactly be sporting of Thrudd to poke me on the nose in my own house at Christmas, would it?"

As Mel agreed that it wouldn't, Lady Colveden appeared from the kitchen to greet her guests, and take their coats. "Do go straight through to the sitting room—but I'd better warn you," she added, with a giggle. "The Admiral brought a pot of honey, and a new recipe for mulled wine. Which means he and George—and Nigel—have been sampling their handiwork for the past half hour or more . . ."

Nigel gurgled. "You could," he said, "say that it packs one hell of a *punch*, couldn't you?"

Which terrible pun brought the expected groans, and despairing references to Christmas cracker mottoes, and chuckles all round.

"Now that," said Thrudd, as they followed their hostess down the hall, "is what I *call* a tree. Talk about an optical illusion! Would there be a trapdoor up there, or did you just saw the top off to look as if it goes right through the ceiling?"

"Not a trapdoor in sight," Nigel told him cheerfully. "And if you don't believe me, I've the blisters to prove it—though my mother did all the decorating. Round the lower branches, anyway. We don't"—he lowered his voice to a conspiratorial whisper—"trust her up ladders, just in case, tonight of all nights."

"I heard that," called her ladyship from the kitchen, above the merry clink of glasses. "I should say I'm every bit as capable as you or your father of climbing a step ladder— and tonight, in my opinion, I'm *more* capable than both of you put together. And why"—she emerged with a tray in her hands—"*tonight of all nights*, might I ask?"

Thrudd, with a quick look at Nigel, stepped forward to take the tray from her ladyship's hands. Nigel, swaying slightly, widened innocent eyes and said, with a grin and another gurgle of mirth:

"Why? Because it's Christmas Eve, that's why—which means it's Christmas Day tomorrow. And if you're in hospital with half-a-dozen broken legs, Mother darling, there'll be nobody else to cook the Christmas goose . . ."

"I'll cook *your* goose for you, if you don't behave," his darling mother told him, as Nigel, a little unsteadily, led the way through to the sitting room.

There were old friends there to greet, and new: the Admiral, busy with spice-bags and spoons and bottles of wine; Sir George, a thoughtful and appreciative gleam in his eye as he stirred the huge glass bowl and savoured the fragrant steam; Mrs. Knight (looking slightly bereft without her husband, Dr. Injecta) from the nursing home, with daughter Anne and son-in-law, Detective Sergeant Bob Ranger of Scotland Yard— and Bob's boss, Detective Superintendent Delphick, whose presence was acknowledged with cries (from Mel Forby and Thrudd Banner) of glee, and with demands to know what on earth he had been doing all day. To which demands Delphick replied that he and his sergeant had been extremely busy, and would now be glad of a few hours' relaxation before he, if not Bob, drove home in time for Christmas Day.

As everyone chatted together, more punch was poured, and pronounced excellent. Mel cast a calculating eye from the amount in Delphick's glass to the kissing-bough, with its evergreens, red ribbons, candles, and paper rosettes; and she resolutely ignored any possible claims of Thrudd or Nigel in favour of the chief superintendent, on whom she turned the full force of her beautiful eyes.

"Come on, Oracle," she begged. "Put us out of our misery—what was all the fuss last night about?"

Delphick, gazing into his glass of punch, knew that he was the centre of attention. He sipped, suppressed a smile of quiet self-satisfaction, looked up, and sighed.

"You're very insistent, Miss Forby. Does a hardworking police officer warrant no holiday, even at Christmas?"

"No," Mel informed him, as he drew breath for another self-pitying sentence. The brief monosyllable punctured his martyred pose, and he chuckled.

"Very well—if you insist. I suppose I may be confident that I'll have no peace until the tale is told . . ."

"Right," said Mel, to a chorus of agreement from everyone except Miss Seeton, who was enjoying the comfortable punch-inspired glow creeping from her tummy to her toes, and who was coming to the equally comfortable decision that yesterday's embarrassment was, well, yesterday's, and there was perhaps no point in worrying any more about it.

"Right," echoed Delphick, marshalling his thoughts as he took another heartening sip. It heartened him so thoroughly that he raised no particular protest when Mel, making great play of taking her notebook from her bag, under cover of the distraction signalled to Nigel to take the Oracle's almost empty glass from his hand and replace it with a full one.

"Right," said Delphick again, as his gaze flicked across in Mel's direction; she could almost have sworn she saw him wink. He cleared his throat with some force, and all eyes were upon him.

"We began," he said, "with the, er, irruption of Miss Seeton into the pantomime proceedings, with the advice that he was not a she, nor she a he—if I have that correctly, Miss Seeton?"

As he raised his glass to her, Miss Seeton, blushing, sipped n her turn, ventured a smile, and murmured (with another ɔlush) that she rather feared he had. Delphick smiled reassur-ɪngly on her confusion.

"Nothing to fear, believe me, Miss Seeton: we're really most grateful to you for bringing the facts to our notice—ɔr should that be the *fact*? Not he, but she: not Cole, but Letty, Green. A real-life Principal Boy—and she almost got ɪway with it . . ."

After Major Howett had seized the escaping Green in one ɔf the arm-locks she had learned during her time in Her Majesty's forces, Delphick had called on reinforcements in the persons of Lady Colveden and Miss Treeves to escort the—he hesitated over the word *prisoner*, as no arrest had yet been made, and he couldn't for the life of him see what charge it would be, anyway—to escort the bank manager to some quiet place where fuller investigation could be carried ɔut. With so many women nowadays wearing trousers, slacks, ɔr jeans, was a charge of transvestism—or whatever the female equivalent might be—a serious possibility? In the days of poor Maria Marten of Red Barn fame, a female might be prosecuted for assuming male attire, but surely not in the 1970s . . .

But *something* was wrong—Miss Seeton's outburst, and Green's attempted flight, had demonstrated that beyond all doubt—and it was up to Superintendent Brinton, on whose patch these stirring events had taken place, to ascertain what it might be. And if Brinton, bemused by what had been stirred up (without one wave, as his Yard colleague laughingly reminded him, of Miss Seeton's umbrella) chose to call in outside aid to the interrogation—well, Delphick and his enormous sidekick Ranger were more than happy to oblige . . .

"It was her husband who'd been appointed to the Brettenden post," the senior Yard man now explained, while his junior colleague, who wasn't driving back to London, allowed Sir George to ladle more punch into his glass as he listened, as enthralled as the rest, to a story he already knew. "They'd been married for years, and she was always on at him to better himself. She nagged him into applying, and even wrote the original letter—*and* filled in the forms on his behalf. When,

thanks to her efforts, he was called for an interview to head
office, naturally nobody knew what he looked like. Letty
guessed he'd lose his head—and the job—when he turned
up in person, and decided to step in."

"Amateur dramatics," broke in Bob, through slices of fruit,
as Delphick paused to wet his whistle. "It was Letty's one
interest in life, apparently, and being so tall—for a woman,"
he added, conscious of his sturdy six-foot-seven, "she often
had to take a man's part if there weren't enough real men to
go round."

Mel was about to say something, then didn't. Thrudd, a
gleam in his eye, enquired:

"How on earth did she get away with it? Surely her husband
would've stopped her when he found out what kind of game
she was playing! How about when she left the house in her . . .
her disguise, for instance?"

"Probably too terrified out of his tiny wits to breathe a
word," said Mel, turning a page. "You heard the Oracle say
she nagged him? Well, there you are, then."

"I'm afraid," said Delphick, accepting the responsibility of
reply as Bob was once more overcome by mulled wine, "it
was rather more sinister than that, Mel. In the first place, she
kept him quiet by—"

"Ah!" For Sir George, the perfect host, to interrupt a guest
in full flight was unheard of. Delphick was so startled that he
almost dropped his glass.

"Sorry," said Sir George, "but—coincidence, y'know.
Delphick—everyone—*quiet*. Listen . . ."

And everyone listened: to the sinister, echoing, clattering
noises coming from outside. Coming up the drive—and coming ever closer to the house.

chapter
-26-

THE CLATTERING WAS accompanied by the crunch of booted feet on gravel, and the murmur of men's voices. Nigel shot a quick, appraising look at his father, exchanged glances with his mother, and rose promptly from his chair.

"I'd better go, I think. Or—will you?"

Such a suggestion was so out of character for Nigel, the nearest to Sir Galahad anyone was ever likely to meet, that several people gasped. From what they could hear, there must be half-a-dozen men approaching the house—and yet the baronet's son, who'd at least had the sense not to volunteer his father, seemed to be proposing that his mother might care to face the intruders alone.

Big Bob Ranger and his tall boss spoke almost at the same time. "If you need any help—"

Nigel, his mother, his father, Dr. Knight's ladies, and— after a pause—Miss Seeton stared at them. Admiral Leighton and Thrudd Banner indicated their willingness to support the defence. Mel Forby, who at first had felt as nervous as her fellow non-Plummergenites—the Admiral, she recalled, hadn't lived in the place more than a few months—suddenly chuckled to herself, and began to sing the chorus of that lovely Christmas song made popular by Harry Belafonte more than fifteen years earlier.

"Gosh, yes!" Nigel paused in the act of hurrying from the room. "Where did you put the scarlet ribbons, Mother?"

Lady Colveden said: "On the chest in the hall, unless they've been moved—one for each of us, remember. And if you *can* keep them out—I know I left the door open, because it seems so unhospitable, and I was expecting the others to get here first—but if they scratch the parquet again, you know how cross Martha will be . . ."

Bob and Delphick, divining that whatever was going on gave no cause for alarm, had subsided, and sat taking puzzled sips of punch as the squire's son vanished through the sitting-room door, and could be heard almost running down the hall, pausing briefly in the general neighbourhood of the mahogany chest before carrying on to the front door. Her ladyship, with a smile, looked round at her guests.

"If Nigel only manages to persuade them to stay on the drive—Oh, dear, I forgot to tell him the money was beside the ribbons—I hope he spotted it—well, we ought to have just as good a view from the window. Shall we see?"

She rose gracefully to her feet, and, followed by some who knew what was happening, by others who didn't have a clue, and by Mel, who was pretty sure she'd guessed, moved across to the far end of the room. Tall, wide-paned windows looked out upon the final curve of the Rytham Hall drive, and the golden glow of electricity illuminated for the interested watchers indoors a truly remarkable sight.

Nigel—was it Nigel? With his back towards them, in the dark, it was hard to be sure—had reached the intruders, and appeared to be remonstrating with—

"A horse?" Delphick, Bob, and the others not in the know took a second, a third look. "It can't be!"

"It can," said Mel. "It is. I'm right, aren't I?" She turned with a grin to the locals as Nigel made a sudden lunge at the strange, blanket-covered beast which reared and pranced, jerking its bridle out of his reach, snapping its jaws with that same uncanny clattering that had heralded its arrival.

"That *is* the Hooden Horse, isn't it?" said Mel, as the man holding its bridle cracked a massive whip, and shouted for his charge to behave. "And that's the Waggoner, with the whip? I read about them when I researched *Pagan Past and Current Customs*, but I've never been in this part of the world around Christmas, so . . ."

The Waggoner cried, "Whoa!" as the Horse plunged to

and fro, tossing its head, clashing its jaws, and presenting a terrifying prospect to those around it. All of them—apart from Nigel, still trying to catch hold of the Horse's bridle, and a woman in a long dress—wore smocks, of the kind not seen in general use since before the First World War.

"Whoa!" Another crack of the whip, as the Horse bucked and whinnied, its heavy draperies flapping. The woman in the long dress darted forward, and was now seen to be holding a besom broom, with which she swept the ground behind the skittering Horse, making little feints towards Nigel's feet as he still made snatches at the bridle, and the Horse again jerked its head out of his reach.

"Yes, it is," said Lady Colveden absently, in reply to Mel's earlier question. "And that's Mollie . . ."

From the non-local guests came exclamations of surprise. The vicar's sister, wearing such a rig? Capering about on the Colvedens' drive with a broom, and with—

"Her face! It's all black!" cried Bob, as Anne beside him stifled a giggle. Her loving spouse had not yet spent Christmas with her family, as opposed to his, and consequently knew nothing of the age-old local customs—older by far than the Victorian celebrations invented almost single-handedly by Dickens—which Plummergen had never abandoned.

"Soot," explained Sir George, swaying slightly as he stood on tiptoe to see above the heads of his guests. "Always reminds me of the war, y'know. Camouflage."

"In some parts of Kent," said Mel, sounding knowledgeable, "it isn't just Mollie who has a black face, but the whole group of Hoodeners—except the Horse, I suppose. He wouldn't bother, would he? With nobody able to see him inside that great head."

"Mollie," said Delphick thoughtfully, as the besom was plied with great vigour by the black-faced person in the floor-length garb. "Dressed as a woman, but—another man, I take it?"

Sir George uttered a sharp bark of laughter. "Catch 'em letting a female in on all this! Seven years' bad luck, at the very least. Could be useful for the Jockey, though," he added, as Nigel still attempted to capture the rampaging Horse "Lighter."

"But it's always," his wife reminded him, "the stronges man in the village inside the Horse, and Dan Eggleden doe a splendid job, you know he does. I don't suppose he'd b so happy to do it every year if he minded having peopl scrambling on and off his back half the night."

"Under the spreading chestnut tree," ventured Miss Seeton "the village smithy stands." Dear Mr. Delphick's remark ha reminded her—even though one had been so interested in th antics of the Hooteners that one had only just realised wha he had said—had reminded her of yesterday's unfortunat incident at the pantomime; perhaps—although one was, o course, among friends, who would, naturally, be far too polit to mention it—a change of subject would not come amiss "The smith," she continued bravely, "a mighty man is he With large and sinewy hands; And the muscles of his brawn arms Are strong as iron bands."

"They certainly are," agreed Lady Colveden. "I only hop he doesn't forget just how strong he is and throw Nigel int my roses—it won't do them any good at all."

Anne, standing beside her quiet mother, giggled. "I be Nigel wouldn't be too happy about it, either—but at leas he's young. His bones should heal quickly enough, especiall if he's treated promptly. With Dad not here . . ." With anothe giggle, she hurried on: "Shall I hunt out your first aid kit, Lad Colveden, to have the bandages ready?"

"Is it obligatory," enquired Delphick, "for a member of eacl household honoured with a visit from the—what did you cal them? The Hooteners?—is everyone obliged to ride the Hors before the, er, attentions cease?"

"Not unless they want to," said Lady Colveden, as Nigel with a sudden spring, seized the bridle and dragged the recal citrant Horse to a halt. "Once he's tied on the red ribbons and handed over the gratuity—oh, dear, I do hope he remem bered—Martha will never forgive me, after last year—but believe some of the younger men see it as a challenge. Rathe like a bucking bronco, I suppose."

"A challenge I, for one," Delphick said, "would prefe

to ignore. That Horse, tamed or not, is a fearsome-looking creature indeed."

The Hooden Horse, almost as if it had heard, wrenched its bridle from Nigel's grasp even as he seemed to be about to tie on the placatory ribbons, made a rush for the house, and could be seen clearly for the first time, curvetting from side to side with its long tail streaming out behind, its teeth glittering, its eyes glaring white, red-rimmed, staring, and wild.

"Hinged jaws," remarked Mel, as the strange clattering could be heard again. "And iron nails for teeth—but isn't it a pity they haven't put a candle inside? They do in some places, from what I've read—"

"Used to in Plummergen," said Sir George, as Nigel made another grab at the bridle, and was almost allowed to catch it. "Bit of an accident a few years back, though. Decided best to leave it out, in future. Great shame. Made it even more impressive, to my mind."

"It's impressive enough as it is." Thrudd nudged Mel as the Horse galloped to the bottom of the Hall steps. "Going to do a circus act and jump on his back?"

"I'm afraid," Lady Colveden said, with a sigh, "that the bareback riding will have to come from Nigel, after all. It doesn't look as if they're going to leave until they've given us a really good show—but oh, dear, I do hope they keep away from my roses . . ."

And so did Nigel, as he finally succeeded in capturing the Horse's bridle again, and managed to add his three red ribbons to those already fluttering among the shining brass ornaments between the leather ears and across the wooden forehead. By the end of the evening, there would be many of these scarlet trophies, but as yet there were very few. The Hooden Horse of Plummergen condescends to call upon only selected establishments around the village: there may be no more than five hundred inhabitants in half as many houses, but most of these are as hospitable as any in Kent. Rytham Hall, at the end of Marsh Road, is either one of the first, or the last, ports of call, depending on where the Hoodeners choose that their ritual should begin; the energies of Daniel Eggleden inside his Horse's costume were far from exhausted, and Nigel, first Jockey of the night, guessed he was in for a difficult ride.

The bucking and rearing were accompanied by wild yells from the future baronet as he entered into the spirit of the occasion, and by the attendant Hoodeners' performance on handbells, a concertina, a tambourine, and (the Waggoner, leaving his whip to fend for itself) a metal triangle. Mollie, the Old Woman, brushed with her besom like a creature possessed; and a loud cheer arose from all as the son of the house finally gave up the struggle to stay on the Horse's back, and allowed himself to be deposited—

"Oh no, not my roses!" cried Lady Colveden in dismay— in the middle of the herbaceous border.

Mel Forby crept away from the crowd watching the departure of the Hoodeners to refresh Delphick's drink, then rejoined her friends in all innocence to add her farewells to the rest. "Well, I've read about it, but the real thing's certainly something else, when you see it. Guess I've the makings of one of the best Plummergen Pieces for quite a while, after that little display— pagan origins, and all that—but I'm darned if I'd ever let anyone kid me it was a good luck charm, the way it looks. Those teeth—and the eyes!"

She gave an artistic shudder, concentrating the attentions of everyone upon her as they returned to their seats, and successfully diverting Delphick's from his glass. With a smile, she went on:

"There was some poor woman dropped dead on her doorstep when she saw the thing—eighteen-something, admittedly, but you have to admit, it's pretty scary. How about the Oracle goes on with his story to cheer us all up?"

Delphick, who was frowning at the level of punch in his glass, chuckled. "Christmas Eve is traditionally a time for ghosts, Mel, not for murder. The shade of Siberius Gelidus Brumalix may, for all we know, have bribed Charon to ferry him back across the Styx so that his story might be told tonight. Think of his disappointment when—"

"Styx, nix," Mel broke in, shaking her head. "A promise is a promise, Oracle, although"—once more, her eyes drifted to the kissing-bough above—"if you're in need of a little coercion, well, in a good cause I guess I could stretch a point or two."

Delphick chuckled again. "The cause being your byline, of course. And Thrudd's," he added, as Mr. Banner brandished his notebook in one hand, waving his drink in the other. Once more, Delphick contemplated his serving of punch, and with a thoughtful air remarked: "As I recall, among the largesse distributed to the Hoodeners after their musical interlude was an adequate share of refreshment, both solid and, er, liquid. I trust that the, er, generosity shown to my humble self has left none of our visitors short . . ."

Mel stifled a giggle, and met his gaze with one of her very best wondering looks. Delphick looked right back at her, and this time his wink was obvious.

"Very well, Miss Forby, since it's Christmas, I'll continue my narrative—if anyone can remind me which point I had reached, that is."

A chorus of voices, those of Mel and Thrudd being the loudest, advised him that when the Hoodeners arrived he had been describing the machinations of Letty Green, particularly her efforts at keeping her husband quiet.

"Except," Mel added, "you never told us how she managed it. If it comes with a guarantee"—with a darkling look in the direction of Thrudd—"I might try it myself some day."

"I sincerely trust," Delphick said, "that you won't pursue Letty's methods to their sinister extreme, Miss Forby. In the first place, she drugged the poor fellow—slipped him a Mickey Finn in his goodnight cocoa that kept him under for the whole of the following day: the day on which she went to the interview herself—and won the branch manager's job—as Cole, not Letty, Green."

Miss Seeton, who had been quietly interested by all that had gone on about her, clicked her tongue, and sighed. Lady Colveden, brooding on Delphick's use of the words *sinister* and *in the first place*, breathed a horrified "Oh, no," and Mel was not alone in echoing the sentiment.

"Afraid so." Delphick nodded grimly. "When Letty realised poor old Cole wasn't willing to go along with the conse-quences of her little plot—that he wanted to confess to the

bank's board the trick she'd played—well, she couldn't bear
to see her chance, the chance she believed she'd earned after
so many years in the lower ranks, slip through her fingers.
Particularly as she had another, even more profitable scheme
in mind, for which it would be of the greatest possible help
to be a reasonably high official in the organisation of the City
and Suburban Bank . . ."

"So she killed him, right?" Thrudd was scribbling with
enthusiasm, even as Mel shuddered to a temporary halt and
pulled a face. "Drastic . . . Effective, though."

"Undoubtedly effective." Delphick sighed. "She's quick—
and decisive. She drove poor old Cole out to the country
and buried him in the first patch of sandy soil she found.
She told the neighbours he'd gone on ahead to sort out
their new house in Brettenden, so nobody noticed he was
missing. His colleagues at the bank never thought to question his disappearance—why should they? And you know
how paperwork can go astray in a large organisation. The
Head Office Personnel Department simply assumed it was
they who'd made the mistake when Cole Green started
one week later in Brettenden than they'd expected—and
the Brettenden staff thought precisely the same thing, as
Letty had guessed they would."

"But," said Mel, as Delphick drew breath, and sipped punch
with an air of near amusement.

He smiled at her. "*But*, Mel, Letty started to give herself away by—I trust the liberated ladies of my acquaintance
won't tear me limb from limb when I say this—by behaving
in a rather too feminine way for the man she'd taken such
pains to resemble. Old-fashioned business clothes—waistcoat,
watch-chain, tailcoat, striped trousers—excessively masculine
moustache, pungent hair oil as preferred by Edwardian gentlemen—oh, she had the *costume* to perfection. But the longer
she played the *part*, the more careless she grew. She started
tidying—which was a big mistake."

"New brooms," announced Miss Seeton, who had finished
her glass of punch almost without noticing. "Rather like the
Mollie, of course, in some respects—but in others, of course,
well, perhaps not." She blinked, frowned, and took a deep

reath. "Brooms, I mean—although, if it is as old a ritual as 'e are given to understand, perhaps not as new as, well . . ." Her cheeks felt suddenly warm—the number of people in Lady Colveden's sitting room, no doubt. "Dear Martha, you know, is of the opinion that no man can ever be as tidy around the house as a woman—and, of course, in her own case she is especially correct."

"Around the house," Delphick said kindly, "or around the bank—it was all the same to Letty. First of all, she unearthed that chest of medals, which put Brettenden, and herself, on the map. Then she sent out those chatty letters of introduction, which were perhaps not quite in the style one would imagine a bank manager to adopt—as Miss Seeton, subconsciously, seems to have recognised." He bowed to Miss Seeton, who turned still more pink, and lowered her gaze.

"But she betrayed herself most noticeably—to those of a noticing disposition, that is—when she went slightly to pieces in dealing with the aftermath of the shotgun robbery—in excuse me, Mel, Anne—ladies) in a manner more feminine than masculine. As Miss Seeton, ah, noticed."

"Oh, dear." Miss Seeton's cheeks were pinker than ever. "Oh, dear, I suppose I did—but not, of course, until last night, when Mr. Jessyp was so cleverly being Instructa—and then it all, well, suddenly made sense. He—she—fussed, you see, and patted me on the shoulder, and looked, well, so much more *upset* than one would expect of a . . . a professional gentleman." Her gaze fell upon Sir George Colveden, in his regimental tie. "It didn't seem . . . well, I peeped through the side curtains, and there he—she—was, sitting beside Mr. estin, who has always been so helpful—and they were both laughing—but not, you see, in the same way. And then I—oh, dear, I'm afraid I acted on impulse. I can't think what came over me . . ."

"Don't worry about it, please, Miss Seeton." Delphick spoke as forcefully as he could, to allay his old friend's obvious distress. "You were, with all due deference to the excellent performance onstage, the evening's star turn, if you don't mind my saying so." A general chorus supported his words, and Miss Seeton blushed again.

"Superintendent Brinton," Delphick went on, "is, believe me, delighted with you—as, I might add, am I. You must realise that, with your usual, ah, talent for seeing to the heart of things, you have not only nailed a murderess—you have also helped Scotland Yard lay its hands on yet another criminal mastermind—the boss of the Night Safe Gang . . ."

chapter

-27-

GOOD—GOOD GRACIOUS," said Miss Seeton, blinking; while the rest of the room exclaimed, and applauded.

"Exactly so," said Delphick, permitting himself a slight bow in acknowledgement of the applause, although he was soon the steady professional again. "You have to understand, you see, that this was Letty's real purpose in wanting the manager's job: she needed access to a list of every branch of the City and Suburban Bank around the country. She was far too practical to waste time hunting in telephone directories, which are in any case never entirely up-to-date—and she was too cunning to risk having questions asked by applying direct to Head Office for the information. Cole, poor chap, would never have betrayed his banking trust by telling her what she wanted to know, and his job was hardly of the level to require his ever bringing home such information in his briefcase. So . . ."

"Clever stuff," muttered Thrudd, busy taking notes. It was a sentiment echoed by everyone except Mel, likewise busily noting, and Miss Seeton, who appeared dismayed by the revelation; but it was left to the Buzzard—Rear Admiral Bernard Leighton of the Royal Navy (the Senior Service, renowned for its efficiency)—to enquire:

"Sound scheme, no doubt, but—how did she recruit the other members of the gang? She'd find it pretty difficult, I should think. After all, as a rule the ladies, God bless 'em, don't care for mixing with the criminal classes." And, raising his glass in salute, he beamed round at every lady of the company, and drank a hearty toast.

215

"Difficult?" Delphick chuckled. "On the contrary. I told y⟨ Letty was practical by nature, remember. And she made adm⟨ rably practical use of the facilities to hand by—incredible, b⟨ true—advertising for them. At the bank's expense," he we⟨ on, above a chorus of amazement, "and in the bank's tim⟨ She even interviewed them on the bank's very premises—aft⟨ hours, mind you, so that nobody who worked there would fi⟨ out what she was doing. She gave out a Box Number to wri⟨ to, rather than telephone in working hours and run the ri⟨ that the wrong person might answer the call; and she to⟨ prospective members of her gang that the bank was workir⟨ on a new security system for the Christmas period, and th⟨ they were to be the couriers for the newly designed nig⟨ safes . . ."

He glanced round, smiling, as the chorus of amazeme⟨ renewed itself. Anne, who'd been as fascinated a hearer ⟨ anyone of a tale she'd already heard (albeit briefly) onc⟨ asked:

"Would she—could she possibly have got away with it, ⟨ you think?"

Before Delphick could reply, Mel looked up. "Get awa⟨ with it? Wow! With a scheme as well-organised as hers—n⟨ that I hold with murdering people, of course, but—I reck⟨ if it hadn't been for Miss S here, she would have."

As Miss Seeton sighed, and clicked her tongue, and th⟨ others regarded their friend with admiration, Delphick said:

"Get away with it—who knows? I'd say, on balance, sl⟨ had a sporting chance—but her chances, as Mel has pointe⟨ out, were indeed, thank goodness, ruined by Miss Seeton⟨ Delphick smiled again, with genuine affection for his elder⟨ colleague: who blushed, and murmured, and lowered her ga⟨ to her fingers: which, twined on her lap, had suddenly begu⟨ to flutter and twitch.

"Thanks also," Delphick went on, his eyes intent up⟨ Miss Seeton's dancing digits, "to whichever members ⟨ the Plummergen Amateur Dramatic Society elected to d⟨ *Cinderella* as a traditional pantomime. If Prince Charmin⟨ had been a young man, or the Ugly Sisters women, th⟨ story could have turned out very different from the way ⟨

did—though our main thanks, as ever, Miss Seeton, must of course go to you. By the way," as Miss Seeton ventured to meet his gaze with another blush, "I'd be very surprised, you know, if you hadn't had some . . . inkling of what was going on long before last night." Miss Seeton's hands tightened on her lap, and he smiled kindly. "Am I right in assuming that, in common with several other villagers, you'd encountered the new bank manager on one or other trip to Brettenden?"

"I normally make a point of transacting my business with Mr. Jestin," Miss Seeton told him, making an effort to still her restless hands by picking up her empty glass, and holding it awkwardly. Delphick, biding his time, nodded encouragement. "Such a very helpful young man," Miss Seeton went on, with a sigh. "But it is true, I fear, that I had observed him—or I suppose I should say *her*—in the background—being naturally interested in one who, as I understood—though not from Mr. Jestin himself, for he is the soul of discretion—but to have been passed over for promotion which, as Martha told me, was so well deserved . . . I fear I may have been guilty of what some might see as unpardonable curiosity, since I couldn't resist a quick peek once or twice as he—I mean she—passed through . . . but not, of course, to *stare*, which would have been . . . unforgivable." And her blush was positively fiery at the very idea.

"Goodness, Miss Seeton," cried Lady Colveden quickly, "it's only natural you should have been interested, when it was your money he—she—oh, dear, the bank—was looking after. I know *I* was—interested, I mean, when I went in to cash a cheque—and I'm sure George and Nigel were too, only catch them admitting it. Men," she added, with a twinkle, "don't. What *we* call plain common sense, and being observant, *they* choose to sneer at, and call female curiosity, and then they wonder"—turning to Delphick in some indignation—"how criminals manage to get away with so many crimes. If there were a few more like Miss Seeton at Scotland Yard, just think how much easier your life would be!"

Flushed both with the success (as she saw it) of her argument, and with the heat of her oratory, Lady Colveden—for all her claims for feminine observation—failed to observe that Delphick and Bob, at the thought of *a few more like Miss Seeton* running riot at Scotland Yard, had turned pale. Sergeant Ranger drained the last of his punch, and held out his glass automatically for more; the chief superintendent—the higher the rank, the stronger the nerves—simply closed his eyes for a few seconds, and took several deep, controlled breaths.

The brief, strained silence was broken by a sudden chortle from the chair nearest the door. Young Mr. Colveden—who, from the effects of punch as well as the aftereffects of his encounter with the Hooden Horse, was more flushed than his mother—said: "You know, Mr. Delphick, you don't look at all well. Neither does Bob, if it comes to that. I really can't think why." Nigel favoured his friends with a knowing wink. "It could always be the mulled wine, I suppose—yes, of course that must be it—but you've no need to worry." With an owlish look, he indicated the sitting-room clock, then nodded towards the still-open door, and chuckled. "If you, er, feel you'd be happier having a doctor take a look at you—well, there ought to be one along any minute now—in a manner of speaking. Isn't that right, Anne? Mrs. Knight?"

With a laugh in her eyes but a perfectly serious note in her voice, Anne agreed that the two policemen had not been misled. Mrs. Knight, with her usual quiet efficiency, nodded quick confirmation of Nigel's intelligence, while the Colvedens and Miss Seeton hid smiles as they, too, nodded.

Thrudd and the Admiral seemed as bemused as Delphick and Bob by the little exchange. Mel, however, a glow in her beautiful eyes, let out a little cry.

"A Doctor? Not a Quack Doctor! Oh, don't," she begged, "say we're going to have Mummers round tonight—not really! That's wonderful! This must be just about the best Christmas I've ever had—and it's hardly started yet!"

"Starting," Nigel corrected himself, his head on one side, "any *second* now, I mean. Not minute, because—"

He was interrupted by a sudden rapping at the Colvedens front door, followed by the sound of heavy steps striding accompanied by a strange, sibilant sound, along the hallway towards the sitting room. Every head turned to stare at the open door . . .

Through which entered a truly remarkable figure.

"In comes I—Old Father Christmas!" announced the figure. It—he—was tall, covered from head to foot in long, shivering strips of crimson paper and lengths of red ribbon, through which a soot-blackened face peered out from under a wreath of evergreen, twined with tinsel, about his head. "Am I welcome, or am I not? I hope Father Christmas will never be forgot!" He gestured wildly with his arms, and the fluttering lengths parted to reveal white linen underneath, coarsely woven. "Now, in this room there shall be shown the dreadfullest battle ever known—"

He whirled to face the open door, and raised his voice.

"Step in, King George, with thy free heart,
  To see if thou canst claim peace in thine own part!"

More heavy, striding, rustling steps, and another figure appeared, as blackfaced and beribboned as Father Christmas, but with paper strips of many rainbow hues instead of plain red. On his head, rather than woven greenery, he wore a high top hat, entirely covered with beads, scraps of coloured cloth, and pieces of silver foil; in one hand he held a sword of blackened wood, in the other a long, narrow shield.

"In comes I, Saint George the King,
  From Old England I did spring . . ."

Saint King George proclaimed, in forceful couplets, his prowess as a fighter, his duty as his country's defender to withstand the infidel at no matter what cost to himself, and his intention to rid the world forever of the infamous Turkish Knight, on whose head he heaped a multitude of curses, all the time ferociously brandishing his sword.

As he finished, a third figure erupted into the sitting room, dressed in similar fashion to King George, but with a turban instead of a top hat, a circular shield, and a curved wooden scimitar. He bounded to the front of the area chosen for a stage, and announced in a strong regional accent:

> "In comes I, Little Turkey Snipe.
> I comes from Turkish Land to fight!"

Throwing back his turbanned, paper-stripped head, striking a belligerent pose, he glared in the direction of the noble saint, and raised his voice in challenge.

> "I'll fight with thee, King George,
> Thou man of courage bold—
> No matter if your blood be hot—
> I'll quickly fetch it cold!"

The ensuing battle was so realistic that Lady Colveden quailed for the survival of her furniture. King George, his eyes wild, pursued the Turkish Knight by leaps and bounds, aiming mighty blows at him with his sword; while the self-styled Turkey Snipe ducked and twirled and parried each blow, until he was chased from the room.

Now another of the Christmas Champions appeared, holding a peeled willow wand in one hand, with his hat topped by a paper crown. Limping into the room, he announced himself to be Old King Cole, with his wooden leg. The paper costume hissed and shivered as, his face as black as those of his fellow mummers, he recited the age-old lines, then retired to stand beside Father Christmas, waiting for the next to arrive: who was the blackest of all, in face as in character. "In comes I, Beelzebub. Over my shoulder I carries my club . . ."

King George and the Turkish Knight now reappeared, and all the Champions played primitive tunes on the musical instruments they carried, concealed beneath the heavy paper thatch of their costume: melodeon, tambourine, mouth organ. They chanted, and sang; and then the battle recommenced, the Turkish Knight falling finally to the ground, skewered by the sword of Saint George through the heart—or, as those seated closest to the action could see, under the armpit.

Nigel uttered a little yelp of satisfaction as the cry now went up for a doctor to heal the wounded. A chuckle ran round the audience as Dr. Knight—could there be anyone else in Plummergen of such bulk?—strode in through the door, as bepapered as the rest, and began to examine the patient. The former neurologist of Harley Street seemed as much at home with the pagan doggerel of life and death and resurrection as any of those who had been bred to it . . .

With much boastful hocus-pocus, the Doctor eventually deigned to raise the Turkish Knight from his living tomb, and the cast was almost complete—almost, but not quite.

> "In comes I, Little Johnny Jack,
>   My wife and children on my back."

The rustling, black-faced form spoke with the voice of Jack Crabbe, and rotated slowly in one spot, so that those watching might observe the row of wooden dolls tied across his shoulders.

> "My family is large, and I am small,
>   So every little bit helps us all.
>   Out of nine, I got but five—
>   Half of they be starved alive."

He put up his hand, removed his hat, and held it out to the audience.

> "We want some money, or else some bread,
>   Or all the others will soon be dead.
>   But one mug of your Christmas ale
>   Would make us all merry and sing:
>   And money in our pockets is
>   A very fine thing . . ."

And, with a few more flourishes, the mumming was over for another year.

The Champions agreed that, as the punch bowl had been so thoroughly refilled, it would be a crying shame not to sample its contents. Sir George dispensed full mugs, while Lady Colveden brought in a tray of mince pies, and Nigel—

still slightly pink of face—hunted out plates, and dropped hints about small change which the guests were not slow to understand. Delphick, Bob, Thrudd, and the Admiral dug deep in their pockets; Mel, Anne, Mrs. Knight, and Miss Seeton rummaged in handbags. With a final brisk flourish on their out-of-tune instruments, the Christmas Champions were gone.

Their departure, with everyone crowding to the main door of Rytham Hall to wave them on their way, prompted some of the Colvedens' guests to take their leave, although the Admiral spoke thoughtfully of Lambs Wool, and the eyes of Sir George began to gleam as he hospitably urged his friend to stay longer. The Buzzard, naturally, needed little urging; but Mrs. Knight and Anne, having seen the head of the family taking part, for the first time, in one of the Plummergen rituals which outsiders were never invited to join, were now happy to hurry back to the nursing home. Major Howett, in command of a skeleton staff over Christmas, must be given her chance to relax . . .

Bob, of course, would accompany Anne: he was, after all, on holiday. Delphick, with the Night Safe Case and two murders brought to a satisfactory conclusion, looked forward to driving home to London over roads which, so late in the evening, would be blessedly free of traffic . . .

Miss Seeton drew on her gloves, nodding and smiling, and thanked dear Lady Colveden for a delightful evening. The fingers in the gloves, Delphick was amused to observe, still danced a restless little dance when their owner hoped nobody was watching: and he knew he was not the only one to watch.

"Give you a lift, MissEss?" Thrudd Banner, his notebook tucked carelessly into his jacket pocket, smiled the wolfish smile of the headline hunter. "We'll be going right past your door on our way to the George—"

"Miss Seeton," interposed Delphick smoothly, before Mel could add her honeyed tones to the persuasion, "will, I hope, allow me to offer her a lift. A small matter of business uncompleted—"

"Hey, that's great! You're heading for Town—well, so are we." Mel's look challenged the chief superintendent to argue this point, although she and Thrudd had said earlier that, with the permission of their editors, they'd planned a short Christmas break in Plummergen. "And you're so right, Oracle, the roads are pretty lonely this time of night. A girl never knows when she mightn't run into a spot of bother. We'd be so grateful for police protection. Guess we could kind of do the trip in tandem—at the very least, until you've dropped Miss Seeton off. What do you say?"

Delphick sighed. "I'd say, Miss Forby, that you had the cheek of the devil and the hide of a rhinoceros—and that if anyone stands in need of protection, it certainly isn't you. Am I never to be allowed any peace?"

"Guess not," Mel told him with a twinkle, as she tucked her notebook, very pointedly, into the outside pocket of her handbag. "But," she added, her eyes drifting to the dancing fingers of Miss Seeton, "talking of peace—and quiet, and letting off steam, and laying ghosts, or whatever it is some of us need to do—at this time of year, I mean . . ."

"I know exactly what you mean." Delphick tried to sound stern, but his heart wasn't in it: he'd known, from the moment he'd seen her walk in with Thrudd, that Mel Forby would have the whole story out of him—and Miss Seeton—if it took forever. And Delphick didn't want it to take forever: he had a home, and a wife, and a holiday tomorrow . . .

"Five minutes," he said. "No more, Mel. Promise?"

But Mel merely winked; and her chuckle was very knowing.

chapter
-28-

BEFORE THOSE WHO were leaving could be allowed to do so, the merits of the kissing-bough must be investigated. Nigel, having duly saluted both Mel and Anne, ventured a peck on Miss Seeton's cheek which left her blushing with pleasure. Bob—who, with Anne, had adopted Miss Seeton as an honorary aunt—was as bold as his friend, although Thrudd Banner was more circumspect in his attentions. The foreign correspondent of World Wide Press could never quite make up his mind about Miss Seeton, and compromised now by kissing her hand with true continental gallantry: a fashion which Sir George and the Admiral were pleased to follow. Lady Colveden came in for her fair share of courtesies; and then it was the turn of the gentlemen, most of whom enjoyed themselves a great deal. Delphick, however, observing Amelita Forby as, having moved out of sight, she reappeared, said hurriedly that until he'd made his report he supposed he must consider himself still on duty, and therefore unable to participate in these festivities in a manner which—

"On duty on Christmas Eve? Nerts!" Mel, moving so fast she was almost a blur, inveigled the protesting chief superintendent under the bough in a matter of seconds, and smacked a hearty kiss on his cheek with a mouth which, as Nigel and the rest could bear witness, had surely not been so heavily lipsticked just a few moments earlier.

"There," she said, with another chuckle. "Wasn't so bad was it?" She handed him a clean paper handkerchief, and winked: whereupon the other ladies of the party—with the

224

exception of Miss Seeton, ever mindful of her professional relationship with the chief superintendent—wished him the compliments of the season in such a manner that, by the time they had finished, he seemed to have been utterly charmed by the experience. Bob Ranger, marvelling from a corner of the room, wondered if they'd ever believe him, back at the Yard. Must be the punch: just as well they weren't going to stay for the Lambs Wool, whatever that was. Sounded pretty potent, from the way the Admiral and the Major were muttering about hot ale, and roasted crab apples, and toast, and nutmeg, and sugar, and eggs, and cream . . .

The cars were brought round from their place of safety well out of Hoodener range, and the appropriate farewells were spoken. The Plummergenites, who would be seeing one another later at the midnight carol service, wished the Town-bound traveller Godspeed; and Miss Seeton, tucked with a rug round her knees into the passenger seat of Delphick's car, was driven the quarter-mile distance through the starlit dark to her cottage at the corner where Marsh Road meets The Street. In the wake of Delphick's car came another, emitting little dragon puffs of steamy breath into the chill winter air; and it did not overtake when Delphick stopped, but dimmed its lights and parked, as he did.

Miss Seeton unwrapped herself from her plaid cocoon. "This was indeed most kind of you, Mr. Delphick, when I can well imagine how anxious you must be to set off for London—after such a long day, and with your wife waiting up for you, no doubt—and it would really have caused me no great inconvenience to have walked, although to carry them, perhaps—my shoes, and the torch, and my umbrella, that is—except that, accustomed as one is to living in the country—oh, dear, it sounds so ungrateful, when indeed I . . ."

"Allow me." Delphick leaned across to assist as she fumbled for the passenger handle, then hurried round to help her to her feet before escorting her through her front gate and up the short path to her door.

"As you're staying up for the midnight service, Miss Seeton, I hope you won't mind my—our—taking up a little of your time now. Just a few minutes, as I mentioned earlier. A mat-

ter of some uncompleted business, that's all," as she seemed
puzzled by the request. "It really is rather important . . ." And
Miss Seeton, once more reminded of her professional relationship with the chief superintendent, blushed, and made haste to
issue the required invitation.

He took the key from her hand as she was reaching for the
lock, opened the door, and bowed her across the threshold.
While she switched on lights and turned up the central heating,
he waited with resignation for Mel and Thrudd to hurry up the
path to join the party.

"Five minutes," he warned the two reporters, knowing it
was up to him to make sure they left Miss Seeton in peace
once his business was finally complete. "At this time of night,
that's more than enough, so no trespassing on Miss Seeton's
good nature, if you please."

"Us?" enquired Mel, wide-eyed; and she smiled as her hostess trotted back down the hall to greet her. Miss Seeton smiled
back, and asked whether—although dear Lady Colveden was a
splendid hostess—anyone would care for some tea, or coffee—
or even, bearing in mind the season of the year, a small glass
of sherry—except, of course, that the gentlemen were driving, when it was, as she understood, advisable to limit one's
intake of alcohol—which left dear Mel, who was more than
welcome, naturally, and if the others would care for a cup of
something . . . ?

Miss Seeton was earnestly assured that they could wish
for no better hospitality than that which they had recently
experienced at Rytham Hall: but they would, if she didn't
mind, very much like to talk to her, just for a few minutes.

"Why, certainly." Miss Seeton, puzzled, nevertheless smiled
at her friends, and led them through to her own small sitting
room. They chose their seats—Mel and Thrudd where they
could rest unobtrusive notebooks to write in comfort, Delphick
in a high-backed armchair—while Miss Seeton, with another
puzzled smile, settled herself on a plump, leather-topped tuffet
beside the fireplace. Although Cousin Flora had done without
central heating for over fifty years, there was no denying
that the discreet warmth of well-plumbed radiators was very
convenient, but an open fire . . .

"Roast chestnuts," murmured Miss Seeton, as her friends prepared to launch into their enquiry. Delphick, catching her words, chuckled.

"Chestnuts? A little late in the year for conkers, Miss Seeton, I think—"

He broke off suddenly. Mel, catching his eye, could barely suppress a giggle. *Especially after all that we've heard about what happened here in October*, said Mel's expression, as clearly as if she'd spoken the words out loud.

Delphick frowned at her, and cleared his throat. "Miss Seeton, it's late, I know, and I'm sorry to bother you—but you could, I think, say that it's on police business." Miss Seeton gave a little gasp, and sat up straight, folding her hands on her lap. "We were saying at the Hall," continued the chief superintendent, "if you remember, that you—like so many other people from the village, Lady Colveden not excepted—had shown a . . . an understandable interest in the new bank manager when you saw first saw him. Her."

"Well," said Miss Seeton, her fingers starting to dance on her lap, "yes, I'm afraid—I'm rather afraid I did."

"An understandable interest," Delphick said again. "And when you came home, you drew his likeness?"

Miss Seeton blinked. Her mouth opened, then shut again as a puzzled expression appeared on her face. Delphick's laugh was kindly. "Don't worry, Miss Seeton, I know the signs of old—and I should very much like to see the drawing, if I may. Better late than never, even if you managed the trick without needing to show it to us. And my curiosity, which I trust you will excuse, is, being of a professional nature, at least as pardonable as your own."

"You mean," cried Mel, as Miss Seeton rose slowly to her feet and headed for the writing desk, "there was a picture we didn't see? Miss S, I thought we were pals. Why didn't you show us?"

"She didn't show us," Thrudd took great delight in telling her, "because you hustled us out of here as soon as you had the answer to the Mosaic Murder, and didn't stop to ask if there was anything else to see. Talking of which—"

"Talking of which," broke in Mel, "now we're on the Mosaic Murder, doesn't Miss S get a pat on the back for solving that, as well?"

"Indeed she does," said Delphick. "I have Superintendent Brinton's authority to administer several pats, in fact—and a titbit for you, Mel, and for Thrudd, which you will, if you please, regard as a Christmas present for your personal use, since it is most emphatically not for publication. As journalists," and he looked pointedly at Mr. Banner, "you must be well aware of the libel laws . . ."

"Okay," promised Mel. Thrudd nodded. Miss Seeton, who had retrieved her portfolio and was hovering nearby, smiled uncertainly, and sat down again on the pouffe, the portfolio on her knees.

Delphick glanced from Mel, to Thrudd, to Miss Seeton. He drew a deep breath. "Professor Caernavon Carter," he said, "didn't come to Plummergen by chance—he was, for want of a better phrase, despatched. As in *on a mission,*" he added, before either of the wordsmiths could point out that *to despatch* has more than one meaning. "Carter was deliberately sent here by someone whose fancy had been caught by the discovery of the Temple of Glacia—someone constitutionally unable to resist the icy charm of the name Siberius Gelidus Brumalix— someone who, like the professor, lives in Alaska, the coldest state of the USA—someone with more than enough money to pay for the relics, and perhaps even the mosaic, once it has been lifted, preserved, and completed as Dr. Braxted intends, to be shipped to his underground hideaway . . ."

"Oh-oh," said Mel, while Thrudd whistled softly. "Chrysander Bullian strikes again!"

"I name no names," Delphick warned her, though he winked. Chrysander Bullian, the American-Armenian megalomaniac multimillionaire, had crossed Miss Seeton's innocent path on more than one occasion in the past. Living in permanent fear of World War III, this reclusive madman, who suffered from chronic cryomania, had built himself a huge bombproof palace beneath the frozen snows of Alaska, and now devoted his time to the acquisition of *objets d'art* and *de vertu* of no particular period or style, provided they had a strong affiliation with his liking for the wintry. The Temple of Glacia, and the silver dinner

service of Siberius Gelidus Brumalix, were simply begging for
him to add them to his collection . . .

"They'd better watch out next spring," said Mel, "when
the mosaic's dug up, or whatever the word is, and taken to
Brettenden Museum. I hope they've got good locks on their
doors, with you-know-who on the prowl."

"Superintendent Brinton will no doubt be glad to detail
his Crime Prevention officer in Dr. Braxted's service," said
Delphick gravely: he could imagine what his old friend was
likely to say—and the staff of the museum, as well. Maybe it
would work out cheaper in the long run to let the chap pinch
it, since he seemed so keen . . .

Miss Seeton was frowning over the identity of she-knew-
who, because she didn't—know, that was to say—who they
were talking about. She'd been too busy worrying about the
picture dear Mr. Delphick had insisted on seeing to pay full
attention—how discourteous—to what everyone had been saying . . . Her fingers plucked at the portfolio fastening, and she
sighed.

"Miss Seeton, I do beg your pardon." Delphick smiled, and
reached across to take the bundle of drawings from her lap.
"You don't mind, do you?"

Miss Seeton's face was troubled. "Oh, dear—I tried to
explain, but . . . Such a waste of time, I fear, on your part,
and such impertinence on mine—that is, it would have been, if
I had, which of course I had not—until later, for some reason,
when dear Martha told me about the burglary . . ."

Delphick blinked, but quickly rallied. "You mean your sketch
of the bank manager wasn't drawn at the time you first saw him
in Brettenden?"

Miss Seeton, blushing, murmured that she feared he was
correct, and that it was all very muddled, and when he must
naturally be in a hurry to go home it seemed a shame—

Delphick broke into her protestations with a smile. "Not
in that much of a hurry, I assure you, Miss Seeton—and
perhaps, while I'm looking at these—art appreciation is very
thirsty work, you know—could you possibly make us, after
all, a pot of tea? It's a long drive," he pointed out, "back to
London . . ."

• • •

Delphick, Mel, and Thrudd together looked through the selection of sketches, drawings, and set designs which currently crowded Miss Seeton's portfolio. The reporters were able to advise the chief superintendent as to which they'd already seen, and he lifted out, as he came across them, the items referring to the Mosaic Murder . . . but Mel and Thrudd were as surprised as Delphick when, leafing his way backwards through the loose sheets, he came upon something else which was clearly no mere sketch, but a cartoon—yet another of Miss Seeton's special Drawings.

At first glance, it appeared to be a roughed-out idea for a Christmas card: but closer inspection showed details which made it much more interesting than that. A sprinkling of snow fell from a cloudy sky upon the roof of a house—a stately residence with large, clear windows, set in spacious grounds. From the rear of the house, a furtive figure crept with a sack over one shoulder, a mask on its face—a burglar, with his swag—or was it "hers?" The figure wore trousers, true— but its form was curvacious, its features (where visible) softly delineated, its hair long and flowing.

"Which last," Delphick pointed out, "means nothing, nowadays. Look at young Foxon, for example."

"As was," said Mel, with a giggle. "Remember, he's had a trim—quite a change, isn't it? In my girlish innocence I complimented him on the improved looks of the Broker's Man. Talk about an illusion shattered! It's nothing to do with Method Acting—seems he's thinking of trying for sergeant, and thought he ought to find out what it was like to be . . . well, respectable. Can you imagine?"

"H'm." Delphick's response was noncommittal. "As a former fashion reporter, Mel, you might venture the suggestion that anyone choosing to wear emerald green trousers with a pink shirt and a crimson tie runs no great risk of being considered respectable . . ."

He studied the picture again. Yes, that burglar's gender was far more likely to be female than male, now that he looked carefully: especially when compared to the figure he could see inside the house—a figure very plainly masculine, dressed in policeman's uniform, a row of medals across his chest, a moustache above his upper lip, a helmet on his head. About his booted feet more snow lay in swathes, blown through the open window; and behind the bobby, as if guarded by him from the fleeing burglar, stood a large, old-fashioned safe, set in the middle of the room in which it was the only furniture . . .

"Looks as if the burglar's sent most of the stuff ahead by Carter Paterson," said Delphick. "I don't think he—she—can have opened the safe, according to this . . ."

"Oh, no, Mr. Delphick," said Miss Seeton, coming in with a pot of tea and two plates of goodies on a tray. She set the tray down, and came to stand beside him, gazing at the picture he held. "Forgive me, but I don't believe dear Sir George has a safe up at the Hall for anyone to open—I'm afraid that was simply my imagination running away with me, after hearing dear Martha's distressing news—my feeling, as it were, that for people such as the Colvedens, with so many valuable heirlooms, a safe would be such a wise precaution. One could hardly, of course, expect dear Mr. Potter to stand guard like that all the time—and Sir George is far too sensible to expect it, I'm sure."

"Ah," said Delphick, pointing to the bemedalled bobby inside the house. "This is PC Potter, is it?"

Miss Seeton frowned. "I suppose it must be, since I was thinking of him—with dear Martha grumbling about the powder for the fingerprints, and saying he was busy at the Hall, which is why she came to clean for me instead of for Lady Colveden—as it would have annoyed her, you know. But Mr. Potter, as I recall, has no moustache—and I'm sure I can't think why I should show him wearing medals, except that it was such a fortunate thing the burglar did not steal those belonging to dear Sir George, of course."

"For *snow,* read *fingerprint powder,* no doubt," mused Delphick. "We also have an emphasis on medals—on a safe— and the moustache you've given this chap looks decidedly phony." He pointed with a careful finger. "And I certainly have doubts about the sexual orientation of the criminal whose attempt to rob this safe has so obviously been thwarted . . . Miss Seeton, I think you must allow me to take this drawing for our files. We'll pay you, of course, at the usual rate—"

"Oh, Mr. Delphick—I couldn't possibly permit it. If," said
Miss Seeton, twining her fingers, "my foolish doodling has
been of any help to you at all—which I confess I find hard
to believe, because you had already established the . . . the
identity of the malefactor before you saw this . . ."

"And the others," Delphick said, ignoring her protests. "Mel
knows where they are in the heap—I'd really like to take all
three, please. I'm afraid, with the holiday, you won't receive
the cheque until the New Year, but it will, once again, be
payment for a job well done—even if," with a wink for Mel
as she studied again the two pictures which she and Thrudd
had been instrumental in decoding, "most of it was done for
us by other people."

"Oh, dear," said Miss Seeton. "I suppose . . ."

"Other people," repeated Delphick firmly, above her protests, "who will, now that they have heard the whole story,
very soon be on their way to London—as will I." He rose to
his full height, favouring Mel and Thrudd with a pointed stare.
"We'll leave you in peace, Miss Seeton, to enjoy a well-earned
Christmas holiday secure in the knowledge that you have, yet
again, played an invaluable part in the solving of a baffling
criminal mystery."

Miss Seeton, blushing, murmured that she had really done
no more than her duty, and in any case could hardly consider
that a few foolish doodlings merited the description dear Mr.
Delphick had been so kind as to—

"Invaluable," Delphick said, in a tone that brooked no argument. "The police are more than grateful to you, Miss Seeton.
As I told you before, Superintendent Brinton—Oh." For a
moment, the Oracle looked as guilty as one of the criminals
he spent so much of his time chasing. "Oh—good Lord, I
almost forgot. He told me to give you something else besides
a pat on the back, if you'll excuse me . . ."

He rose from his chair, hurried into the hall, and went
outside for no more than a couple of minutes, returning with a
long, slim, flat parcel, gift-wrapped, beribboned, adorned with
a spray of berried holly and a tumult of gold tinsel. Smiling,
he handed the parcel to his hostess.

"From Chris Brinton, in recognition of your recent loss (courtesy of Major Howett) undergone in the course of duty at Brettenden Bank . . ."

"A new umbrella, I bet," exclaimed Mel, delighted.

"Oh, dear—really, he shouldn't—when he has already so kindly insisted on having the other repaired at his own expense . . ."

Delphick shook his head to silence her, and pushed the package into her hands.

"On my old friend's behalf, and with his admiration and thanks—sentiments in which we all, believe me, share—a very merry Christmas, Miss Seeton—"

"And a Happy New Year," chorussed Mel and Thrudd in conclusion. Then, as Miss Seeton blushed, and bent her head to unwrap her present, Amelita Forby caught Delphick's eye. In her own enchanting orbs, the light of adventure began to sparkle. Here was Miss Seeton, with another umbrella to add to the fray—and Chrysander Bullian still on the loose, not to mention others as yet unencountered . . .

And headlines to go with them . . .

Mel grinned.

"A happy and *prosperous* new year," she said.

HAMILTON CRANE

HAMILTON CRANE IS the pseudonym of Sarah J[ill] Mason, who was born in England (Bishop's Stortford), went to university in Scotland (St. Andrews), and lived for a year in New Zealand (Rotorua) before returning to settle only twelve miles from where she started. She now lives about twenty miles outside London with a tame welding engineer husband and two (reasonably) tame Schipperke dogs, in a house with an undemandingly small garden. Under her real name, she writes the mystery series starring Detective Superintendent Trewley and Detective Sergeant Stone of the Allingham police force.

Miss Emily D. Seeton . . .

Retired art teacher Miss Seeton steps in where
Scotland Yard stumbles. Armed with only her
sketch pad and umbrella, she is every inch an
eccentric English spinster and at every turn the
most lovable and unlikely master of detection.

Miss Seeton has been enchanting mystery
fans for years. Now she appears in her most
delightful adventure yet.

Turn the page for an excerpt from an all-new
Miss Seeton adventure . . .

MISS SEETON
UNDERCOVER

Coming soon in hardcover from
BERKLEY PRIME CRIME

Detective Chief Superintendent Delphick smiled, and held out a hand in welcome. "Miss Seeton, good afternoon. It really is kind of you to have come up to Town at such short notice. I do hope, though, that you didn't let us disturb you in the middle of anything important."

Miss Seeton, courteous as ever, hurried to reassure him. "Oh, no, only the garden—which is there all the time, of course. Except that after last night's rain it needs rather a lot of tidying to suit dear Stan . . ."

Bob politely relieved her of her handbag and umbrella; Delphick took her light tweed coat and hung it on the stand. Miss Seeton's eyes held a shamefaced twinkle as she went on: "He is a little vexed with me, I fear, for having allowed the garden roller to split the handle of my besom so that we have nothing with which to sweep away the worms—when the telephone rang—or rather their casts, all over the lawn, as well as the leaves. Such surprisingly high winds, for October, though one can always make compost with them, and the earth is of great benefit—and the worms, of course."

Delphick ushered her to the most comfortable of the visitors' chairs, and she sat down, still trying to explain the unimportance of her doings that afternoon when duty called her elsewhere. "To the compost. Of course, it was an accident—the telephone—and naturally I have promised to take greater care in future. Besides, it can always be used for stakes, and to stop the birds eating the seeds, so it won't be as much of a waste as I had at first feared—and he will not be coming

239

again until the day after tomorrow, which gives me plenty of time to buy a new one, since you did, I believe, say—" she paused, her head slightly to one side, a questioning note in her voice—"that it would be merely a matter of this afternoon when you required my services."

"Just this afternoon," Delphick agreed, crossing mental fingers as he added the silent rider *deo volente*. With Miss Seeton, he knew, you could never be sure . . .

Miss Emily Dorothea Seeton stands five foot nothing in her stockinged feet, weighs no more than seven stone fully clothed, and is in her mid-sixties. With her grey hair, sensible shoes, and restrained (apart from her hats) attire, she is the epitome of the English spinster pensioner, having taken early retirement some seven years ago from the post of art teacher at Mrs. Benn's little school in Hampstead. There is, clearly, nothing in her appearance or general demeanour to explain why even experienced police officers such as Scotland Yard's own Oracle are apt to view any dealings they might have with Miss Seeton with a degree of circumspection. Who, after all, could be supposed more circumspect in her behaviour than a retired teacher of art?

She was, perhaps, (Miss Seeton will regretfully admit) not the most inspirational of instructors. Her enthusiasm for her subject she will never be so foolish as to deny; but her ability to impart to her pupils both her enthusiasm and the skill necessary to express their own were—and indeed, when she emerges from retirement to help out from time to time in Plummergen's little school, still are—sadly (she will sigh) limited. One did, of course, one's best to help people to look at things properly: to *see* things, and then to express what they saw on paper so that the seeing might be communicated to, and enjoyed by, all. . . .

Miss Seeton, even judged by the exacting standards of an English gentlewoman, is too modest: she was, and is, a very good teacher. She will coax and encourage the most unobservant pupils to produce work of a standard far higher than anyone would suppose possible. She is a very good teacher: but she is not, in this respect, unique; and it is for Miss Seeton's unique talent for communication that she is so very highly regarded by the police—her ability to See, and to show in her work what she has Seen in so unique a fashion.

This unique ability she does her very best to suppress. She has the strongest possible feeling that one should only draw what is really there: she is always embarrassed when what she has drawn, or sketched, or painted proves her to have noticed far more than that—to have seen what, in philosophical terms, might be regarded as *really* there: the Ultimate Truth of that which has been painted, sketched, or drawn. She would blush to be considered psychic: she would think it not quite right: and perhaps, indeed, it is too strong a word, though it is hard to find another which will adequately sum up Miss Seeton's qualities. Her vision of life is . . . different. It is clear, and uncluttered; it is instinctive, and cannot be explained—but it can, by those who understand something of its value, be harnessed. And harnessed it has been: by the police.

When Miss Seeton, walking through Covent Garden one evening after enjoying a performance of *Carmen*, remonstrated with a young man behaving in an unacceptable manner towards his female companion, she did so by applying the ferrule of her umbrella to the small of the young man's back. She had no idea, as she did so, that she had interrupted the notorious Cesar Lebel, drug dealer and thug, in the act of knifing to death a prostitute—had no idea that such a person as Lebel existed, and certainly knew nothing of his name. But his name was only too well known to Superintendent (as he had then been) Delphick of Scotland Yard, and his face, when at Delphick's request Miss Seeton sketched it, was instantly recogniseable.

At Delphick's further request, Miss Seeton sketched again—and again: faces, scenery, impressions. All showed aspects of the case which had not previously occurred to any of those involved in the investigation: it was as if a new light, a new vision had appeared in the drugs-riddled darkness. With Miss Seeton's help, Scotland Yard had managed to curtail the activities of certain of the drugging fraternity, arresting Lebel, among others, and leaving the air of London a little sweeter for those arrests. Miss Seeton, in recognition of her contribution to that sweetness, to her delighted surprise received the gift of a gold-handled black silk umbrella from Superintendent

Delphick as a token of his gratitude and esteem. Seven years later, Chief Superintendent Delphick had lost count of the number of reasons he had for being grateful to Miss Seeton, the number of cases her remarkable insights had helped him (and his colleagues both at the Yard and in other forces) to solve. So grateful were they for her efforts that they had officially retained Miss Seeton, on a modest salary, as an art consultant.

A pity, though, that so much of what happened in the vicinity of Miss Seeton wasn't always as clear and uncluttered as her invaluable insights. Was often anything but clear and uncluttered. Could be (to say the least) confused . . . exasperating . . . bewildering . . . exhausting.

"Just this afternoon," agreed Delphick, feeling exhausted at the very idea of trying to work out what she'd been trying to tell him about the garden roller, the besom, the worms, the stakes, and the compost. Worn out when they'd barely begun—their official business yet to come—and he wanted to see her safely on the homeward train well before midnight, if remotely possible.

He cleared his throat. "Yes, just this afternoon, with luck, and once we've had tea and biscuits—be a good chap, Bob, and chivvy the canteen, will you?—we'll be off on our guided tour, as I explained on the phone. And afterwards, a proper tea—at the Ritz, if you'd like it, or the Savoy—no," as Miss Seeton seemed about to protest at this lavish invitation—"you must allow Scotland Yard to treat you, please, without questioning our motives too closely." He smiled. "Although I'm sure you, of all people, will understand those motives only too well, and realise that we expect you to sing—or rather, draw— for your supper. You have, of course, brought your sketchpad with you."

It was not a question. Miss Seeton smiled back at him, nodded, and reached down for the enormous handbag Bob had placed by the foot of her chair. "And my pencils, and my eraser—plain, I thought, rather than coloured—the pencils, I mean. Autumn in the country," said Miss Seeton, turning a little pink, "is undoubtedly gold and copper and fading red but in London, I always feel . . . except, that is, in the parks of course, with the trees in silhouette, and the reappearance of form and line—my favourite season, and of course one notices such things so much better in the country, where there are so many more—and certainly more than we are likely to see today, of course, as you said we should be visiting only the shops and galleries which have been so disgracefully robbed. Trees, I mean. And although one appreciates that antiques and objets d'art are certainly not without colour, and the patina of the years"—the pink returned to her cheeks at this fanciful notion—"it is perhaps more—more rich than I feel mere pencils could in any case do justice to. And a paintbox," said Miss Seeton, recovering herself with a twinkle, "would be somewhat out of place at the Ritz or the Savoy, don't you think?"

Delphick said that he certainly did, adding that he was pleased she'd decided to accept his, or rather the Yard's, hospitality without worrying about it any more. It would, he reminded her, be on expenses—

"And fully deserved, I've no doubt," he added, as there came a tap at the door, and a uniformed constable appeared with a tray in his hands, a look of awe on his face as he gazed at the renowned Battling Brolly, maker of headlines, solver of crimes, sitting just like anyone ordinary—apart from the hat—in the Oracle's chair. Could almost be someone's old auntie up for the day, except that people's aunts didn't drop in on top-notch Yarders for a gossip over tea and buns the way everyone knew MissEss did.

"Thank you, Constable." Delphick, divining something of the new arrival's emotion, waved at Bob to grab the tray before it tilted to disaster and soaked MissEss sitting so unknowing underneath. MissEss! A quiet smile quirked Delphick's mouth as he recalled the argument he'd had with the Yard's base-ment computer, which considered itself infallible—how it had insisted that the abbreviated Miss Seeton, misheard, was first of all Delphick's Missus (the imagination boggled) and then, after much wearisome explanation, Delphick's MissEss, which seemed the best anyone was ever going to manage.

Bob reached for the tray. Shining buttons, their wearer still staring with fascination at the living legend in front of the

Oracle's desk, moved forward to effect the handover. A booted foot caught, tripped, stumbled. The tray leaped, cups clattering, and was caught just in time by big Bob Ranger, stalwart of the police football eleven. Breathing heavily, he swooped the tray past Miss Seeton's innocent nose by just half an inch to set it, with shaking hands, on top of Delphick's blotter.

Miss Seeton, bending to retrieve her umbrella, babbled apologies, oblivious to the recent risk of boiling tea or falling china. Blushing, babbling his own apologies, the bobby beat a hasty retreat. Delphick said:

"Shall I pour, Miss Seeton, or will you?" No point in asking Bob: his hands were still visibly shaking as he sat down, without invitation, on the other visitors' chair: Miss Seeton, his dear adopted Aunt Em, had rattled his normal composure. Come to think of it, Delphick didn't think his own voice sounded too steady, either . . .

"I know you like it weak." He forced himself to pour as Miss Seeton fumbled with the clasp of her handbag, settled her tumbled umbrella safely—*was* there ever such a word, if you were dealing with the Battling Brolly's brolly?—across her knees, automatically adjusted that incredible hat, and dutifully prepared to be given her latest assignment.

"You'll have read more details than we had time for on the phone in the press, I expect." Not that Miss Seeton was known to pore over Fleet Street's daily output with particular interest for all it so often featured her activities in blazing headlines but she had, he knew, the local paper once a week, and the milkman delivered a daily *Times* (if it arrived from London at the Brettenden distributors before he left on his rounds) or—since acquaintance had blossomed with Amelita Forby—the occasional *Daily Negative*, out of loyalty to a friend.

Miss Seeton, sipping tea, sighed, and nodded. "A great pity that so much intelligence—for such, from the little one reads it appears is used to plan these . . . these raids—could not be put to better use: and a real tragedy for so many works of art and pieces of genuine historical interest to be lost to the nation if, as one has been led to understand, the items in question are being . . . being stolen to order on behalf of some who live abroad. Although even if he lives in this country, of course the fact that he will have to keep them hidden in future means that they are, to all intents and purposes, still lost. If they are of such a size as to fit inside a car, it will be regrettably easy for him to do so. And very selfish . . ."

She sighed again. "And very callous, too, as well as thoroughly dishonest—that someone with more money than, I fear, moral responsibility should, so to speak, simply write out a—a shopping list, and hire people to fulfill his requirements. In other words"—Miss Seeton sat upright, the cockscomb ribbon above her right eye bristling—"deliberately encouraging those who might originally be merely *weak* to become true criminals. Not just stealing the pictures and the porcelain, but even the cars with which to—to ram their way through the shop windows—and it is, as I understand it, no more than good fortune that so far nobody has been hurt in these disgraceful robberies . . ."

She looked at Delphick in sudden dismay. "Oh, dear—am I to understand that the reason you have asked me to—"

"No, no, Miss Seeton." Delphick forgot courtesy and interrupted before she could distress herself further. "No, you're right in your understanding—nobody's been hurt in any of the Ram Raids, not even the one early this morning." He paused; he met her eye with a look as knowing as her own.

"Nobody," he emphasised, "has been hurt—yet. But I have the feeling, Miss Seeton, as does Inspector Terling of the Art Squad, that it may only be a matter of time. . . ."